Praise for Rose B

"...her characters seem fully capable of walking away from the particulars of whodunit and engaging the reader in other aspects of their lives." – *Lambda Book Report*

"When Jennifer Fulton writes mysteries, she writes them as Rose Beecham. And since Jennifer Fulton is a very fine writer, you might expect that Rose Beecham is a fine writer too. You're right...On the way to a remarkable, and thoroughly convincing climax, Beecham creates believable characters in compelling situations, with enough humor to provide effective counterpoint to the work of detecting." – *Bay Area Reporter*

"A well-written blend of subplots and well developed characters... An intriguing mystery which introduces a competent and complex cop to the ever-growing lesbian detective genre." – *Washington Blade*

"...Rose Beecham certainly can write! Grave Silence is set in the remote Four Corners area of the Southwest, and Beecham's descriptions of the landscape rival Nevada Barr's. Detective Jude Devine, lesbian and ex-FBI agent, brings some secrets of her own to the Montezuma County Sheriff's Office. When the body of a teenage girl is discovered with a stake through her heart, Jude finds ties to a fundamentalist Mormon sect that practices polygamy. The story involves graphic, but not gratuitous, violence and abuse. With social consciousness, a believable plot and strong characters, Grave Silence is an exemplary thriller..." – Nan Cinnater, *Books To Watch Out For* v.3 # 1

"[Grave Silence] is by far the most unique and intriguing murder mystery I have ever read. Why? Because of the backdrop. Sheriff's detective Jude Devine finds herself balancing two calls of duty as she investigates the murder of a teen. As the investigation deepens, the two duties begin to entwine resulting in a conclusion no reader can foresee. The entire story is set against a backdrop of Utah and religious zealots who believe in plural marriage. And, there's romance, too..." – Patricia Pair, publisher, *Family & Friends* January 2006

SLEEP
OF REASON

by
Rose Beecham

2006

SLEEP OF REASON

ISBN 1-933110-53-8
This Trade Paperback Is Published By
Bold Strokes Books, Inc.,
New York, USA

First Edition, September 2006

Credits

Editor: Shelley Thrasher
Production Design: J. Barre Greystone
Cover Graphic: Sheri (graphicartist2020@hotmail.com)

By the Author

MYSTERIES as Rose Beecham

Amanda Valentine Series
Introducing Amanda Valentine
Second Guess
Fair Play

Jude Devine Series
Grave Silence
Sleep of Reason

ROMANCES as Jennifer Fulton

Moon Island Series
A Guarded Heart
Passion Bay
Saving Grace
The Sacred Shore

Heartstoppers Series
Dark Dreamer

Others
Greener Than Grass
True Love

CONTEMPORARY FICTION as Grace Lennox

Chance

Acknowledgments

I belong to that species of author for whom writing a novel is a lonely, antisocial affair. Family and friends are excluded, the phone is ignored, and the espresso machine works overtime. My dear ones, especially my partner, put up with all of this and still love me. Puzzling, but I cannot thank them enough.

I worked on this novel with the support and encouragement of the women who make my life make sense: Fel, Sophie, and JD. In particular, I thank my mother, Wyn, who spent the first part of her big overseas vacation looking after me and my home so I could write much of this work without disturbance.

Lori L. Lake has my thanks for being unfailingly generous with her advice and skills, and only letting me stay precious for twenty-four hours at any time. Shelley Thrasher edited this book with insight and sensitivity, for which I am extremely thankful because it was extremely late to her desk. And Radclyffe, as usual, was the perfect publisher—a patient tyrant and a writers' friend, without whose mentoring and encouragement I would be a lesser author.

DEDICATION

To the memory of Jaidyn
and all the children who share his fate.

When I was living in Melbourne, Australia, a toddler named Jaidyn Leskie vanished in bizarre circumstances, sparking the biggest manhunt in the history of that nation. After Jaidyn's body was found, his mother's boyfriend was tried for his murder, acquitted, and was recently alleged to have made a jailhouse confession to the crime.

This novel is not a fictionalized account of Jaidyn's story, but I was inspired to write it because of that sad case. There are a few superficial similarities to his story, for many common elements can be found in the stories of countless children who die every year at the hands of those supposed to protect them.

"The sleep of reason produces monsters."

– Francisco Goya

CHAPTER ONE

At ten in the evening on a freezing Saturday in Cortez, Colorado, Tonya Perkins was chugging a beer and planning to fuck a total stranger when her night on the town was interrupted by a phone call from her boyfriend, Wade Miller.

Wade had bad news. Tonya's two-year-old son Corban had burned his hand on the stove, and Wade had to take him to the hospital.

"Shit," said Tonya. She never went out drinking with her friends anymore. She couldn't pay for a sitter. Now, finally, she had a boyfriend who said he'd mind Corban, and this happened. "Okay. I'll come home."

"Nah. You don't have to. Just thought you should know what happened."

Tonya heaved a sigh of relief. If Corban was okay then she could stay at the bar. She gave her sister Amberlee a thumbs up and checked out a hot guy across the room. "You sure you don't need me there?" she asked as someone shoved another pitcher of beer in front of her.

"Yeah. Don't worry. He's got himself a sore hand, that's all."

"I don't get it. I just hit him yesterday for reaching up on the stove."

Wade mumbled something that sounded like, "This time he learned."

A tightness in his voice registered with Tonya. Guessing at the reason, she took a swig of beer and asked, "What'd you have to pay them at the hospital?"

"It's fine. I got some extra work."

Didn't sound like the Wade Miller Tonya knew. Since he'd started saving up for his new car, he was even stingier than usual. That's why he didn't care about missing Amberlee's party. He acted like he was a hero for babysitting Corban, but Tonya knew he just wanted to avoid buying a round.

"You sure?" She gave him a last chance.

"No sweat. You're my old lady."

"I love you, ding dong." Tonya let her eyes return to the man-meat across the room. She tried to remember his name. Something foreign. Andre. No, Vincente. The guy had his own car repair shop. He looked like Ricky Martin. She decided if she couldn't get him, she would check out one of the salesmen in town for the agricultural show. They were always married, so no one would make annoying phone calls the next day and start calling himself a boyfriend like Cortez males were in the habit of doing.

"You gonna be much longer?" Wade asked.

"We're going back to Amberlee's after this."

"Right. I forgot. Want me to pick you up later? Like in a few hours or something?"

The stud was looking her way. Tonya sucked in her stomach. "Yeah, okay," she remembered to answer. She was already fucked up, and she'd only been drinking since eight. Laughing, she said, "I can't drive. No way. I'd take a wrong turn and end up in the reservoir."

❖

Sitting at a table a few yards away, Matthew Roache had a pitiful look on his face, and his eyes were glued to Tonya. His sister, Heather, felt sorry for him, but this had gone on long enough. He'd been living at her place since he broke up with that slut, and Heather had had it. She was fed up with him and his loser buddies camped on her sofa and eating her food with the TV blaring day and night. And she was fed up with that dirty goat tied up in her yard, causing a problem with the neighbors.

When the heavy snows came a few days back, Matthew brought the disgusting animal into the house, and he was keeping it in the guest bathroom now. He never cleaned up after it. Heather had to scrape droppings off the soles of her best boots on her way out the door tonight.

"What do you think you're doing?" she asked. "She dumped you and she's with someone else. Forget her. Just walk away and forget her. She's not worth it."

"I love her."

"Well, she doesn't love you."

Heather had decided recently that you had to be cruel to be kind. Matthew was her little brother and she loved him, but he was letting Tonya Perkins ruin his life. He'd even lost his job. His boss got fed up with him calling in so-called sick. Heather knew exactly where he was on those supposed sick days—parked outside of that bitch's house.

Unable to help herself, she stared past a sea of bodies to the peroxide blonde perched on a bar stool and thought, *I hate that woman. I hope she dies.* Normally she would feel ashamed of herself for thinking such a thing, but as Tonya dropped her cell phone into her purse and leaned back against the bar trying to look sexy, Heather could only marvel at the stupidity of males. How could they be sucked in by such a whore?

Tonya wore fuck-me pumps and a denim miniskirt no one a size XXL should wear. Black fishnet stockings strained over her fat thighs. They couldn't hide the cellulite, and she must have spent hours with the curling iron, getting her big hairdo coiled into long ringlets. Someone should tell her strawberry blond wasn't her color.

As if anyone could possibly miss her double Ds, Cortez's number-one home wrecker tugged her pink crop top down so her staunch, pale breasts bobbed over. This drew attention to the tidemark at the base of her throat where her tan foundation began. She wore candy pink lipstick, baby blue eye shadow, and eyeliner flicked up slightly in the corner of each eye.

Heather almost laughed. How yesterday was *that* look? Turning away before Tonya caught her staring, she could barely stop herself from slapping Matthew upside the head. He was slouched over his beer, sniffing noisily.

"We were supposed to be getting married today," he choked out.

"As if I could forget. I was supposed to be in Cancun, remember? Has she given you back that ring yet?"

"I don't care about the ring," he blubbered.

"Well *I* do. You owe me four hundred dollars." By rights that engagement ring belonged to her. Matthew had been paying her back the seven hundred she lent him to buy it, but after he lost his job the payments dried up. "I worked hard for that money," she reminded him.

"I know. " Matthew snatched her hand and flattened it over his pounding heart. "I'll pay, I swear. God's honest truth."

"Even if you just got the ring back, I could live with that," she said generously. "I could sell it on eBay."

"How am I supposed to do that?"

"Try asking. If she says no, then stop by her place when she's not expecting you and get it off the dresser in her bedroom. She keeps it in that music box I gave her for the engagement."

"How do you know?"

Heather rolled her eyes. "Duh. I only organized her bachelorette party. I've been in her room."

Matthew seemed to be thinking. He gave a small harsh laugh. "While I'm there, I'm gonna take back that stuffed panda I gave her, too."

"Oh, that's smart. You walk out with your hood over your face and carrying a big, huge stuffed animal. Just in case no one noticed you burglarizing the house."

"I never thought of that." He snuck another look at Tonya and rifled his fingers frantically through his hair as if that might dislodge the trashy slut from his brain.

"Lovely," Heather said. "Now you've got dandruff in your beer." Why she bothered trying to make him think with his brain instead of his dick was a mystery. He was never going to ask Tonya for the ring, and if he tried to steal it he would probably get caught. At this rate, she would be spending her next vacation in Kansas, not Cancun.

Predictably her brother acted like everything was settled, promising, "I'll get a job and pay you back. Twice as much. You'll be able to go to Mexico just like you planned."

Heather had heard it all before. The fact was, that woman had cast a spell on Matthew, and until he snapped out of it, he would be unemployed and eating everything in her fridge. "That's all well and good, but I'll tell you something you can do for me now. Okay?"

Her brother dragged his arm across his face. "Okay."

"I want that goat gone by tomorrow. I refuse to have it polluting my home for one more day."

"He doesn't hurt anyone. And we don't have to mow the yard with him chewing on the grass. You'll be glad when it's summer."

"Oh, really? You think I enjoy listening to the neighbors complaining about their kids putting goat poop in their mouths because they think it's raisins? The joke's over. It's you or him."

"A week," Matthew begged. "Jason'll be in town next weekend. He'll take him."

"No."

Their older brother, Jason, hadn't shown up for months. He had some land in Jackson County, and he was always promising to drive down and visit, but he never got around to it. Heather seriously doubted he'd want the goat anyway. Matthew was kidding himself. He thought he was so funny when he got the animal after 9/11, telling everyone how he was naming it after *My Pet Goat*, the children's book the President was reading when he was told about the terrorist attack. He just made himself look stupid calling it Bush's Homeland Security adviser and asking it what color the terror alert should be.

Heather didn't see the big joke, and she didn't appreciate her brother disrespecting the President. She'd voted Bush/Cheney both times because she didn't believe in abortion. She'd tried to talk to Matthew about the unborn and about how the gay lifestyle was being taught in schools as close as Boulder. But even with the sanctity of marriage in direct peril, he'd been too busy running around after Tonya to get to a polling place. That woman had lowered his IQ, which—let's face it—wasn't right up there to begin with.

Leaning closer to him, she said, "Listen to me. I'm trying to help you, but you have to start doing stuff for yourself. Get rid of that goat. Get a haircut. I'll buy you some new pants and a shirt, and you can start applying for jobs. That's the best revenge you'll ever get. Show her you don't care and you're a success. My boss is looking for guys to help out with a big roofing contract in the spring. That's good money."

"Roofing? Oh, man. It'll be all Mexicans and me. I don't speak Mexican."

"It's better than laying around all day watching the soaps. And think about it, you'd be one of the only white guys so you'd be boss of your own gang pretty quick. Mr. McAllister needs men who can communicate with the client."

Matthew whined, "Do we have to talk about it now?"

"Yes, we do!" Heather seized his chin and forced his head in Tonya's direction. "Look at her pawing Vinnie Russo when she's supposed to be with Wade Miller now. She's a slut, Matthew. She stole her sister's husband, and then *he* left her—guess why?"

Matthew looked guilty. "It was love at first sight. We couldn't help it."

"Oh, that explains why she seduced Wade off of Brittany Kemple while you two were engaged. If you *had* gotten married, trust me, she'd be cheating on you right now."

Her brother stiffened. His light brown eyes glittered with fury, and his chest rose and fell like he was palpitating. "I'll fix her." He stood up and shoved his chair back.

Heather grabbed his arm. "You can't fight Vinnie Russo! He'll kill you."

"I'm not going to fight Vinnie." Matthew looked her dead in the eye. He was pale and his mouth shook. "I'm going to do what you said. I'll show her. I'll take that job and get a decent car and my own place, and she'll wish she'd never dumped me for that asshole Wade fucking Miller. And when you get home later, no goat. Okay?"

Before Heather could say thank you, he stalked out of the bar.

CHAPTER TWO

S heriff's Detective Jude Devine untangled herself from her sheets, groped for the phone, and peered at her digital clock. 4:30 a.m. Normally, she got up at 5:30 so she could work out for an hour before she drove to work. A phone call this early meant she wouldn't be bench-pressing anything bigger than a coffee mug.

"Get in here, Devine," her boss demanded as Jude licked her furry teeth and tried to formulate a greeting.

Dragging herself upright, she located the bottle of water she kept on her nightstand. After two years away from Washington, D.C., she was used to dealing with the Colorado altitude. Anyone who didn't drink plenty of water could expect a permanent headache.

"What's up, sir?" she asked after a few protracted gulps.

"We have a situation." Sheriff Pratt's grim delivery made it clear she would not be staying in her nice warm bed much longer.

"How bad?"

Pratt coughed wetly into the phone. "Bad enough for me to be freezing my balls off down here instead of doing what the doctor ordered and staying in my goddamned bed for another week."

"Bummer."

Jude slid her feet into the chill air and groaned. She turned the heating down when she went to bed, so her room wasn't even fifty degrees. Shivering, she stumbled across her cold floorboards to the window and twitched the curtain aside. It was still dark, but her yard glowed winter white with the first serious snowfall of the season.

No one could believe they'd had to wait until March to see the usual high country snowpack. Even the most earnest devotees of denial, of which the Four Corners had more than its fair share, were suddenly wondering aloud if global warming was not just a liberal fiction invented to destroy the American way of life. Hurricane Katrina and the cost of gas had unleashed a rare storm of doubt about the wisdom and pronouncements of the demigods on Capitol Hill.

"Snow's coming down pretty heavy out here," she told Pratt, gloomily resigning herself to shoveling her driveway in darkness so she could get her Dodge Dakota out.

"Weather report says we're expecting another nine inches," he said unsympathetically. "The sooner you leave, the less you'll have to shovel."

Jude hit the lights and squinted until she could relax her eyes. "I hear you. So, what have we got?"

"Hard to say exactly. Just do me a favor and haul ass, Detective."

Surprised by this masterful directive, Jude juggled the phone as she located underwear and warm clothes. The sheriff seldom took that kind of tone with her. Although he had never wanted her on his staff and was antsy around her at the best of times, he usually managed to conceal his feelings behind a mask of professional respect. Whatever was going on had to be big for him to drag her in right off the bat.

Intrigued, Jude asked, "Sir, any special equipment requirements?"

No answer. She surmised Pratt had his hand over the phone while he was coughing. He'd caught a bad case of the flu a week earlier and was so feverish at work he collapsed on a bed in one of the detention cells. The staff panicked, imagining a terrorist attack, maybe anthrax in the mail. Homeland Security closed the office for a day and sent in a team in hazard suits while doctors ascertained the cause of Pratt's symptoms. He'd been at home in bed ever since.

Jude could hear nose-blowing in the background. Finally her boss croaked, "We'll be needing the K-9 unit. There's a kid missing."

"A kid. Now? In this weather?"

"Looks like it. And we have a felony animal-cruelty incident tied in, so you might want to prepare yourself before you get to the scene."

What he really meant was for her to prepare Tulley. Her deputy at the Paradox Valley substation was stoic in the face of crimes against persons and property, but anything involving a four-legged friend derailed him.

Jude buttoned her shirt. "I take it we're talking about a search-and-rescue op."

"Yep, assuming we don't find the little guy on the property. I got a team down there now combing the neighborhood, and I've called out the posse. Everyone's asking for that hound."

Tulley would be ecstatic. He'd taken their bloodhound, Smoke'm, on a course recently to learn new techniques for tracking in snow. Pratt had bitched about the cost.

"Is it an abduction?" Jude asked.

"Too soon to say for certain. We're not getting a whole lot of sense out of the mother. I don't want to guess at her blood-alcohol level." His voice became a thin, breathless rasp as he added, "Of course, if you want to call your buddies in right now, I can't stop you."

Jude sighed. If a nonfamily child abduction was indicated, the Feds would have to be involved and Pratt would want her to make that call, given what he liked to refer to as her "secret goddamn identity" as an FBI agent working undercover. Jude had been gathering intelligence on domestic terrorist groups based in the Four Corners region for two years now, and Pratt seldom let her forget her "real mission."

For some reason her masters at the Bureau had thought that sending her into the area as a sheriff's detective was a stroke of genius. They hadn't bothered to consult Pratt about their brilliant plan, but had simply converted a schoolhouse in Paradox Valley to a substation, hired a secretary, and ordered Pratt to appoint Jude to head up this remote outpost.

The Valley was not even in Pratt's jurisdiction, so he was forced to enter into an unwelcome joint arrangement with the Montrose sheriff, who knew nothing about the real rationale but was happy to score some extra guns in the canyon region. In most of the surrounding counties, the big preoccupation for local law enforcement was the annual Telluride Film Festival. As long as Jude didn't start busting celebrities, no one cared what she got up to. But Pratt never missed a chance to whine about the invidious position he was in, thanks to her. He clearly expected her to unearth a vast conspiracy at any moment, one that would play right into the hands of his chief opponent in the forthcoming elections.

"I'll see you in an hour, sir. We can discuss other agency involvement once we know what we're dealing with." She slid her belt through the loops of her black wool pants. "We'll probably want to go the CBI route right off, then bring in the Bureau. That would be diplomatic."

Pratt audibly released a breath. Like a lot of local sheriffs, he was queasy about bringing federal agents into any investigation in his jurisdiction. Even aside from his personal gripe with the Bureau, Jude knew he pictured the usual scenarios—slickly dressed Feds take over, state and local law enforcement get cut out of the loop, the Feds claim the credit for any success and blame the locals for every failure. Jude had heard the same complaints time after time when she worked in the Bureau's Crimes Against Children Unit. But when a child went missing there was no gain in playing politics. Most serious cases went multi-agency from day one.

In recent times, the Amber Alert system had helped iron out a few problems, giving state and local response a higher profile and more media attention. The Colorado Bureau of Investigation coordinated the system statewide and worked closely with all the national and local clearinghouses for missing-children information. They would send in a Major Crimes Unit, if requested, and once they knew what they were dealing with, they could call in the FBI. The simple fact was no small regional police or sheriff's department could fully resource a major investigation, and everyone knew it.

Jude was about to end the call when Pratt asked, "Detective, would it be fair to say you're familiar with tactical interrogation techniques?"

Cautiously, Jude said, "Federal agents get some extra training."

These days, the "tactical interrogation" methods employed by the military and intelligence communities were gaining traction in law enforcement, and the term was being tossed around by training providers like it was a magic bullet. Forget the standard time-consuming behavior analysis and interrogation techniques that had worked for decades—there was now a shortcut, a fast-food approach to getting confessions. Jude wasn't sure what was new about police officers beating information out of a suspect; it had been a pretty popular "tactic" until the eighties. But Iraq had breathed new life, and new euphemisms, into disgraced ideas, and all of a sudden departments could send their staff for training so they would know how not to drown a prisoner or leave DNA all over an interview room. No one used the word "torture" for any of this; it made a poor impression.

Sheriff Pratt got to the point. "Can you tell when a subject is lying?"

"No one can be sure about that, sir, and I doubt my instincts are any better than yours." She pulled on two layers of socks and shoved her feet into snow boots. "Got a subject in mind?"

"There's a boyfriend in the picture. Wade Miller. One prior for misdemeanor assault. Had a protective order served on him a couple of years back."

"And he's not the missing kid's biological father?"

Jude automatically ran the odds as she loaded her duty revolver, a Glock 22. The statistics were all too familiar from her years in the CACU. Eighty percent of violent crimes against young children were committed by a parent. If a baby made it through the first day of her or his life without being murdered by the mother, the father then posed the greater risk. A stepfather was about fifty times more likely to kill a small child than a biological father. Missing-baby-plus-mother's-boyfriend was an equation well-known to anyone in law enforcement.

"The real dad is on an oil rig," Pratt said. "We put a call in to his employer as soon as the missing-child report was filed."

"How's the boyfriend acting?"

"Like he got lobotomized at birth."

"Keep them apart." Jude stated the obvious. "And get his clothes off him and bag them. I don't care what you have to tell him. Get him clean ones and make him change."

She felt bad telling Pratt his job, but small town law enforcement sometimes tried to be human in cases like this. A panicky mother could be left with her partner for comfort. If Pratt was expecting any reliable data from interviewing this couple, she didn't want them getting their stories straight before she talked to them.

"Don't worry." Pratt sounded pleased with himself. "We've had Miller in his own interview room since they walked in the door with their bullshit story. I'll see about his clothes."

Jude holstered the Glock and gazed out into the lethal cold once more. "How old is the kid?"

"Not even two. A baby."

"So, we're looking for a body." She spoke her immediate thought aloud.

"Worst-case scenario, yes."

She started assembling her blizzard gear. "I'll be in as soon as I can. Don't let the boyfriend use the bathroom."

"You got it." Pratt hung up.

Jude collected her car keys and called Tulley on her cell phone. "Harness that hound of yours," she instructed, "and get down to Cortez."

Tulley's voice came back fuzzy, and something crashed in the background. He said, "Hang on, Detective. Knocked the lamp over."

She heard him mumble something to whoever was in bed next to him. It sounded like: *How many times I gotta tell you? Don't slobber on the phone.*

"Hurry it up," she said. "There's a toddler that's missing."

"You got it." Jude could make out the sounds of drawers opening and closing. "I'll take Smoke'm out hungry. That'll make him keen."

"Good thinking. Oh, and something else. The sheriff says we have an animal-cruelty issue, but I'll handle it. Okay?"

"Have they arrested someone for that?" Tulley's voice went up a few notches.

"I don't have any details. I'm just warning you."

"I want five minutes alone with the guy that did it," her subordinate said darkly.

Jude picked up a snow shovel from next to the garage door. "We both know that isn't going to happen. See you down there, Deputy."

❖

"The seductively clad female is the boy's mother," Sheriff Pratt informed Jude as they both observed several people seated in the beige waiting area at the recently built Montezuma County Sheriff's Office.

Unlike most mothers of missing toddlers, Tonya Perkins was not pacing the floor, weeping uncontrollably, or verbally abusing cops who could not join the search for her baby. She had discarded her black high-heel pumps and was lolling back in her chair, snoring. Someone had draped a blanket over her lap.

"Where's the boyfriend?" Jude asked.

Pratt indicated the interview rooms along the hallway. "Locked up and pestering to use the facilities."

"What's he been saying?"

"He claims he collected Ms. Perkins from a party at the home of her sister, Mrs. Amberlee Foley, at two and some time after that discovered the boy was missing."

"He reported this when?"

"Four fifteen. Just before I called you in."

"What took him so long?"

"Good question. He said he couldn't wake Ms. Perkins up. He also said he thought the kid had wandered out of his bed, at first. Maybe fallen asleep somewhere in the house. Later, he notices the front windows have been vandalized and the boy is missing."

"He didn't hear this vandalism happening?" Jude marveled.

"He claims it must have transpired earlier in the night when he was picking Ms. Perkins up from the sister's place, but he didn't see the damage when they arrived home. Too busy getting the mother of the year into bed after her drinking binge."

Jude went over to Tonya Perkins and woke her up. The woman smelled like a bar.

"What am I doing here?" Perkins gazed at her dully. "I want to go home."

"Ms. Perkins, you're here because your son Corban is missing."

Perkins began to laugh. The sound was slurred and uneven. "No, he's not. Ding dong's just playing games. Where is he?" She cast a wavering glance around the room.

"Where is who?"

"Wade."

"Your boyfriend is being interviewed."

"Tell him I want to go to bed. This is stupid."

"Do you know where your son is?" Jude asked.

Perkins squinted at her like she was a figment of a bad dream. "Isn't he at home?"

Jude summoned patience. There was no point getting frustrated with a confused, drunk woman. "No, he's not, Ms. Perkins. If your boyfriend was playing a trick on you, where do you think he might take Corban?"

Slowly an idea registered on Tonya Perkins's face. "He's in the hospital," she announced.

"Why would he be in the hospital?"

"He burnt his hand. Wade took him to the hospital last night."

"First we've heard," Pratt murmured from a few feet away. "Which hospital?"

Perkins shrugged. "I don't know. Hey, where can I get a cup of coffee round here?"

Pratt waved a deputy over and ordered the refreshment. Jude glanced at the wall clock. 6:30 a.m. Corban had been missing for at least three hours, maybe longer, depending on whether this woman or her boyfriend were telling the truth or covering up a crime.

"I'll call the hospital," she said.

Pratt met her eyes. The doubt in his own was transparent.

❖

Southwest Memorial had no record of Corban Foley. It had been a slow night, and no one could remember a man coming in with a small child. A couple of deputies were analyzing the security tapes.

So far, there was no sign of the toddler in his own neighborhood, either. The preliminary canvass had generated only a few leads worth a dime. At 2 a.m. when Wade Miller claimed he'd left to pick up his intoxicated girlfriend, the residents of Malafide Road were tucked in their beds sound asleep. No one could say with any certainty that they'd heard a vehicle drive past their home.

Earlier that same evening, they'd been snugly ensconced in front of their TVs watching *Nancy Grace* and *Deal or No Deal* while the snow came down outside. No one had noticed Wade Miller's truck arrive or leave the Perkins house. Everyone whined about the price of gas and the amazing March snowfall that had terminated their dry, warm winter. An elderly man several doors down shared his unflattering views on Tonya Perkins's appearance and morality. And Tonya's next-door neighbor, a single mother of three, said Tonya had "bad taste in men." She'd seen "that loser she's dating" shouting at the missing child, calling him names like "retard" and telling him to shut up.

According to her, they'd been out in the yard one day just before Christmas playing with Miller's big dogs, and Corban was howling up a storm and trying to escape from the animals. Miller kept calling him a "dumb little faggot" and looked like he was going to start belting the kid. The neighbor went to the fence and made her presence known.

Miller called off his dogs then, and took Corban into the house.

The woman concluded her comments with the statement, "If anything's happened to that poor little kid, he did it."

"Only problem is," Pratt told Jude as they approached the Perkins house, "her sister was dating Miller before he took up with Perkins, and there's some bad blood there. Girl named Brittany Kemple. We're bringing her in."

Jude crunched her way through a foot of fresh snow to Tonya Perkins's driveway. The Perkins house was a fixer-upper no one had bothered to fix up. It stood out, even among the surrounding low-priced real estate, as the one house in its street with paint so badly flaked that the timber beneath was exposed. It also stood out because the front yard was secured by crime scene tape and in the dead center the snow had been blown aside to reveal a gory crimson halo surrounding the decapitated head of a goat. Compounding this macabre spectacle, the goat wore a baseball cap emblazoned with the slogan Don't Blame Me! I Didn't Vote For Him. Someone had tried to cross out "For Him" with a black marker pen. The goat's ears were fed through a couple of holes cut in the cap.

"This sick ticket thinks he's a funny guy," Pratt wheezed.

"Sir, I can walk the scene," Jude offered. "Why don't you go back home and get warm. I'm sure Mrs. Pratt must be worried sick knowing you're out here."

Pratt seemed genuinely torn. "You're right, but the way this is shaping up, I should be at the scene."

Jude knew what he was saying. With elections looming in less than nine months and the political climate being what it was for Republican incumbents, the race for sheriff was heating up. It hardly seemed possible that a Democrat former deputy was looking like a real contender, but Pratt was as neurotic as Jude had ever seen him. He wanted his face plastered all over the TV screen at every possible opportunity, and he saw every open case in the county as a personal slight. Arrests, even dubious ones, were the order of the day.

"The broken windows," she asked, "these happen last night?"

"So we're told. One of them belongs to the kid's room." Pratt singled out a narrow casement-type window about four feet from ground level. They ducked under the yellow tape and padded carefully around the perimeter of the yard to inspect it.

"No one got in or out of that hole," Jude said.

The entry point smashed in the window wasn't big enough for a child, let alone an adult kidnapper in winter clothing. There was no sign of fiber or blood on the deep jagged shards and no way anyone could have squeezed past them without leaving part of their anatomy at the scene. The pane had been smashed from the outside, and some kind of dust coated the tips of the shards.

"Brick through the window." Pratt gave voice to Jude's immediate conclusion.

She pulled on a pair of latex gloves. The sensation was like sliding her hands into a second skin of frigid Jello. She allowed her eyes to roam slowly around the scene and realized she wasn't the only intent observer. A solitary raven, wings held low and close against the cold, was perched on the guttering of the house next door, wearing its sleek black feathers like a mourner's cloak. It angled its head quizzically, as if in response to Jude's gaze, and took several slow sideways steps in her direction. Staring pointedly down at the goat's head, it released a soft, guttural "quork" that sounded like a question.

"I guess you're hungry," Jude said. Winter in the Four Corners was usually harsh, and most Colorado birds flew south. They started returning to their nesting territories in March. The raven had probably made the flight from Mexico some time in the past few days, reaching its destination just in time for the worst blizzard of the year.

Jude examined the torpid sky. There was no sign of sunlight through the snow squall. Drifts of big feathery snowflakes had replaced the wind-driven deluges of the past twenty-four hours. Falling snow had long since covered any footprints or tire tracks on the Perkins property, and the white hush of morning was broken only by the sounds of voices, car engines, and horses snorting.

A few yards down the road, the sheriff's posse had assembled, ten riders in black felt cowboy hats, black bandannas, and heavy snow vests. Surrounding them, members of the SAR team coordinated a steady stream of volunteers. News spread quickly in a small town like Cortez. By noon half the town's able-bodied adults would be involved in the search-and-rescue operation.

Uncomfortable with the foot traffic milling about, Jude said, "We need to relocate everyone. They're already compromising the scene."

"It's in hand. As soon as we've combed the neighborhood again, we're shifting the command center to the posse hall," Pratt said. "Maybe the town hall if we get a big turnout."

Jude began photographing the surroundings. "We'll want pictures of the crowd, too," she said.

As Pratt relayed these instructions over his radio, several members of the Crime Scene Unit emerged from the house. One of them waved Jude and Pratt in, saying, "You gotta see this."

They traipsed indoors to the entrance of a cheaply furnished living room. A green Formica dining table was jammed into the corner behind the door, and a dated sofa was parked about six feet from a television that was too big for the room. Between the two, a plain mint-toned rug lay across the floor. Standing to one side was a CSU technician Jude had worked with a few times, Belle Simmons, one of several Montezuma County deputies trained in crime scene processing.

"Must have been a heck of a drive for you this morning, Detective," Simmons said. Her drawl was pure Louisiana. She'd married a Mancos man who ran an online shoe sales business. He seemed to do okay and was held up as a big success story in the Four Corners, where not too many people lived the American Dream.

"Made me think fondly of the D.C. commute," Jude remarked.

She liked what she'd seen of Belle Simmons. The deputy was mature, intelligent, and methodical, and she had a warm way about her. This morning, her manic red curls were restrained in a ponytail, and she wore her customary makeup—foundation, coral lipstick, carefully applied eyeliner and mascara, subtle bronze blusher across the cheekbones. Jude had her pegged for the kind of woman whose husband had never seen her without the works. However, Simmons's job mattered to her. Everyone knew she'd sacrificed her acrylic nails for it. That was the kind of commitment that made the front page of the *Durango Herald*. A celebratory puff-piece was pinned to the staff bulletin board at the sheriff's office in Cortez.

Jude took a few careful steps into the room. "What have we got?"

"Blood splatter."

Radiating out from the rug was a low-velocity pattern. The trajectories indicated a source of origin roughly at the rug's center, but there was no sign of anything on the pale green pile. It looked brand-new.

Jude snapped a few mid-range images, then asked, "Have you lifted the rug yet?"

Simmons shook her head. "Thought you'd want to take a look first."

"I appreciate that."

Jude was pleasantly surprised that the scene had been so well preserved. In a situation like this, where the initial investigation was macroscopic and its focus still uncertain, it was not unusual to find a scene virtually ransacked by the first responders. This was especially true in small town environments where the local police and sheriff's departments didn't have a wealth of experience dealing with serious crimes.

However, Jude had discovered that law enforcement personnel in Colorado were sensitive about any shortcomings in this regard. Crime scene mishandling had been a significant factor in the still-unsolved Jon Benet Ramsey murder, and no one wanted their officers accused of incompetence if a big-deal slaying like that one ever happened in their bailiwick. From the faces Jude could see, a missing two-year-old and a boyfriend with a history of violence had set off serious alarms bells in the MCSO.

She crouched on her heels and shone a flashlight across the underside of the rug and the heavily scratched wood floor. Even with some smudging and fiber transfer, a wipe pattern and a couple of shoe prints were evident on the boards. Transfer marked the underside of the rug.

"We need a blood-pattern analyst in here," Jude said. "Seal the room."

"I'll call Grand Junction." Simmons took out her cell phone. "It'll take a while."

Jude almost offered to do it herself, but stifled the impulse. "No problem," she told Simmons and wondered if the strain in her voice was audible.

Yes, she could phone Grand Junction; it would give her an excuse to talk to Mercy for the first time in a month. Was that what she wanted as a major case was unfolding—to exchange pointless civilities with a girlfriend whose idea of commitment was that she was faithful to both her lovers? Jude couldn't think about that sordid reality without wanting to kick something across the room.

She should phone Mercy some time soon, she thought, if only to prove she wasn't sulking because Elspeth Harwood was in town. Mercy only slept with one of them at a time, and because Elspeth had to travel from England, Jude was expected to be considerate during her visits. Every time these happened she would tell herself not to tolerate this crazy situation for another day. Then, a prisoner of her hormones, she would slink back to kiss the hand that maimed her. Already, she was counting the days until Elspeth was due to leave and she could yet again nourish her self-abasing passion.

Not this time, Jude promised herself beneath her breath. This time she was going to tell Dr. Mercy Westmoreland to find herself another lonely, weak-willed stud.

"Ready to bag this?" Simmons asked, indicating the bloodstained rug.

"Go ahead," Jude said, hoping her lapse in concentration wasn't obvious. "And once the analyst has been in here, lift the boards whole. I want those footprints intact."

"Size nine. Male," Simmons noted with impressive accuracy. Jude guessed the same, and she'd had years of practice. "I'll confirm that once we have exact measurements."

"Do you have a Hexagon OBTI kit nearby?" Jude asked, taking notes. "There's one in my truck if you don't."

"As a matter of fact, that was one thing I did remember to pack." Simmons slipped out of the room and returned with the test cassette and reagent bottle, which she passed to Jude.

"Can't beat instant gratification," Jude remarked heartily. She lifted some blood with the collection stick, then returned it to the bottle.

Simmons administered the test, slowly shaking the contents before depositing a couple of drops into the small cassette. A few minutes later a single blue bar showed in the result window.

"It's not human." Simmons sounded both relieved and puzzled.

They would have to wait for a full lab analysis to determine the origins of the sample, but Jude had a species in mind. "*Capra hircus*," she murmured.

Both Simmons and Pratt stared at her blankly.

"Goat." Jude swung her attention to the shattered windows. "That head was in here before it was ever out there."

CHAPTER THREE

S even hours had elapsed since Corban was reported missing by the primary suspects in his disappearance. That was a problem. Three-quarters of the children murdered in stranger abductions were killed in the first three hours.

Tonya Perkins, sober at last and a credit to the TV makeup people, was all set to plead for her son's life. Fluffy booms hovered like so many drunken moths around her big hair. For the occasion she wore tight low-rise jeans and a white knit crop top she kept pulling down over her navel. That was the good news. The bad news was sitting in the chair next to her, combing a jet black mullet that was teased over the balding center of his head. The rest of his hair was growing out mouse brown at the roots. Wade Miller. The boyfriend.

Miller had a gift for crying on cue when the reporters asked him how he felt about little Corban. At least that's how every law officer in the room saw it, if their hard eyes and locked jaws were anything to go by. Jude was no exception. She'd interviewed Miller for two hours, so far. The guy couldn't give a straight answer. And his feet were size nine.

On first impression, he seemed dim as a ten-watt bulb, but after a while, when he got impatient waiting to be taken to the bathroom, he'd dropped the ingenuous routine and revealed flashes of a more aggressive, cunning personality. He seemed conscious of these lapses and would immediately take cover behind a whiny, apologetic outburst. During such melodramatic interludes, he would invariably proclaim his love of little kids, Corban especially. Jude wasn't the only interviewing detective who thought an innocent man would not need to make the point so emphatically.

Miller's story had already changed. He'd signed an initial statement saying he was looking after the baby while his girlfriend was at her sister's party. Around ten that night he'd phoned Tonya to tell her Corban had accidentally burned himself but was okay. Later, Corban was in his bed asleep when Wade went out to pick up Tonya. That was the last time he saw him.

The trip there and back to Amberlee Foley's house took thirty minutes. Wade's theory was that whoever abducted Corban must have been watching the place and they struck while he was out. When he returned, he was so busy getting the drunk Tonya into the house that he didn't notice the broken windows or the goat's head in the front yard. After he'd got her settled, he had a quick look in Corban's door and saw he wasn't in his bed. But Corban often went into the living room in the middle of the night and fell asleep in front of the fireplace, so Wade was not concerned.

That was version one.

In version two, after Jude read aloud Tonya's statement about Wade taking Corban to the hospital, Wade acted like the stress of the moment had made him forget all about that journey to Southwest Memorial through heavy snow in the dead of night not long before he made the call to Tonya. He amended his statement, saying the doctor just took a quick look at Corban and said there was nothing to worry about. The burn was minor. Wade stuck a Band-Aid on it when they got back home and gave Corban a few teaspoons of Jim Beam to help him get to sleep.

What he didn't mention in any of his statements was that he had left the house some time after his phone call to Tonya. His truck had been spotted by the state patrol slightly after 11:00 p.m. about fifteen miles north of Cortez on the Devil's Highway near Cahone. Things were so quiet, they'd run the registration for something to do. So far, Jude hadn't confronted Miller with this information.

"What do you think?" Pratt murmured in her ear as Tonya outpoured to the cameras.

"He's got to be the worst liar I've ever interviewed."

"Look at him. All that weeping and gnashing of teeth." Pratt sounded disgusted. "Who does he think he's kidding? He's only known the kid for a couple of months."

"Most people are going to buy it," Jude said. "The media's eating it up. Just watch—this is going to be a big story."

They'd agonized over the TV plea, but even with Miller's

suspicious behavior, they could not afford to make assumptions. He could simply be feeling guilty because his girlfriend's child had vanished while in his care. If a stranger had, in fact, taken Corban, there was no time to be lost.

Tonya swept a cluster of brassy blond ringlets back from her face and leaned forward just enough so that the viewer's eye would be riveted to her fulsome cleavage.

"So please," she begged with every sign of genuine distress. "My baby needs his mom. It's real cold out there and I'm afraid for him. Please, if you know anything at all or if you have Corban. Please. Phone the number on the screen."

As she broke down, Wade took her in his arms and they sobbed on each other's shoulders. Reporters immediately started shouting questions, and Pratt moved away from Jude's side to take the microphone. A deputy walked them backstage and Jude followed, wanting to resume her interviews before the two of them got a chance to compare their stories. Wade was mumbling into Tonya's ear while they were embracing. Jude took his arm and propelled him a few steps away toward a stern-faced deputy.

"I need to speak to Ms. Perkins," she said firmly. "The deputy will take you back to the interview room and bring you some lunch, Mr. Miller."

Tonya pointlessly wiped mascara from around her eyes and protested over shaky sobs. "I've told you all I can tell you. I want to go and look for him like everyone else. He's *my* baby."

"I understand," Jude said gently. "I know you're worried sick. But I need to go over your statement again to be sure we didn't miss any important details. You were intoxicated during the first interview, so some things might have been kind of fuzzy."

Tonya flushed and lifted both hands to her face. "Why is this happening to me? I haven't been out in weeks, and the first time I have some fun…"

Jude walked her back to an interview room. "Would you like something to eat? Coffee?"

"Just a Diet Pepsi. Oh, God. Where is he?"

Jude asked a deputy to bring the soda and showed Tonya into the room. "I'm going to read you your rights again," she said as a second detective set up the interview to record. The woman had been virtually catatonic the first time they spoke and didn't seem to understand her son was really missing until she saw the first television reports.

"I don't know why you're wasting time talking to me." Tonya sniffled. "I wasn't even there. You should be out looking for Corban. It's freezing. What chance does he have—he's so little."

Before she could work herself into another emotional free fall, Jude touched her arm and said, "Ms. Perkins. The best way you can help Corban is to answer my questions as fully as you can."

Tonya blinked at her. "I don't understand how he got hurt anyway." Her puzzled frown suggested she was starting to fret over Miller's account of events. "He can't even reach the burners. How'd it happen?"

Good question. Jude Mirandized her and reminded her the interview was being filmed on video, then asked, "What was Wade talking about with you back there?"

"He said he loves me and he didn't mean for anything like this to happen. He thinks I blame him."

"What does he think you blame him for?"

"Not being there when they took Corban." She sobbed anew. "It wasn't his fault he had to pick me up from Amberlee's."

"What time was that again?"

Jude gestured for Detective Pete Koertig to join her at the table as he had during her first interview with Tonya. Koertig had recently been promoted to detective and was very much one of the boys. He seemed mystified that Sheriff Pratt had chosen Jude to lead the interviews. When he sat down, he shuffled in his seat and ran a hand over his sandy buzz cut, making it clear he thought it was time for a real investigator to take over.

"I don't know," Tonya said. "About two."

"How did he seem when he arrived?"

Tonya shrugged. "He was wet and dirty from being out in the snow. He had to park the truck down the road some."

"Anything else?"

"I don't remember."

"What happened then?"

"Next thing I woke up in bed. He was taking off my shoes and everything." She smiled. "He's good like that. Sensitive."

Koertig rolled his eyes.

"You don't remember arriving home?" Jude asked. "Pulling into the driveway? Seeing the house?"

Tonya shook her head. "I was out of it."

"You didn't go check on Corban?"

"No."

"Even though you knew he'd been burned and Wade had taken him to the hospital, you didn't look in on him?"

"I didn't think about it. I mean, Wade said he was okay."

"So you went to sleep right away, without going anywhere else in the house?"

"I went to the bathroom is all."

"Your bathroom is directly across the hall from Corban's bedroom, isn't it? You didn't just open his door a crack and look in on him?"

Tonya's cheeks bloomed dark red, and she stared at Jude as if it had just dawned on her that most mothers would have wanted to reassure themselves that their injured toddler was really all right.

Defensively, she said, "I was drunk, okay? I couldn't even stand up. Wade had to hold me on the toilet seat. Anyway, everything was quiet. I didn't want to wake Corban up."

"So it *did* cross your mind to wonder how he was?" Jude asked softly.

"What kind of a mother do you think I am?"

Jude refrained from giving an opinion; she also tried hard to resist a rush to judgment. Tonya Foley had a well-equipped bedroom for her son, with inexpensive but carefully thought-out nursery décor, plenty of toys, a musical mobile of angels suspended from the ceiling, and a clean, comfortable bed. Pictures of the little boy around the house showed a smiling baby who looked healthy. He was a beautiful child with a mischievous Cupid's smile, big dark blue eyes, and a mop of white-blond curls. There was no question a certain type of pedophile would consider him a prize, certainly enough to have targeted him.

It was too soon in the interview to make Tonya defensive; Jude didn't want her to clam up or suddenly demand a lawyer. So, in a soothing tone, she said, "I know this is a nightmare for you, Tonya. Please understand, we're only asking you all these questions in case there's something in the back of your mind that might give us a vital clue, something you might have forgotten all about. We want to find Corban, just as much as you do."

Tonya nodded and wiped her eyes. The door opened and a deputy brought in a couple of cans of Diet Pepsi and a sub. Tonya took one of the cans and cracked it open.

As she gulped down the contents, Jude said, "Tell me about your relationship with Corban's dad." She referred to her notes. "Dan Foley—correct?"

"Yes."

"And Mr. Foley was previously married to your older sister Amberlee?"

"They're divorced now." Tonya pushed the sub aside without inspecting it.

"When did Dan and Amberlee separate?"

"They weren't happy from the start. Ambam...that's what I call her from when we were kids. She was only sixteen when they got married. "

Jude did some quick math. Corban was nineteen months old. Tonya was only twenty-one. She would have been pregnant at eighteen with the child of her sister's husband.

"I understand Dan is suing you for custody of Corban."

Tonya gasped. "Do you think he took him?"

"Do you?"

Tonya concentrated on her Pepsi can. "He would never hurt Corban. If he's got him, that means my baby's okay." Hope could not quite displace the doubt in her tone.

"We're still trying to contact Mr. Foley using the number you gave us," Jude said.

Tonya's mouth shook. "He doesn't have him. He'd never do that to him...break windows... and that goat's head. Dan's a vegetarian. "

She fell silent and glanced sideways as Sheriff Pratt knocked and entered the room. He signaled Jude and she strode over, leaning close so they could speak quietly.

"Just finished interviewing the rest of the night shift at Southwest Memorial," he said grimly. "Miller's story is bullshit. No one remembers him bringing Corban in, and he's not on any of the security tapes."

Jude steered Pratt outside the interview room. "Why in hell make up a story like that in the first place? And why tell the mother?"

"Not the sharpest crayon," Pratt suggested.

"Something obviously happened," Jude thought aloud. "And he

was trying to tell her, but he chickened out. The guy seems to make everything up as he goes along, so maybe he started down the track toward telling the truth, then realized he'd be in trouble and backed off."

"Wanted to make it seem like things were under control...but it's a psychological slip," Pratt suggested. "I'm guessing the baby was injured by then and Miller was looking to cover his ass so she wouldn't think he was negligent when she got home."

"But something went wrong with his plan...something else happened, and he had to hide what he'd done."

"Highly likely." Pratt sounded keyed up. He could smell a big arrest, Jude thought. One that would involve saturation media.

"Do we have results back for the clothes yet?" she asked.

"I'll chase it," Pratt said. "Want us to take another run at him while you work on the mother?"

Jude shook her head. "He'll keep. But turn up the pressure." She glanced around until she spotted the meanest-looking simian-built deputy in the department. "Deputy Linebacker over there...send him in. Tell him to make Miller nervous."

"Gotcha."

"Miller's truck. What kind of state is it in?"

"Looks like your Dakota," Pratt replied. "Packed with fresh snow underneath."

"So he took it out of town around eleven, then didn't do much driving once he got back—not enough to shake off the new snow."

A drive in the mountains during a big snow fall packed heavy but relatively clean snow in every hollow beneath a vehicle. Around town, the roads were shoveled and the pack was dirtier and wetter, spraying up beneath a vehicle in layers over days.

Pratt's cell phone rang and he took the call. Putting his hand over the mouthpiece, he told Jude, "Gotta go."

She took a moment to gather her thoughts. If Miller had lied about taking Corban to the hospital, what did that mean? Did Tonya know something she wasn't saying? Had the two of them come up with a story to hide a crime?

Jude stalked back into the interview room and summoned Koertig. In a low, rapid murmur, she told him, "The boyfriend definitely lied about the hospital. Let's see if she knows more than she's letting on."

"Want me to take over for a bit?"

"Have at it."

Predictably, Koertig marched up, banged on the table, and leaned over Tonya. "Your shithead boyfriend lied about taking your kid to the hospital. Did you know that?"

Tonya's head jerked up. "What are you talking about? He phoned me when he got back. Corban saw the doctor."

"So what you're saying is, the doctors and nurses at the hospital got it all wrong. They said they never saw Corban, but they're lying. Why do you suppose they'd do that?"

"I don't know." Tonya's voice wobbled. "Maybe there's been a mistake."

"You bet there's been a mistake. You made a huge mistake when you went out drinking and left your baby with a violent man."

Tonya's eyes widened with dismay. "You're wrong. Wade would never hurt Corban. He took him to the hospital. Maybe it's another hospital. I don't know."

"Listen, Ms. Perkins. Every hospital in this state has surveillance cameras and fancy computer systems with records of every single person a doctor breathes on so they can ring up those charges. Do you seriously think anyone walks in there they don't know about?"

"But why would he say he took him if he didn't?" Tonya cast a pleading look toward the door where Jude leaned casually against the frame.

"Well, that's the question, isn't it?" Koertig said. "What do you think?"

"I don't know," Tonya answered meekly.

Wanting to capitalize on her uncertainty, Jude moved toward the table and asked, "Tell me something, Tonya. How does Wade discipline your son?"

Tonya's rapid blinks gave her away. "He doesn't hit him, if that's what you're thinking. Just spanking when he's naughty."

"When he's naughty?" Koertig maintained his intimidating proximity. "How often would that be?"

"I don't know." Tonya fought a losing battle with her tears. The mascara applied for the TV cameras coursed down her cheeks. "He's good with Corban. You can ask anyone."

"Oh, we will," Koertig promised darkly.

"So, if Corban was naughty and burnt his hand," Jude conjectured, "he must have been in pain and crying. Maybe even screaming. That would have been stressful. Is Wade the patient type?"

Tonya fell silent, staring into space, her expression a painful testimony to the direction of her thoughts.

"That would be a 'no,'" Koertig surmised.

"If Wade didn't take Corban to the hospital, what do you think happened?" Jude asked.

Tonya seemed to grapple with the question, then her focus sharpened. "He put a Band-Aid on Corban's hand. He told me about that. Maybe he just made up a story about the hospital so I wouldn't worry. That's typical. He's really considerate. Not like most guys."

CHAPTER FOUR

"What were you thinking?" Heather Roache cuffed her brother Matthew around the ear. "If you took that little kid and did anything to him, so help me I'll—"

"I didn't, I swear." Matthew seized her wrist before she could strike him again. "I don't know anything about it. Jesus Christ, what do you think I am?"

"An idiot. A fucking unbelievable idiot." Heather stared at the television as the cameras zoomed in on Tonya Perkins's house. "That goat is wearing your baseball cap. Think no one's going to remember seeing him in our yard with that same cap on all summer?"

Matthew dropped her arm and studied the screen, slack-jawed. "What the fuck…It's in the yard? Oh, man, what are we going to do?"

"*We*?" Heather picked up her purse from the coffee table and fished out her car keys. "*You* are coming with me to see the sheriff."

Matthew shook his head rapidly. "Nah-uh. No way. I'm not getting involved in this shit."

"You *are* involved, and if you don't tell the cops first, they're going to hear it from someone else. How's that going to look?" Heather watched *Law & Order*; she knew her brother's only chance was to come forward and help with inquiries. If they waited for the detectives to find him, he'd be a suspect. "Go take a shower and shave that fuzz off your face," she ordered. "I'm not taking you in there looking like America's Most Wanted."

"I didn't do anything to that kid," Matthew reiterated as Heather dragged him to his feet. "You gotta believe me."

"It's not me you need to convince." Heather shook him hard, furious that he'd been so stupid and that their family name was about to be dragged through the mud all over again. Like it wasn't bad enough that their mom ran off with a high school kid and their dad made a public spectacle of himself by dying in the act with a hooker.

Heather was eighteen when that happened, so she could handle it. But Matthew was four years younger. He'd had a rough time of it. Heather often thought that was why he'd flunked out of high school and ended up parked on her sofa, watching reruns of *Friends*.

Well, she wasn't ready to write him off yet, and she believed him about the missing toddler. If Matthew had taken a baby, it would be here in her home, waiting for her to feed it; Heather had no doubt about that. No—her little brother might be many things, but he wasn't a child kidnapper. People like that wanted ransoms or were filthy perverts. Heather had seen the porno magazines Matthew kept under his mattress. They were the normal kind with naked women in crude poses.

Close to tears herself, she marched him along the hallway and deposited him outside his bedroom. He was crying, repeating over and over that he was sorry and he never touched that little boy.

In the end, she took pity and hugged him, saying just like she did when they were younger, "Everything's going to be okay. You made a stupid mistake, that's all."

Sniffling into her shoulder, he mumbled, "It wasn't my idea."

Heather suspected as much. It was impossible to imagine Matthew coming up with anything as creative, or nasty, as killing his pet goat, smashing up an ex's house, then leaving the goat's head in the yard like a Satanic symbol.

"Then whose bright idea was it?" Not that she needed to ask. She already knew exactly which of her brother's loser buddies would come up with a crazy scheme like this one.

Matthew confirmed her suspicions. "Gums said I needed to teach her a lesson."

"You know better than to pay attention to Gu…Hank Thompson. He's crazy, or did you forget that?"

Matthew stared at the TV screen. "Maybe people will think a biker gang did it."

"A biker gang is going to ride their Harleys into town in the middle of a snowstorm, come here, kill your goat, then go vandalize Tonya's house, and leave the goat's head as a warning like with the horse in the *Godfather*?"

Matthew nodded as if the cops might actually buy this ridiculous story. "We can say someone stole him from out back."

Right out of patience, Heather shoved him in his bedroom door. "You are going to tell the sheriff the truth. And you're going to tell him it was all Hank's idea and you just went along with it."

"Fuck. He'll kill me with his bare hands."

"You should have thought about that before you left a whole mess of evidence on that slut's property."

❖

Wade Miller took out his comb and ran his thumb slowly along the prongs. "You gotta understand. I couldn't tell Tonya. She'd go nuts."

"So there never was a hospital visit?"

"It was her sister's party. I didn't want to spoil it."

"How did Corban burn his hand?"

"I was cooking his dinner. Had him up next to me on a stool. He goes and touches the skillet. Dunno how many times I told him not to do that, but he always has to learn the hard way."

Jude remained silent, just to see if he was going to embellish this account any further. So far, it was the longest answer they'd had from him.

"What time did that happen?"

He picked a pimple on his chin as he contemplated the question. "Maybe nine."

"You were cooking a baby's dinner at nine o'clock?"

"Could have been eight, I suppose. Don't wear a watch." Miller flashed his hands as evidence.

"And what happened then?"

"He cried some but I fixed him up. Put on a bandage."

"Did he stop crying?"

Miller hesitated. "Not for a while."

"You must have been worried," Jude said sympathetically. "In charge of your girlfriend's baby and he hurts himself. How big was the burn area? Can you draw it for us?"

She slid a sheet of paper and pen across the desk, and Miller sketched out an image about an inch long and quarter of an inch wide.

Jude gave a low whistle. "Pretty nasty on a little hand like his. It would have stretched right across his palm."

Miller's mouth tightened, and for a split second a flash of anger displaced the dopey solemnity of his manner. He said, "Yeah, well, it wasn't deep. Nothing serious."

"It didn't bleed?"

"No."

"Well, that's puzzling," Jude said. "Because I was just told that our lab found blood on your clothing. Is it Corban's?"

He blinked. "Guess it could be. He's always getting nose bleeds and shit."

Jude stared at him. As the seconds passed, he grew restless and picked up the comb he'd dropped on the table a few minutes earlier. His stringy black mullet didn't need the extra attention, but he worked on it anyway.

In a town like Cortez, Wade Miller was what passed for tall, dark, and handsome, Jude supposed. Lean and well built, he wore boot-cut jeans, a flashy belt buckle, and a flannel shirt. A dark stubble shadowed his jaw; clearly he hadn't shaved that morning. He dealt with a surefire unibrow, probably by plucking, and he seemed self-conscious of both his balding head and his teeth, which were uneven and slightly discolored. Jude figured his mumbling speech pattern was a habit he'd cultivated to avoid displaying them.

Looking uneasy, he wiped his comb on his pants, then dropped it on the table. "So, you guys through with me now?"

Jude smiled pleasantly. "Actually, I was wondering why you didn't take Corban to the hospital? You must have thought about it or you wouldn't have made up that story for Tonya."

Miller avoided looking at her. "I was going to. But they were parked outside. I heard them. Tonya's ex and his buddies. They're always pulling stunts like that."

"Like what?"

"They follow me sometimes, like they're trying to get into something. You know, to make me mad. Road rage. Shit like that. And they've done stuff to my place. Painted obscenities on the wall, left dog turds on my doorstep... Matt Roache was real pissed that Tonya dumped him. They were engaged."

"I'll need some names," Jude said. Obviously Miller was expecting her to construe from these subtle hints that this ex and his pal were principal suspects in the window smashing and goat's head symbolism, and, by inference, Corban's disappearance. "What time did you notice them out there?"

"Ten thirty, maybe." Miller finished jotting names on the notepad she'd provided and added, "If I didn't have the kid to look after, I'd have gone out there and taken care of it."

"So, you saw these men parked outside Ms. Perkins's home before or after you called her at the bar?"

"After."

"Was Corban still crying then?"

Miller frowned like he was straining to remember. "Can't say exactly. He calmed down after I gave him the Jim Beam."

What would it take to put a two-year-old in a coma—a few ounces of 80 proof? Jude's mind ran with the scenario. Corban crying relentlessly after burning his hand. Miller dosing the child with bourbon a few times until he falls asleep. Eventually he realizes Corban is unconscious. He panics...

"How much bourbon did you give him?" She kept her tone bland.

"Dunno. A few spoonfuls."

"When was the last time you saw Corban?"

"I told the other deputy."

"And now you can tell me."

Miller looked restless. "Right about when I phoned Tonya."

"Which makes it around ten?"

"If you say so." He didn't lift his voice to reply, but Jude sensed it was a close thing.

"How was he then?" she asked.

"Asleep."

"You sound very sure about that. A moment ago you couldn't be certain if he was crying at ten thirty. Yet now you're telling me he was asleep at ten, when you called Tonya. Which one is it?"

Again a brief flare of anger sharpened his dopey stare, and his mouth compressed. "He was asleep."

Jude produced a slightly puzzled smile. "You seem tense with this line of questioning, Mr. Miller. Is there something you're not telling us?"

"No." A belligerent glare.

"Mr. Miller," Jude prompted softly. "We know things can go wrong with kids through no fault of the adults caring for them…tragic, unintentional accidents. If something happened to Corban, now is the time to tell us."

Miller stared down at the desk for several seconds, and when he lifted his head Jude could not read his expression. Blank blue eyes met hers and Miller said, with disingenuous confusion, "Are you accusing me of something? Do you think I hurt him?"

"Did you?" Jude asked, watching for the fleeting, quickly suppressed microexpressions that could betray what Miller was really feeling.

"Why would I do a thing like that?"

"You tell me," Jude said mildly. "I heard you don't like him much."

"That's bullshit."

Jude growled softly, "Let's not play games, Mr. Miller. You live in a small town. You think people don't notice things? We have Brittany Kemple in the next room giving us a statement right now. Telling us all about your violent temper and how you once told her the only thing Corban Foley was good for was feeding to your dogs."

Miller lurched to his feet. "Brittany Kemple's a fucking crazy woman and so are you if you believe anything that bitch tells you."

Jude rose instantly and ordered him to sit down. For a few seconds it seemed Miller might actually take a swing at her. If he'd had a gun in his hand, he'd have used it. Or tried to.

She almost hoped he would try to land a punch, but if Brittany Kemple was any indication, the women he liked to slap around were former cheerleaders who weighed 100 pounds soaking wet. At 5' 10" with muscle she didn't bother to hide, a badge, and a large colleague standing a few feet away just waiting for a nod from her, Jude was a whole different ball game.

She stared him down, noting with interest that all trace of dopey innocence had left his eyes. Miller looked downright menacing when he let the harmless hick veneer slip. But, apparently, he could control his hotheaded impulses when he needed to.

His mouth twisted faintly, and he dropped his butt back onto the seat. "Hey, dude, I get it," he announced. "You're the cop and I'm the witness. You gotta know if I'm for real, so you wind me up and wait and see what happens."

"He watches TV," Jude commented to Koertig. It was her cue for him to join the interrogation. Facing Miller again, she set up the topic. "That goat's head. When did you first see it?"

"After I noticed Corban was missing."

"You went outside at that point?" She gave Pete Koertig a nod.

He read ponderously from Miller's earlier statement, "I walked around the house looking for him, but he likes hiding in places. I thought he'd gone to sleep in a cupboard or something, so I went back to bed."

Koertig bent down next to Miller and said with mocking disbelief, "Now you're telling us you went outside and saw that goat's head, *then* you went back to bed?"

"No. I saw it after I got up again." Tiny beads of perspiration gathered across their subject's forehead.

"What time was that?"

Miller pointed at the statement Koertig was holding. "I already told you."

"I want to hear it again." Koertig spoke slowly and patiently, like he was talking to the learning-challenged.

He did pleasant menace very well, Jude reflected. Koertig was a stocky, well-scrubbed, Nordic-looking man whose youth and single-minded preoccupation with his wife's marathon training program prevented him from declining into the pink and white chubbiness that seemed to prevail in his family. Two of his siblings ran a local bakery Jude patronized. Both looked like they sampled the wares too frequently.

Most days Koertig ran at least six miles with his wife before he showed up to work. This feat engendered awe at the Montezuma County Sheriff's Office, where folks found something odd about any guy organizing his life so he could throw wet sponges at his spouse during the Bolder Boulder race. Certainly if Jude had to pick from among the MCSO officers the man most likely to be his wife's chief coach and support crew, Pete Koertig would have been at the bottom of her list.

Miller had reverted to whiny defensiveness once more. He said, "Guess it must have been around four when I saw it."

"What were you wearing?" Koertig asked.

With a bemused frown, Miller said, "T-shirt and shorts."

"So, what you're saying is you woke from a deep sleep and decided maybe the kid wasn't hiding in a cupboard after all. You went outdoors in minus twenty degrees wearing your Jockeys, walked around to the front of the house, and saw the goat's head?"

"Yeah."

"Now see, that doesn't make any sense to me." Koertig glanced toward Jude. "How much snow did we have last night, Detective?"

"Here in Cortez, it must have been a foot. Enough to cover that goat's head."

"So you saw a lump in the snow," Koertig concluded. "You went out there and dug the snow away with your bare hands. Is that how it went down, Mr. Miller?"

"Yeah."

"What did you do then?"

"I saw the broken windows, and I went in the house and woke Tonya up."

"You left the goat's head where it was?" Jude asked.

"Yeah." Miller's eyes flickered. Smugly, he said, "I knew it was evidence."

"Evidence of what?"

"That fucking Matt Roache and Gums Thompson were there and they did something."

"Something to Corban?" Jude prompted.

"What else? He's gone, isn't he?" Miller grabbed a tissue and blew his nose, overwhelmed with emotion all of a sudden.

The tears could easily be genuine, Jude conceded. He could be feeling sorry for himself, aware he was in deep and seeing no way out. Or he was innocent, exhausted, and genuinely distressed over the child's disappearance and the stress of being interrogated for hours. But she doubted it. Although Miller presented as an emotional subject, she had a sense that he was much more calculating than that.

She deliberated on his reply for a few seconds. They had just caught him out in a lie. The blood evidence from Tonya Perkins's living room showed that the goat's head had been in the room, probably hurled through the broken window. Someone with Miller's foot size had subsequently removed it and covered the bloody area with a rug. Trace suggested that the rug was previously situated in front of the dresser in Tonya's bedroom. The head was then transported outdoors and placed in the middle of the yard.

No one could have gained access through the broken windows, and the doors showed no signs of forced entry. Who else but Miller could have moved the goat's head and rearranged the scene? Jude concluded he'd staged what he hoped would come across as sinister and symbolic. Did he imagine the police would speculate that Devil worshipers killed a goat and stole a baby for some kind of sick ritual?

She decided to hold back what they knew about the goat's head and see how many more lies Miller would tell. Signaling Koertig to work with her, she softened her tone and said, like she was buying the Satanic angle, "It sure sounds like these individuals are mixed up in something nasty."

She watched Miller closely and caught a faint relaxation in the line of his mouth and jaw. He tapped a name on the list he'd written. "Talk to him first. He's the ringleader."

"Gums Thompson. Do you know him, Detective?" she asked Koertig.

"Local mental patient," he confirmed.

This seemed to please Miller, who got cocky all of a sudden and announced in the manner of a man who'd just added two and two, "Come to think of it, he made some threats a while back. I told Tonya to ignore him. But now…"

"Could you be more specific?" Jude asked like she'd taken the bait.

"He told her to stop seeing me or she'd be sorry, and so would her kid."

"When was that?"

"Dunno. Three weeks ago, maybe."

Jude nodded sagely and told Koertig, "Get these individuals brought in. I want them dragged out of their beds and scared shitless."

Miller seemed to be trying to keep the glee off his face as Jude and Koertig got to their feet and made a show of losing interest in him.

"We'll continue this interview later, Mr. Miller," Jude said, moving toward the door.

"Can I get a burger or something?"

"No problem." Like it was an afterthought, she added, "One more question. We have a report from state patrol that your truck was seen on Highway 666 at around eleven last night. Care to explain that?"

She waited for an outright denial, but Miller said, "Oh, yeah. Right. I forgot about that. Tonya was out of disposables so I went to pick some up from the late-night gas station."

"You needed to change Corban?"

"No, but Tonya would have been pissed at me. She asked me to get some at the supermarket before I came over to her place, but I forgot."

"Why travel so far?"

"Couldn't find anything open in Cortez, so I thought I'd try Dove Creek."

"I see. And did you find the diapers in the end?"

He shook his head solemnly. "No, but I tried. That's gotta count for something."

Jude managed to keep her tone completely bland. "Would you mind if we searched your truck?"

"Sure. Corban rides with me all the time. He loves that truck."

Jude smiled faintly. Miller was letting them know that any evidence they found would mean nothing. All the same, Jude was amazed he'd agreed to let them take a look. If he had something to hide, the guy was either genuinely stupid or arrogant enough to believe he'd covered his ass.

She wondered if arrogance had factored into his acknowledgement about the Triple Six. Whatever the motivation, if they uncovered anything in the vicinity of Cahone, Miller had just put himself there by his own admission. It was probably his biggest mistake yet. She could tell Koertig was thinking exactly the same thing as they left the interview room.

He said, "Ate a bowl of stupid for breakfast."

"We need to know everything about this guy," Jude said. "Interview all his buddies. I want behavior patterns, a full history of acts of rage, a record of every word he ever spoke about Corban. And find out if he's ever had a girlfriend with kids before Ms. Perkins. If he has, bring her in."

Pratt collared her as she and Koertig exited the hallway into the main office area. "What do you think?"

"Opportunity and motive," Jude mused. "Plus statistical likelihood and odd behavior. And Cahone...that's in close proximity to several bodies of water. "

"I got three teams lined up to search the Dolores and the reservoir up there first thing in the morning," Pratt said, hot on the case. "Your boy and his hound ready to start in again at first light?"

"No problem. Are you considering divers?"

"Not if I can help it." Pratt pulled a man-sized tissue from the box beneath his arm and grumbled, "Ka-ching, ka-ching."

After he'd turned aside and blown his nose, Jude asked, "Think there's any chance he's alive?"

Pratt chewed it over for a few seconds. "Times like this, I get to thinking what the job does for your mental outlook."

"I know what you're saying."

"You jump to negative conclusions."

"It's hard not to."

"What's wrong with people?" Emotion altered Pratt's voice. "He's just a baby."

"Do you want me to arrest Miller, sir?" It had crossed Jude's mind that the pressure of charges being filed could net a confession. It often did with domestic offenders who hadn't been in the system. They tended to believe what they were told about getting a better deal if they came clean, and the guilt-stricken ones were usually desperate to unburden themselves.

"What have we got on him?" Pratt asked.

"It's all circumstantial so far."

"I don't want him lawyering up."

"Then we'll have to send him home some time soon, and we need for Perkins to play ball. I want her to wear a wire."

Pratt looked startled. "Can we do that?"

"He's a suspect in a child abduction and possible homicide. If he's going to confess anything to his girlfriend, it's probably going to happen as soon as they're back together alone."

"Think you can talk her into it?"

"Let's give it twenty-four hours," Jude said. "He's told enough lies for us to hold him a while longer."

"He's going to ask for a lawyer," Pratt warned.

"I'm not so sure." Jude was still trying to get a fix on Miller's psychology. "I think he's holding off so he can paint himself as a poor dumb schmuck caught up in events outside his control. He's arrogant enough to believe he can pull off an act like that. Maybe he thinks a lawyer might make him look smart. And guilty."

Pratt barked a hoarse laugh. "Like he isn't."

CHAPTER FIVE

"A re you going to join the search?" Debbie Basher asked the woman at the opposite end of her sofa.

Lonewolf, whose real name was Sandy Lane, took a break from cleaning her twelve gauge to reply, "I thought about it."

"I'll come, too, if you want."

"I'm not sure what the point is. My money says the kid's dead." Lonewolf set the shotgun aside and returned her attention to the evening news. "Check out the boyfriend. That's one guilty sonofabitch."

Debbie tried to imagine how she would feel in his shoes. "He must be a wreck. I mean, he was supposed to be looking after the baby and now this."

"My point exactly. Two-year-olds don't just up and wander off in the middle of the night," Lone said. "And when something like this happens it's almost always the stepfather or the boyfriend."

"He doesn't seem very bright."

Lone's eyes came to rest on Debbie, and her expression softened. "Do you always think the best of people?"

"I try to."

"That must get pretty disappointing."

"Sometimes." Debbie looked away, wanting to hide the emotion she knew was written on her face. Lonewolf could read her with disturbing accuracy. It had been that way since they first met.

Debbie liked to think about that early fall day because it reminded her that life could deliver gifts as unexpectedly as blows. She had been hiking in the LaSal Creek Canyon, on the Utah side of the state line, stopping every so often to take photos of the astonishing red rock formations. When she first heard the terrible screams, she panicked, running this way and that, trying to fathom their direction. She wanted to persuade herself she'd only heard the shrill delight of a young woman

ROSE BEECHAM

cavorting with friends along the trail, but another more bloodcurdling shriek pierced the still mountain air, and this time the woman was screaming for help.

Debbie threw off her backpack and started running. The sound was close, just past a rock formation and down into a gully off the track. Terrified, her mind swapping one scenario for the next—a bad fall from the rocks, a rape in progress—Debbie almost tumbled over a mountain bike lying across the track. At the same exact moment she saw a sight she would never forget as long as she lived. A mountain lion was dragging a woman by one foot up toward a rocky overhang.

Debbie had been warned about wilderness hazards like this before she'd moved to the Southwest, but she'd never expected one to happen to her.

The woman saw her, too, and they shared one frozen instant of horror before she sobbed, "Help me! For God's sake, help me. Oh, Jesus."

Debbie grabbed the bike and plunged down the slope, yelling at the top of her lungs, "Get off her, you monster. Go!"

She struck the big cat a clumsy blow across the head with the front wheel of the bike. It growled at her from deep in its chest, but kept hold of the woman's foot. Debbie hit it again as hard as she could and started yelling for help in case anyone could hear her.

The woman was sobbing and begging her not to leave. The lion's mouth was red with blood.

Debbie threw the bike down and was looking frantically around for something that would make a better weapon, when a low, emphatic voice commanded, "Stand where you are and don't move."

Adrenalin and terror made it almost impossible for Debbie to do as she was told, yet the sight of a figure in army fatigues, standing atop the outcrop, a rifle trained on the lion, rooted her to the spot.

"Now back away," she was ordered. "One step at a time and keep looking at the cat, dead in the eye."

Debbie hadn't taken two steps when the soldier opened fire. Several shots in rapid succession echoed across the red wilderness, and the mountain lion slumped over the woman.

Telling Debbie to stay back, the soldier quickly descended. It was only then that Debbie realized the rescuer was a woman. She was not as tall as she'd seemed, standing high above with the rifle braced against her shoulder, but she was strongly built and radiated the kind of controlled power and confidence Debbie couldn't imagine ever possessing.

She probed the lion with her foot as she kept her rifle trained towards its head. "It's dead."

Debbie didn't know what to say. She felt frozen with shock. She bent down and touched the lion's flank, horrified, yet sad for the creature. Humans had intruded so far on its habitat that it had lost most of its usual prey. Now it had been killed for doing what its nature dictated.

"Stay calm." A firm hand landed on Debbie's shoulder. "I need your help."

Debbie's teeth were chattering but she managed a timid smile. "What do you want me to do?"

A pair of glittering Windex-blue eyes locked with hers. "Take off your T-shirt. We need to see to her leg so she doesn't lose any more blood."

Debbie didn't think twice. She pulled her top over her head and handed it to the woman, who tore it effortlessly into strips. The lion's victim was unconscious, which was a blessing, Debbie thought, as they extracted her mangled leg.

"Oh, my God," she said, gazing down at the hamburger mess of blood and bone. "How are we going to get her out of here?"

But the soldier was already on her cell phone, calling for a search-and-rescue chopper. She even gave coordinates. Squatting down, she removed her camouflage shirt, folded it, and placed it beneath the injured woman's head. Underneath, she was wearing a close-fitting khaki tank that revealed powerful, deeply tanned arms and muscular breasts that barely gave contour to the cotton fabric. Several chains loosely encircled her neck with various medallions suspended from them. Debbie recognized a St. Christopher, a gold wedding ring, and what looked like dog tags.

"It's the shock that'll kill her," she told Debbie. "I think they can save the foot."

Debbie promptly burst into tears and blabbed out her thanks. She was shaking all over, and her teeth chattered so badly she couldn't even finish a sentence. The soldier took her firmly by the shoulders and shook her once. "Listen to me." The voice was laced with authority. "We have a job to do until the medics get here. This woman is counting on us. Do you understand?"

Debbie wasn't sure if she was just too terrified to do anything but obey, or if she had some steely inner core she'd never known about. Squeaking, "Yes," she pulled herself together and asked, "What do you want me to do?"

Ten minutes later, the woman was still alive and Debbie had learned that the soldier was not National Guard as she'd assumed, but a veteran who'd recently been honorably discharged after her second tour of duty in Iraq. By sheer good luck she happened to be in the vicinity keeping herself combat-ready when the attack happened. Her name was Sandy Lane.

She said, "You can call me Lone. All my buddies do."

"Lone?"

"Short for Lonewolf." The terse line of her mouth relaxed a little. This was, Debbie guessed, her version of a smile. "I got the nick because I'm the one always living on the edge."

"Do you miss it?" Debbie asked. "The army?"

"I miss my buddies."

"When did you leave?"

"A year ago."

Debbie wanted to ask why, but she sensed a contained emotion in this woman that she couldn't interpret and guessed the subject was sensitive. She asked, instead, "What's it really like over there in Iraq?"

"Well, let's see. You don't know who's a friend and who's an enemy. You see your best friend blown to pieces in front of you when he's trying to carry a child to safety. Nothing makes any sense. Not to them and not to us." Her face registered a flicker of surprise, as if her emphatic response had taken her aback. She fell silent.

"I think you're very brave," Debbie whispered. "I could never do what you did."

Lone gave her a long hard look. "Yes you could. You proved it when you were whacking that lion over the head with your bike. You were defenseless, yet you took on an enemy twice your size. You risked your life for a complete stranger. If that isn't courage, what is?"

Heat rushed to Debbie's cheeks. "I guess no one knows what they're really capable of until something like that happens."

The intensity left Lone's gaze and she seemed to be looking straight through Debbie. In a tone that was flat and detached, she said, "People are capable of almost anything. Good, and bad."

It struck Debbie then that Lone was damaged. Over the six months they'd been friends since then, she'd glimpsed the same injured spirit a few times in sharper focus and realized that she didn't know Lone at all; she only knew the part of her she chose to show the world.

Theirs was a strange friendship. Debbie thought it probably filled a gap for both of them. When she'd moved to the Four Corners region from Denver two years earlier, she'd assumed some of her city friendships wouldn't survive the distance. But as it turned out, the breakup of her relationship was the factor that changed everything. Her friends were really Meg's, she'd learned, and when they'd had to choose, they chose Meg.

In a way, it made sense. Meg had a new partner to share in the couples outings they'd always enjoyed. Whereas Debbie was single and lived in the middle of nowhere. Paradox Valley. Who could even find it? No one from her former life had bothered to try.

Meg was still living in their house in Park Hill; Debbie had walked out when she discovered Meg was cheating on her. They'd had a couple of conversations about Meg buying her out, but so far nothing had happened. Whenever Debbie mentioned it, Meg said she needed time to get in a position to pay the higher mortgage. Debbie knew her excuse was weak, but she didn't have the money or the stomach to go to a lawyer and fight. She was depressed, and that sapped her energy and confidence. She'd promised herself that when she felt better she would do something about her financial situation. But time had passed and she had drifted along, feeling kind of lost.

How did you get to be thirty-five and suddenly find you were friendless? For a time, Debbie had determinedly kept up the phone calls and emails, but then she embarked on one of those experiments that reveal more than you want to know. She stopped writing and phoning and waited to see who would contact her. After a year, when the silence got truly deafening, she gave up making excuses for everyone and faced reality. Nobody cared. She was more alone than she'd ever realized.

Her mother would call it poetic justice. Debbie had let her former friends drift away in her midtwenties when she left her job and apartment in Greenville to move to Denver and be with Meg. Now, a decade later, she had no lover, and, apart from her parents, no one gave a damn if she was dead or alive. Only Lonewolf.

They spoke almost every day and Lone often showed up

unannounced, sometimes in the middle of the night. She would always have some plausible reason for stopping by—there was a bear in the area, or the snow was going to be extra heavy, and she would stay over and help Debbie shovel the driveway the next morning. That had been her pretext tonight.

Debbie thought the real reason for most of her visits was that she liked home cooking and wasn't gifted in the kitchen herself. Tonight she had slapped a couple of packs of meat on the counter as she came in the door, premium fillets, the kind Debbie's budget didn't stretch to. Debbie worried about accepting these gifts, but she appreciated the gesture and didn't want to insult Lone by turning her down. Besides, Lone ate at her table often enough that it was only fair she contributed. Debbie would have done the same.

With a quick sideways glance at her guest, she asked, "Is that a new sweater? It looks homemade."

"Yeah. My mom sent it. She bought it from an old lady she knows who knits for extra income."

"You should invite her out here in the spring." Lone was an only child with divorced parents. She seemed close to both of them.

Debbie envied that. Her own mother lived for her grandchildren and regarded Debbie as a failure for her lackluster breeding performance. Maternal phone calls revolved around Debbie's older brother, Adam, and his ever-expanding family. Not only was he heterosexual and fertile, he was also a pastor at the Harvest of Hope Evangelical Church in Greenville. It just didn't get any better than that, and Debbie's mom needed to remind her of this fact at every opportunity.

She had always stopped short of insulting Debbie over her sexuality, preferring to ignore the topic entirely, and to be fair, she told Debbie she loved her "no matter what your father would have thought." Debbie sent her flowers on Mother's Day and drove home to South Carolina once a year for Thanksgiving, otherwise known as purgatory, where she got to see proof of Adam's procreative talents firsthand. She couldn't even remember the names of all her nieces and nephews, and she'd lost count of how many there were. Ten, last Thanksgiving, or was it eleven counting the newest baby? None of them was named after her. Huge surprise.

"Mom's not big on wide-open spaces," Lone said. "She gets antsy if there's no shoe stores nearby."

Debbie laughed. From the descriptions she'd heard, Lone's mom was the glamorous type. She'd dumped two husbands so far and was now dating a personal fitness trainer half her age who had his own workout video. Lone's dad had been a drinker and a wife beater, and he was gone before Lone was even born. Husband number two was the man Lone called "Dad." He had managed to stay married to her mom for almost twenty years. After he retired from the military, he bought a car dealership in Abilene. Lone got all her vehicles from him at cost. She said if Debbie ever wanted to trade up, she'd get her a deal.

Lone raised the TV volume when the Montezuma County sheriff started talking about the missing child. They were going to pull out all the stops tomorrow, according to the news anchor. The search would kick off at first light to take advantage of a break in the weather.

"I am making a personal plea to every able-bodied man or woman in this and surrounding counties to join us," the sheriff said. "Little Corban Foley is out there somewhere, and I have personally promised his mom we are going to bring him home."

"He thinks the kid is dead," Lone said. "And he thinks the boyfriend did it."

"How do you know?" Debbie protested. "He says he's going to bring him home."

"Notice how he didn't say the word 'alive.'"

"You're being paranoid."

"Doesn't mean I'm wrong."

"I'm going to join the search," Debbie announced after thinking things through for a few seconds. "I don't think I could ever forgive myself if they found that little boy too late…if extra people would have made all the difference."

"Okay, we'll both go." Lone sounded resigned. She ran one of her sinewy hands over her hair and Debbie imagined, as she often did, how good she would look with blond highlights.

Debbie couldn't understand why anyone would put up with boring old mouse brown if they didn't have to. Bleached streaks would make Lone's unusually blue eyes even more arresting than they were. The thought unsettled her and she stared at Lone more intently than usual, trying to figure out if she felt queasy because she found her sexually attractive, even though they were just friends, or because going on the search meant she would have to be outdoors. Since the mountain lion incident, Debbie wanted to throw up every time she was in an open space.

She let her eyes wander from Lone's attractive profile down her body to her thighs. Even the heavy khaki of her pants could not hide their muscularity. Lone kept herself fighting fit. She told Debbie it was essential to be prepared—you never knew when you could be called upon to take action. The mountain lion was proof.

Debbie pictured Lone as she'd looked that day, stripped down to her T-shirt, a fine sheen of perspiration accentuating the play of muscles beneath her smooth, tanned skin. Debbie wished she was in such great shape herself. She had a treadmill in the spare room, but she only used it after she saw heavy women on TV talking about their weight. She wondered what Lone would think of her pale, ordinary body, naked. The idea made her draw a jittery breath.

Lately she'd been going down that path too often, imagining how it could be, making love with Lone. She fought off the idea. Sex changed everything, and their friendship meant too much to risk destroying it. She lifted her eyes and gave a small start to find Lone watching her. Embarrassed that she'd been caught staring, Debbie gave a nervous giggle.

Lone's expression held the usual mix of wariness and concentration. "Everything okay," she asked, and for once Debbie wished there was something in her eyes other than gentle regard.

But she didn't know if Lone was even a lesbian; she'd made an assumption about that based on her looks and the fact that she'd been in the military. Feeling awkward, she blurted out, "I was just wondering…" The words eluded her.

This was not the right part of the country to ask someone about their lifestyle preferences. What if Lone took offense? What if she was straight and then wondered about Debbie? Her part-time hairdresser job was already precarious in the tough economic conditions; she'd have no customers if people knew she was a lesbian. It was hard living in the closet after so many years being out in Denver, but she wasn't going to take a stand if it meant throwing her one source of income away. Political statements were for those who could afford the consequences.

Lone angled her head and gave a small encouraging nod. "What were you wondering, Debbie doll?"

Debbie couldn't help but smile over the pet name Lone had taken to using for her. "It's not important." A roundabout approach occurred to her then, and she added, "I was just wondering if you were ever married."

"Do I look like the marrying type?"

Debbie caught her hands together in her lap so her nerves wouldn't show. "Not really. I was just curious."

"Are you asking if I'm gay?" Lone inquired with a directness that startled Debbie.

She blushed and risked a darting glance at Lone's face. What she saw there made her mouth even drier than it already was. The kindly regard had been replaced by a frank, sensual gaze. Debbie found herself held captive by those eyes, fascinated by the mosaic of blue and green studding each iris, and the way the pupils pulsed, pooling limitless black into the tiny oceans that encircled them.

"It's none of my business," she said weakly.

Lone reached for one of Debbie's hands and lifted it to her mouth. With surprising softness she brushed her lips over the knuckles. "Does that answer you?"

"Yes." Debbie thought her lungs were going to burst. "Me, too. I mean, I'm a lesbian, as well."

"I know."

"You do?" Alarmed, Debbie stared down at her dusty rose corduroy pants and floral shirt. She'd always thought she was the last person anyone would mistake for a lesbian.

"Don't worry. No one would guess unless you had it tattooed on your head."

"But you did."

"I pay attention and I've been in your house." At Debbie's frown, Lone said, "Two cats. Crystals in the kitchen window. Melissa Etheridge and the Indigo Girls in the CD rack. *Desert Hearts* inside the *Sleepless in Seattle* case on your DVD shelf. Copies of *Lesbian Connection* facedown under the trash basket in your bathroom—"

"You searched my house." The accusation fell out before Debbie could think twice.

Lone released her hand. "I didn't have to. You left it all out there."

"I'm not used to hiding."

"I can tell." Lone seemed very serious all of a sudden. "Look, I don't want to scare you, but these days even our basic liberties are under attack. If you don't think a minority could ever be rounded up in this country, think again. People like us need to take some basic precautions."

"But we haven't done anything."

"That's not the point. The point is, the signs are already there. The military industrial complex doesn't want the American public noticing what's really going on in Iraq, so their flunkies at the White House are blowing smoke up our asses every day. They own the media, remember."

Debbie thought that was an overstatement, but she didn't want to argue. Besides, what did she know about politics? As far as she was concerned everyone in Washington was equally disinterested in the lives of ordinary people. She had registered Republican, like her parents, when she first voted, but these days she supported Independents or Democrats. Meg had been the one who was interested in politics.

Lone was still talking, mostly about oil, the dollar, and OPEC. Debbie only understood every third word until the conclusion, "So, you see, homosexuals are the perfect target."

"You're right," Debbie agreed. "But the Marriage Amendment Bill won't pass. It's just a political stunt."

"That's not the point," Lone said patiently. "The point is that propaganda feeds the social climate. We are at greater risk because the government is sending a message that it's okay to discriminate against us. Hitler didn't declare war on the Jews overnight. He softened the public up first with propaganda and changes to the law. Sound familiar?"

"I never thought about it that way."

Debbie felt a little defensive. She and Meg had volunteered at Pride events sometimes and had gone to a few fundraisers, but most of the people they knew thought the gay marriage debate was a phony issue and the government would let go of it when they found something else to scare conservative voters with. Meg always said the best way to deal with prejudice was to set a good example and don't look for trouble.

Trying to lighten up the conversation, she said, "I can't believe it took us six months to come out to each other."

This raised a faint smile. "There had to be trust."

A lightbulb flicked on in Debbie's head, and she suddenly understood why she'd avoided seeing Lone as anything but a friend. The breakup with Meg had damaged her trust so badly she didn't want to be vulnerable again. Another thought intruded. Lone had known she was a lesbian all along, and yet she'd never tried to change the footing of their relationship. Why? Wasn't she interested?

Filled with apprehension, Debbie asked, "Lone, do you think I'm attractive."

"You're beautiful. Inside and out."

The answer wasn't exactly what Debbie wanted to hear. She took another stab at the question. "I guess I'm trying to ask if *you're* attracted to me."

Very romantic. Debbie sighed. She'd never been any good at chatting up women; she hadn't had much opportunity to practice. Meg was her very first girlfriend, the only lover she'd known. Even now, she couldn't allow herself a mild fantasy about Lone without feeling guilty.

To her surprise, Lone got to her feet and extended a hand. "Come here."

When Debbie allowed herself to be drawn up, she was immediately in Lone's arms, and a bewildering flood of emotion engulfed her. She wanted to laugh and burst into tears all at once; it had been so long since anybody held her like she mattered. She felt very small against Lone's powerful body, and even smaller when she was lifted from her feet and Lone held her in the air so their faces were level.

Lone looked her dead in the eye and asked gravely, "Permission to kiss my Debbie doll."

Debbie giggled. She felt breathless and giddy, flabbergasted by this turn of events. "Permission granted."

The kiss was everything she'd imagined and more. And every passionate caress that followed reminded Debbie that she was not only a woman, but a desirable one. Lone took her to bed and made love to her with such hungry intensity, Debbie had no idea how she'd managed to hide her cravings for so long. She couldn't imagine having that much self-control, but she supposed it was something the army must have taught.

That, and astonishing stamina.

For which she silently thanked the U.S. government as she lay cradled in Lone's arms in the still of predawn. More exhausted than she'd been in her life, she trailed a hand over the hard contours of Lone's torso and belly, down her hip and thigh, and marveled that they'd begun the day in one relationship and ended it in another. And it felt so right that her fears seemed silly. Tilting her head back, she looked up, wanting to see her new lover asleep. But a pair of night-dark eyes drew hers.

Lone asked, "Can't sleep, baby?"

"I was just laying here thinking how everything can change so fast."

Lone rolled onto her side and cupped Debbie's chin with her hand. "I promise I'll take good care of you."

Debbie sighed contentedly. "I'll take care of you too, Lone."

A knee parted her thighs, and yet again she was on her back with Lone's weight descending on her. Debbie managed a half-hearted protest, "I'm sore."

In her ear, Lone said, "Tell me to stop and I will."

Debbie lifted her hips and clasped her hands behind Lone's neck. Faking a big sigh, she murmured, "Stop."

"Too late," Lone said and kissed her into heaven once more.

❖

"Thank you for coming in, Mr. Roache. I'm sorry we kept you waiting so long."

Jude sat down opposite a nerdy-looking, slightly built man of twenty-three whose older sister claimed he was involved in the goat's head incident. She'd read him his rights, then had to provide him with several Kleenex after nerves made him throw up. The guy was a basket case and the interview hadn't even begun.

He said, "You can call me Matt."

"Okay, Matt."

"I didn't do it," he feverishly declared. "I never touched that kid."

"Okay." Jude decided to adopt a narrative interrogation method, letting him unload whatever was on top before she moved into more structured questioning. With an emotional individual like Matthew Roache, the best way to get results in an interview was to build empathy. By having him repeat his story several times over, various different ways, she could compare the versions and catch him on any lies.

Sympathetically, she said, "You must feel terrible about all this. People are going to think you took that little boy."

"I know. Jesus." His shoulders shook, and he distracted himself by combing his fingers through his nondescript brown hair. "Man, what are the odds? So, we did a dumb thing, no question about it. But that kid disappearing…that's got nothing to do with us."

"Your sister seems very angry."

"Fuck, she's like…lost her mind. I don't know what else I can tell her. Like we'd ever take a little kid and…do stuff. Fuck. We're not animals." He paused, lost in self-pity. "I'll never get a job now. It wasn't even my idea. I didn't want to kill My Pet Goat. That was Gums. Him and his fucking crazy ideas. I'd have never listened to him if I hadn't been drinking."

"People make mistakes under the influence," Jude said, intentionally letting him off the hook. "They do things that are out of character."

He nodded emphatically. "That's exactly what happened. I just wanted to break into the place and get back this ring I bought her, but no. We had to make a fucking statement. Gums was like…scare the bitch. Show her she can't mess with you. God hates faithless whores… shit like that."

"Gums" certainly sounded like a person of interest, so far. "You were engaged to Tonya, weren't you?" Jude asked.

"Yeah. Until she started screwing that asshole Miller. I broke up with her soon as I found out. But she wouldn't give back the engagement ring, and the problem is, I borrowed the money to pay for it off Heather in the first place."

Jude nodded. "Sounds like Tonya caused a problem between you and your sister."

"No kidding."

"Matt, I can see you didn't mean for anyone to get hurt. Or for the animal cruelty."

"No way. Fuck no! I'm sorry. I'm really sorry." He started sobbing noisily again and rambling on about his goat and 9/11.

Jude let it run for a while, then steered him back on track, "Your sister says you and she had some words in the bar and you left. What time was that?"

"Maybe twenty past ten."

"What did you do then?"

"I went and picked up Gums, and we drove around town drinking tequila for a while. That's when he got his bright idea about smashing Tonya's place up and leaving blood or something to scare the shit out of her. We went round there, but Wade's truck was in the driveway, so we just shouted some shit and left."

So far the story confirmed Wade Miller's. Jude asked, "You kept driving around?"

"Not for long. I was telling Gums how Heather was all pissed about the goat and everything, and he had one of his fucking brain waves. So we went back to my place and…you know…dealt with the goat. A couple of our other buddies got back from the bar then, and they wanted to join in. So Gums wrapped up the head in a towel, and we got some bricks and drove back to Tonya's."

"What time did you get there?"

"Maybe half past eleven."

"Half past eleven." Jude kept her voice very even, not wanting to reveal how important the next questions were to the investigation. "Was Mr. Miller's truck in the driveway then?"

"No."

"What did you do?"

"We got out of the car and got the bricks and smashed the front windows."

"What did you do with the goat's head?"

"After we broke the windows Gums took the towel off it, and we threw it in the front room."

"You threw the goat's head into the living room?"

"Yeah."

"What then?"

"One of the neighbors was turning on lights so we got the fuck out of there."

"Which neighbor?"

"Across the road."

"I hope you're not lying to me, Matt," Jude warned.

"No. This is the God's honest truth, I swear. I don't know how the fuck that head ended up in the yard, but we didn't put it there."

"Did you go inside the house to get the ring?"

He shook his head, bemused. "Weird thing about it...I forgot. With all that was happening and I was upset about my goat and all, I just plain forgot."

"That's perfectly understandable." Casually, she asked, "While you were there, did anyone happen to look inside the middle room?"

"That's the kid's bedroom, right?"

"Yes."

Roache shook his head. "The curtains were closed in that room. I looked in Tonya's room, right at the end. Don't know why. You'd have thought I'd remember the ring then. But I didn't."

"I'll need to speak with all your friends." Jude pushed a notepad and pen across the desk toward him and asked him to jot down their names. "Casting your mind back, is there anything else you remember seeing? Anything unusual?"

Roache frowned. The demands of this open-ended question clearly strained his limited imagination. "Like what?" he asked finally.

"Anything that made you look twice."

He dug deep. "A hat. One of those elf-type ones little kids wear."

"Where was it?"

"In the driveway, lying in the snow."

"What did it look like?"

"Hard to say. It had snow on it."

"A lot of snow?"

"No. It wasn't buried or anything. Just covered with flakes. Looked like Denver Broncos colors. Dark blue and yellow."

"You're certain this was a child's hat?"

"Well, I sure wouldn't wear it."

"Any idea who it belongs to?"

"No. Sorry." With agonized expectancy, Roache asked, "Am I under arrest?"

"Not right now. You did the right thing by coming forward. You'll probably face felony charges for criminal mischief and animal cruelty, but because you're a witness assisting us in our inquiries, I'll wait and see what the sheriff says about that."

With a huge sigh, he sagged forward, cradling his head in his hands. "I wish I'd never got involved with Tonya Perkins. She's a piece of work." He raised his head. "Fuck, this is exactly the kind of stunt she'd pull just to get attention."

"Why would you say that?"

"She was always going on about getting a job doing the weather on TV in Denver or trying out for *American Idol*. She blames that kid for ruining her life."

CHAPTER SIX

Agatha Benham had almost removed her snow boots, out front of the sheriff's office in Paradox Valley, when one of those climate-warming SUVs crunched through the snow and rolled to a halt beneath the huge Marlboro Man sign that dominated the parking area. The car windows fogged within seconds, so Agatha couldn't see inside. But she knew who the driver was. Dr. Mercy Westmoreland from the medical examiner's office in Grand Junction, a woman far too elegant for her repugnant occupation.

The pathologist descended from her gas-hog car and raised a kid-gloved hand to Agatha in a pretty greeting. She looked like Grace Kelly from *Rear Window*, a film Agatha would have liked better if James Stewart had not been stuck in a wheelchair. She thought his morbid voyeurism gave the disabled a bad name.

"Miss Benham. Good morning."

The full-cut ivory cashmere coat she was bundled into only made her skin seem more flawless. Her cheeks glowed pink, stung no doubt by the cold. Her honey-silver hair was contained in a tight chignon, and a black beret clung at a jaunty angle to her head. She belonged in Paris.

"Good morning, Doctor. What a pleasant surprise." Agatha unlocked the front door and the security door.

She was usually the first to arrive on the days she worked. Detective Devine and Deputy Tulley came in after seven, which gave her time to make coffee and straighten up the office. Like most law enforcement personnel, the officers she took care of were incapable of neatness in the workplace. They hid mess exactly the way children did, crammed in the bottom drawers of their desks, stuffed into the cherrywood wall console, and piled high in important-looking stacks of files on their desks.

Agatha had spent thirty-eight years working in this schoolhouse before it was converted to a joint substation for the Montezuma and Montrose county sheriffs. She still couldn't see the sense in that initiative, despite the employment it provided her. There wasn't enough crime in the canyon area to keep a detective busy, and Devine was always being called into Cortez to work on this or that case, leaving Agatha to mind the station and make sure Deputy Tulley kept his weapon holstered when the occasional misguided felon poked fun at Smoke'm, the bloodhound.

"How are things out here?" Dr. Westmoreland asked, kicking her boots against the steps to dislodge snow.

"We're doing fine apart from this weather." Agatha was about to continue the chitchat with an equally trivial remark when her jaw locked and her concentration faltered as a second woman emerged from the SUV and picked her way across the crushed snow toward them.

Tall and willowy, brilliant Titian red hair tumbling about her shoulders, she walked with a silver-topped ebony cane. As she reached the bottom step up to the porch, she clutched her black leather trench coat to her and exclaimed in a perfectly modulated British accent, "Where in God's name are we? Fargo?"

Agatha's laughter rose like vomit. Tears splashed the lenses of her reading glasses. In her seventy-one years, she could not have imagined the day would ever dawn when she would stand on the schoolhouse porch next to one of the great actresses of the generation, for that's what Elspeth Harwood was destined to become. Agatha could hardly believe the star was right here in Paradox Valley, looking even more luminous than she did on the big screen.

"Miss Harwood," she squeaked. "What an honor."

"You remember my name—how sweet." The radiant one pressed Agatha's quivering hand in hers. "I'm always amazed when anyone across the pond knows who I am."

Agatha laughed over this absurdly modest comment. She could not have felt more giddy if she were meeting the President. "I've followed your career since you played the psychopathic nun in *Unveiled*."

"Oh, dear God. You saw that?"

"I have it on video. And I bought a signed photo of you in the nun's habit on eBay last year. That's on the wall in my living room."

Dr. Westmoreland said, "Elspeth broke her leg shooting in

Wyoming, and she decided to recuperate here. We just spent a few days in Moab."

"A broken leg. How terrible. I hope you're feeling better." Agatha suddenly became aware of the freezing air and urged belatedly, "Please, come in out of the cold. My goodness, what was I thinking?"

She could already hear herself recounting the anecdote at the next Paradox film circle meeting—how she kept Elspeth Harwood standing on the front porch while she gushed over her like a starstruck adolescent. Mortified, she led her visitors indoors and showed them to seats in front of Detective Devine's desk.

Miss Harwood unfastened her leather coat and slung it over the back of her chair before sitting down. Agatha could not stop staring at her. She had always imagined screen beauty to be nine-tenths mirage; everyone knew lighting, makeup, and camera angle could hide the flaws in a face. But sitting right in front of her was an actress whose skin looked well scrubbed and who was not even wearing lipstick. If anything, Elspeth Harwood was even lovelier in person than she was on camera.

Awed, Agatha confided in an embarrassed rush, "They should have given you the role of Elizabeth in Shekhar Kapur's film. Cate Blanchett has that voice, but her face is horsy, don't you think?"

At this, Dr. Westmoreland stifled a giggle. Agatha guessed that she probably shared the opinion but, being a personal friend of Miss Harwood's, would not want to seem like a cheerleader.

Miss Harwood modestly said, "I respect Cate enormously. She is utterly dedicated to her craft."

Agatha knew this was code for *She only does nudity for the art.* "Well, it's just my opinion," she said. "But you look like the real thing…like you have genuine royal blood."

"We should visit you more often. It's good for my ego." The star gave a warm smile that was so natural, Agatha could almost see her as just anybody.

Sweeping this ludicrous idea aside, she asked, "May I offer you both a refreshment? I'm making coffee."

"Excellent. Thank you." Miss Harwood ran her hand cautiously over the leg stretched before her and asked, "Would you happen to have a couple of aspirin?"

"Will Advil suffice?" Agatha rushed to the medicine chest, thrilled to be of help to the star in a time of need.

"When are you expecting Detective Devine?" Dr. Westmoreland asked. "I thought we might catch her on our way back to Grand Junction."

"I'm not sure if she's coming in this morning." Agatha shook pills into a small paper cup and poured a glass of water. She handed these to Miss Harwood and noticed, with a small flutter of delight, that she could smell the star's perfume. It was a heady but subtle floral, so appropriate for her English beauty. "You probably haven't heard the news if you've been in Utah. There's a little boy missing, and Detective Devine was in Cortez all yesterday conducting the investigation."

"There's no body yet?" The doctor looked pensive. "I wonder if I should go down there and make myself available."

"It might spare you the longer drive when they find him," Agatha said.

It seemed only right to encourage her for Detective Devine's sake. Although the detective did not share Agatha's passion for the art of cinema, she had recently remarked on the media excitement that surrounded Miss Harwood's purchase of a ranch in Taos. Agatha could picture her disappointment once she learned the actress had graced the station house in person, and she'd missed the occasion. How often did anyone get an opportunity to shake hands with a woman who would get an Oscar one day? Agatha didn't have any grandchildren to tell, but if Detective Devine ever accepted Bobby Lee Parker's marriage proposals, maybe she would.

Dr. Westmoreland took out her cell phone. "I assume they suspect homicide."

"I'm not sure," Agatha said. "There's a big search-and-rescue operation today. Our K-9 was called in."

Miss Harwood indicated one of the framed pictures on the wall. "Is that Detective Devine?"

Agatha took it down, happy that someone appreciated one of the small touches that made the station house less impersonal. She'd framed the photograph herself. It showed Detective Devine ready to ride out with the sheriff's posse the previous summer. What a day that was. After three women hiking alone in the canyon area had almost been raped, they finally had a suspect and he'd made a run for it, trying to hike across state lines into Utah. The posse had run him to ground north of

Dove Creek, and they brought him back to town the old-fashioned way, walking roped behind a horse. Detective Devine said it was the kind of thing that would never fly in Washington, D.C., which explained a lot about the state of the union, Agatha thought.

"She looks good in uniform," Miss Harwood observed with a brittle edge.

Agatha instantly regretted her constant chatter. Celebrities had to listen to people like her all day every day. Miss Harwood probably came to this remote part of the country for anonymity and a break from playing the role of herself. Now she was being forced to admire snapshots of law enforcement officers.

Self-consciously, Agatha took the picture back and was about to hang it when Dr. Westmoreland strode over and said, "Let me see that."

She swiped the picture from Agatha's hands and stared down at it. Then, without a word, she gave it back, her face drawn. The wind chimes on the back stoop sounded like warning bells between rounds of boxing. Agatha clasped her hands so they wouldn't shake. She sensed she'd aggravated the doctor somehow and was not sure what she'd done wrong.

"More coffee?" she offered anxiously.

"No, thanks, Miss Benham. We should get going." Dr. Westmoreland helped her friend to her feet and handed the ebony cane to her.

Elspeth Harwood was several inches taller than the doctor, almost the same height as Detective Devine. Agatha was sorry again that her boss wasn't here. She could have taken a photograph of the three women to add to their small gallery. In her mind's eye, she composed the ideal portrait—the fair pathologist in the center because she was shorter, Detective Devine on one side with her dark hair and her square face, and Miss Harwood on the other in ethereal red-haired contrast. Quite the threesome.

"Are you driving down to Cortez?" she asked as Dr. Westmoreland straightened her beret and guided Miss Harwood down the steps.

"I think I should," the pathologist replied. "I'm sure Detective Devine has all the excitement she can handle, but she's always very good at exceeding limits."

Agatha thought about that comment as her two breathtaking visitors got into the doctor's crime-against-the-environment vehicle and drove shamelessly into the flurrying snow. Dr. Westmoreland was right. The detective had no idea what it meant to stop and smell the roses.

❖

"You're saying there was a dead body on the backseat of this truck?" Jude asked Tulley.

"The whining and the ear flapping…that's his alert for residual scent."

The deputy gave his bloodhound a liver treat and led him away from Wade Miller's pickup. His expression was one of determined dignity and embarrassed pride, a look he wore when he wanted to wax lyrical about Smoke'm's accomplishments but was worried he'd be mocked by the boys for his devotion to his dog. At such times he liked to display his grasp of impressive forensic terminology.

Lifting his voice so the officers a few yards away could make no mistake about his K-9 credentials, he told Jude, "That signal indicates preputrefaction essence, ma'am."

"So we're talking about what—a body less than twelve hours deceased?"

"Correct. In the event there was decomposing remains, he'd paw the ground and bark." With a covert glance toward the crime scene technicians, he added, "He can tell the difference. That's how come he was the champion cadaver hound and best in his year. Juries—they believe a dog like him."

"I want that truck taken apart," Jude told the forensic team. "Look under the paint if that's what it takes. And get that hound on video making his signal. Can he do the same thing again?" she asked Tulley.

"Sure can." With a smug expression, he walked Smoke'm back a few more yards and adjusted the dog's working harness. "Soon as you're ready with that video camera, I'll set him loose."

"You did fear-scent work with him on that last training course, didn't you?" Jude asked once the video was rolling and Smoke'm was performing for the camera.

"I see what you're getting at." Tulley whistled and Smoke'm froze in position, standing on the backseat of the truck, a mournful whine rising from his flabby throat. "The problem is, we have to figure out what the fear is about. He can't do that for us."

"So, you could walk him by a suspect and he could detect adrenalin, but that could mean anything. The suspect could be innocent, and just stressed about being questioned?"

"Yes, ma'am. Only time I think the fear-scent detection is real useful is right after a crime is committed and the perpetrator is trying to make his getaway. A good dog can smell that fear and track him." Tulley stared past Jude to the patient hound. "Only thing gets Smoke'm more excited is the smell of roses. Can't say what that's about. If he had to choose between going after human remains or shoving his nose in a bouquet, I sure wouldn't want my money riding on the DOA."

At that moment, Smoke'm lifted his head and sucked in the breeze. His tail wagged.

"Settle," Tulley commanded, walking toward the truck. "Go to work."

The dog seemed to be having a dilemma. He backed out of the truck and descended, staring eagerly toward the doorway. Tulley told him to sit and asked the guy with the video if he had all he needed. The whole time drool descended like icicles from Smoke'm's dewlaps. Jude thought someone outside probably had a burger. The idea distracted her, too. She was starving, and she couldn't face another slice of cold pepperoni pizza.

"I think we're done here," she told Tulley.

"Can I get back to the search now?"

"Yep." Tulley had been trolling the banks of the Dolores since first light and wasn't happy when Jude ordered him to the garage.

"The sheriff's thinking the McPhee reservoir, right?" he asked.

"I'd say it's a no-brainer. Miller's truck was sighted in the vicinity, and he admitted to being in Cahone."

Smoke'm howled. Tulley told him, "Quiet, boy."

A crisp English voice cut across the room, "My God. Is that a genuine bloodhound?"

Jude wasn't sure who looked more stupefied: she, Tulley, or Smoke'm. The dog immediately dropped to his belly and tracked the progress of the two women who entered the garage and carefully traversed the plastic-covered floor. The Brit who'd spoken was walking with a cane. Jude only needed a single glance to confirm her identity. Elspeth Harwood a.k.a. The Other Woman.

Tulley had the presence of mind to answer the actress's question. "Yes ma'am. He's purebred. A hundred million olfactory receptors. That's a whole lot more than a salamander."

Jude's breathing grew hopelessly uneven. The sight of Mercy Westmoreland invariably made her gulp air like a stranded fish, and today the pathologist looked so hot Jude had trouble assembling a sentence.

"Doctor," she said, conjuring the smell of rotting flesh so she wouldn't blush.

Mercy looked her up and down and smiled the smile of a woman who knew the body beneath the clothes. Mischief flashed in her blue-denim eyes. "Detective Devine, I thought I should drive down in case you locate the missing child's body."

"He's not presumed dead, yet," Jude said coolly.

Mercy smiled. "You know as well as I do that we'll be lucky to find him rotting in a shallow grave."

Jude detected a faint start in the glamorous redhead standing a foot away. Evidently Elspeth was accustomed to a gentler side of Dr. Westmoreland.

"Do you have a suspect in the disappearance?" Mercy asked, staying on point.

"We're looking at the mother's boyfriend." Jude congratulated herself for keeping a straight face. The redhead was actually fidgeting, no doubt waiting to be the center of attention. Instead her work-obsessed girlfriend hadn't even introduced her.

"Huge surprise," Mercy responded. "What's with the mother? She makes an appeal for her son looking like she's auditioning for a porn movie?"

"Excited to be on TV, maybe," Jude said blandly, loving that Mercy was displaying her judgmental side. The English girlfriend looked like she'd just found a snail in her salad.

Mercy chose that moment to make introductions. "Oh, by the way, this is Elspeth Harwood."

Jude got the mandatory handshake out of the way like it was nothing to touch fingers that had been between Mercy's legs. She even managed a polite remark about the weather. Beyond that, she didn't have to worry about making nice. Tulley was all over it.

His ears turned cranberry as he shook Elspeth's hand. "Ma'am.

It's a privilege. If you don't mind my saying so, you were awesome in *White Orphans*. I've seen it six times."

Jude called to mind a wooden film with gray skies up the ying yang and characters who never smiled. Tulley periodically insisted she would enjoy this foreign masterpiece if she concentrated on the plot and the symbolism instead of griping about the subtitles. She hadn't even realized one of the stars was Elspeth Harwood. Who could tell with the weird white paint everyone had on their faces?

The actress looked thrilled. "Thank you. It's such an underrated film. Really, I think the semiotics are lost on today's audience. Nuance is wasted on some people."

Tulley responded to this arcane pronouncement like he'd just found his soul mate. "World cinema's my hobby," he said happily. "I've got maybe three hundred foreign-language DVDs."

It wasn't a boast Jude would use to impress girls, but it seemed to go over big-time with Elspeth. She looked like she'd have kissed him if no one was around. Instead she draped a pale hand over his arm and said, "We simply must have coffee, darling. Tell me, who's your favorite director of all time?"

Tulley pondered. "That's hard. Sometimes I watch everything by Fritz Lang. Other times it has to be Kieslowski."

They both sighed and, almost in unison, pronounced with mock swoons, *"The Double Life of Veronique,"* then laughed like they had just invented a secret language of their own.

Jude muttered, "Oh, Christ."

Even Mercy seemed a little rattled. With a defensive edge, she told Jude, "It's not like there's anyone she can talk to around here once Telluride is over."

"Us being such hicks, you mean?"

"That's not what I'm saying."

"Uh-huh."

Jude could tell that Mercy wanted to slap her. Instead they both stared as the culturally deprived girlfriend stepped even closer to Tulley and touched his cheek with the air of an artist appraising a model.

"You know, you have an incredibly photogenic face, Deputy Tulley," she said, patently appreciative of his black-Irish good looks. "Have you ever been screen tested?"

Jude almost gagged. Was her competition bisexual, too? She didn't know whether to be disgusted or perversely pleased. Grimly, she drew Mercy aside and walked with her to the far end of the garage, leaving Tulley and the actress to their mutual lovefest.

"What were you thinking?" she demanded once they were out of earshot. "I haven't seen you in a month and you come in here with *her*?"

"I didn't plan it that way." Mercy's irritation showed. "We dropped by the schoolhouse and Miss Benham told me what was happening, so there didn't seem much point driving back to Grand Junction."

"Do you have any idea how much media we have in town? I thought your…guest was trying to keep a low profile."

"Elspeth thought she might be able to help."

"Help?" Jude laughed without humor. "Oh, yeah. I can see it now. The search party has to turn back because she's worried about her hair."

"She's not like that at all."

"I don't want to know." Jude stared past Mercy. The crime technicians had converged on Elspeth, forming an eager audience that hung on her every word. Jude wanted to yell *Suckers! She's a dyke!*

"You have to get beyond this primitive jealousy," Mercy hissed. "You can't keep pretending she doesn't exist. She's bought property here. She's going to be around much more."

"Oh, that's just perfect."

"I was hoping the three of us could be friends."

"Are you crazy?"

"I care for you, Jude." Mercy struggled on. "I don't think it's healthy for you to be so angry about this."

"I don't think it's healthy for you to have two girlfriends."

"Let's not play tit for tat. Elspeth was fine about coming here. She wanted to meet you."

"Well, I didn't want to meet her," Jude said tersely. "But you didn't bother to find that out. How did you expect I'd react to this…ambush? Don't you know me at all?"

"I expected you to behave like an adult." Mercy's voice shook.

"Define adult. If it's a passive butch plaything you want—and, for the record, that doesn't seem to be the case when we're fucking—then you picked the wrong person."

"This is not about how we have sex." Mercy's face was a study in frustration. "And please keep your voice down. I'm not ready to take out a public notice about my love life just yet."

"And I'm not ready to pretend this is okay with me just to make you comfortable."

Mercy sighed. "I knew this was a mistake."

"Then why come?"

"I don't know. I guess I thought if you met her, you'd see how wonderful she is and you'd understand why I can't just let her go."

Jude felt like someone had just slammed a baseball bat into her gut. "Are you telling me you're *in love* with her?" Not once had Mercy ever mentioned the L-word to her. Not even in the throes of passion. Jude thought she was allergic to it.

"I'm not sure." Color rushed to Mercy's cheeks. "She's been so good to me. I had a hard time when my father died. It made all the difference knowing she was there for me."

Was Mercy *trying* to hurt her? Jude was assailed with memories of her own futile attempts to offer support and consolation during that time of loss. Mercy had kept her at a distance, not once opening up. Jude had respected her privacy. Was she now condemned for that? A suspicion flashed across her mind: Mercy found Elspeth safe. Jude had long ago learned to respect these whisperings from the unconscious, so she gave the thought some room, and the anger drained away.

Trying to build some kind of bridge, she asked gently, "What do you want that I'm not giving you?"

Mercy's face showed nothing, but her pupils gave her away. The question had hit home. She skirted around it, all the same. "Jude, you're an excellent lover."

"That wasn't what I asked." Jude moved closer, shielding Mercy from the room. She ran her fingertips over the inside of Mercy's wrist. It was as close to a kiss as she dared in public. "Please talk to me."

Mercy looked pointedly past her to the others in the room. "This is not the time or place. We both have work to do."

Jude swallowed her frustration. There was never a time when Mercy was willing to discuss where their relationship was going. Every time Jude raised the topic, she found a way to avoid it. Yet, apparently she had the intimate, personal connection with Elspeth that she denied Jude.

It dawned on Jude that this was a form of fidelity. Mercy could be sexually intimate with two partners, but she was only emotionally intimate with one...with Elspeth. Something raw and hot rose from deep inside, and for several seconds she couldn't breathe. She felt stricken. Blood rushed in her ears. Tears prickled and she looked down at her boots, humiliated and willing herself to get a grip. No one had hurt her like this for a long time.

"Let's meet." Mercy's code for getting together to have sex.

Jude's hands shook. She shoved them into her pockets and said casually, "That would be pleasant, but I don't have the time right now."

Mercy looked her dead in the eye. "I don't desire anyone the way I desire you. Isn't that enough?"

Jude wanted it to be enough. She let herself think about Mercy naked and slippery, rocking against her, begging for release. Her body immediately let its needs be known, flesh and skin at odds as a chill of desire spread goose bumps over the heat of her limbs. She wanted Mercy desperately. She ached for her, and she hated how it weakened her resolve. This yearning was like an illness. The more she tried to treat it by giving in, the more barren she felt every time they said good-bye. She loathed her helplessness. She hated that she'd allowed Mercy to dictate the terms of their relationship from day one. What was *that* about?

Angry at herself as much as Mercy, she said, "Whatever," a response she knew infuriated her fickle lover.

Predictably, Mercy responded, "That's not an answer!"

Jude shrugged. "As you said, this is not the time or place. We're investigating a possible homicide, and Ms. Harwood is not authorized to be here. I need for you to escort her out."

She started walking. Mercy kept pace with her.

"Don't do this," she implored in a harsh whisper.

"Do what?" Jude asked.

"End us."

Jude stopped, far enough from the others that they would not be heard clearly. Facing Mercy, she rolled the dice one last time. "Does it matter?"

The question hung between them, imposing a leaden calm the way an earthquake did before the tremors began.

Tears sparkled in Mercy's eyes. "This is pointless. You'll never understand."

"You're right," Jude conceded bitterly. "I never will."

CHAPTER SEVEN

Known to his buddies as Gums, owing to party tricks involving his false teeth, Hank Thompson was older than the other losers he ran with, a man whose claim to fame was that he had been struck by lightning and lived to tell the tale. He wasted no time sharing this God-given reprieve with Jude, whose luck it was to be taking down his statement at 7:30 a.m. when she hadn't had coffee.

"The Big Guy strikes you down—you sit up and take notice," he announced with blinding logic. "Right after that, I made a pledge."

Jude could hardly wait.

"I live a monastic existence," her subject confided. "No worldly distractions. Neither of the flesh, nor a material nature."

Jude interpreted this to mean he was unemployed, lived in a dump, and couldn't get laid. She said, "So, you're on welfare?"

Gums sucked a breath noisily past the thinnest lips Jude had ever seen. "The Big Guy sees to it that I have the time needed to study on His word."

"Where does the tequila drinking fit in?"

"The elixir helps me receive my visions."

Jude pictured the defense wetting themselves when they got their first look at this witness. Inwardly groaning, she went with the flow. "Did you have a vision on the evening of Saturday, March tenth?"

"I was tasked with a foul duty." He smoothed his thinning salt-and-pepper hair. "The slaying of a minion of Satan himself. I speak of a goat that caused offense to a virtuous lady."

"I see." Jude flipped through her notes, buying a little time to think about her line of questioning. She needed to confirm Matthew Roache's story and find out if Thompson had an agenda of his own that could have led him to kidnap a small child from a woman who had no money. "Who is this virtuous lady?"

"Heather, sister of Matthew. He is unworthy, but she is radiant in God's eyes."

Jude contemplated the possibility that this witness had abducted and probably murdered Corban Foley and was busy setting up his insanity plea. On the other hand, it seemed plausible that someone who'd survived being struck by lightning might be missing some key brain cells.

"Why did you vandalize Tonya Perkins's home?" she asked.

He got worked up and started along a deeply nutty track in which all women, with the exception of the fair Heather, were sent to tempt weak mankind, and Tonya was a demon in disguise. When he got really loud and flecks of foam began to gather in the corners of his mouth, Jude handed him a glass of water, insisting, "Calm down and drink this, Mr. Thompson."

He took the water and lifted his gaze heavenward. "The Big Guy has his eye on me," he said with satisfaction. "I thirsted and He sent water."

Once his breathing had slowed down, Jude asked, "Mr. Thompson. Are you on any medication? Pills?"

"I can't take those. God stops talking to me."

"I see." A delusional individual off his meds is at the home of a missing child on the evening of his disappearance. Reasonable doubt didn't get any better than that, assuming they could make a case against Wade Miller in the first place.

Gloomily, Jude surveyed her subject. Every instinct she had told her Miller was responsible for whatever had happened to Corban Foley, but she knew better than to conduct an investigation with an attachment to any one theory of the crime. Foregone conclusions spelled trouble; it was fatally easy to overlook important clues if you couldn't see past your own beliefs. Twenty years ago, a guy like Thompson wouldn't have made it out of an interview room without signing a confession. Death row had seen plenty like him over the years. She had to find some way to rule him out unequivocally, or back up any confession they extracted with a mountain of hard evidence.

"Tell me, how do you think God feels about a woman like Tonya rearing an innocent child," she asked in a conversational tone. "Do you think he might be concerned?"

"Certainly."

She framed a hypothetical; these often yielded insights, especially from offenders deep in denial. "If you were God, what would you do about that?"

Thompson grew restless, wringing his hands and shifting in his seat. "I don't know. I'm not God."

"Mr. Thompson, did God ask you to take Corban Foley from his mother's home?"

His wild eyes stilled momentarily and he said with conviction, "No."

"Tell me what you did when you arrived at Ms. Perkins's house."

"We smashed the windows, and I cast forth the head of Satan's minion."

"Where did you cast it?"

"Into that she-devil's lair. I threw the hat in there, too."

"What happened then?"

"We drove away and I took more of the elixir of truth. Then God delivered a message unto me."

"What was that message?" Jude prompted.

"I wrote it down." He reached into his pants pocket and produced a grubby piece of paper folded into an origami swan.

Jude unfolded it and flattened it out on the table as best she could. The note said, *Admit yourself.*

Hank Thompson stared down at it, apparently mystified. "Do you know what it means?"

Jude felt sad. What it meant was that her subject, once a successful builder and candidate for local office, as described by the deputy who'd briefed her earlier, was still in there somewhere. Lost. Trying to find a way back to his sanity.

She took one of the hands he could not keep still and said, "Hank?"

Something calmed once again in Thompson's eyes, and for a split second Jude thought she glimpsed a rational being.

He said, "Heather calls me Hank, too."

Jude smiled at him. "Listen, Hank. I think God wants you to go to a peaceful place where you can rest. I have a feeling that's what the message means. If you like, one of the deputies can drive you to a place I know about. A hospital."

Alarm jammed his expression. "Is Heather there?"

"No, but I can speak to her about visiting you." Trying once more to reach the part of him that could still reason, she said, "Hank, please think carefully. Do you know where Tonya's little boy is?"

He shook his head. "Want me to ask God?"

Why not give the troops something to snicker about when they reviewed the interview tape? "Knock yourself out," she invited.

Thompson got down onto the floor and prayed in the *sudjood* position of a Muslim, his forehead on the floor. The deputy standing at the door mumbled something about domestic terrorists. Jude thought, *Not even close.*

When their subject had communed with the Big Guy long enough, he scrambled back up and sat at the table once more.

"Well?" Jude asked.

"I need elixir."

"God only answers your prayers when you're drunk?"

Thompson gave her a look. "He said you'll find him."

"Did he say where?"

"God doesn't answer for the Devil," Thompson informed her snippily. "Make no mistake. This is Satan's work."

❖

"Tell them to go away," Tonya complained. Media vans and reporters waving big fluffy microphones had her sister's place surrounded. She wished she'd never come here after the police sent her home, but she couldn't afford a motel.

"Are you crazy?" Amberlee poured herself into her tightest black jeans, tucked in her white stretch lace top, and started trying on different pumps. "Everyone's out there. Channel Nine News. Channel Four. CNN. MSNBC. No way are you hiding in here for the rest of the day. Get dressed."

"What for? I'm not going out there."

Amberlee fastened the ankle straps of the cherry red platforms she'd picked out. "You can blow this chance if you want, but I'm not that stupid."

"What are you talking about?"

Amberlee wobbled over to the bed and dragged the covers off Tonya. "Don't you get it? They're here to see you. This is a big story."

Tonya stared at the phone. Any minute it would ring and someone would say Corban was safe and they were bringing him home. There was still time for him to be okay. She started crying again. She was a mess. She only had to think about her baby and she couldn't control herself.

"I should be out there looking for him," she sobbed. "It's been a whole day. What if he's hiding somewhere like in a log or a cave. Maybe he'll get scared if he hears the searchers. He's shy. Sometimes he only answers to me."

Amberlee looked impatient. "You're getting yourself all worked up over nothing. He'll answer."

"Oh, God. Why did I leave him?" Tonya rolled onto her stomach and hugged one of the pillows against her. "I shouldn't have left him."

"I suppose you're going to blame me next." Amberlee plugged in the flat iron and set about straightening her hair.

She'd spent most of the morning with Saran Wrap around her head to make her home bleach kit work faster. Her hair was now the exact shade of platinum Tonya had wanted for her own hair, only she'd been afraid to use an extreme lightener in case her hair broke off at the roots. So she ended up with a color Amberlee said was light strawberry blond, but was really a pinkish yellow that made her skin look weird no matter what foundation she used.

"Why would I blame you?" Tonya wiped her face and thought about taking a shower. She didn't know what to do with herself. One minute she felt like throwing up, the next she was crying, then she felt far away. And in between all of those, she got so panicked all she could do was walk up and down the house so she wouldn't lay in a ball and scream.

"Well, it was my birthday party," Amberlee pointed out. "I starved myself for months and lost forty pounds so I'd look good. How do you think *I* feel?"

Tonya hadn't thought about it. She supposed she should have. Amberlee was her sister and she hadn't even noticed the weight loss. Forty pounds. Tonya wished she could take off the weight she'd put on having Corban. Last time she looked, the scale said 180. She didn't even want to think about it.

"I'm sorry," she said.

"I'm gonna be down to two hundred by Thanksgiving."

"You don't even look fat, Ambam. Guys think you're hot."

"Thanks, baby sis." Amberlee was quiet for a few seconds, then she said with a frown, "What's taking them so long down at the sheriff's office? I thought Wade would be here by now."

So did Tonya. "Well, he was the one looking after Corban. The detective said they have to rule him and me out first."

Amberlee opened the flat iron and stared down at her hair. "Fuck. My hair's fried. It's snapping off. Oh, God. This is a nightmare."

"I told you not to leave that thirty volume on so long." Tonya got out of bed and found a sweater. "Sit down. Let me see."

Obediently, Amberlee plunked herself on the velvet-covered stool in front of the dressing table. She met Tonya's gaze in the mirror and said, "Your eyes are all puffy. You better put some ice on them before we go out there."

Tonya turned down the heat and slowly worked a strand of her sister's hair through the flat iron. "Keep it on this setting," she announced. "Then it won't break."

"Thanks. I love you." Amberlee smiled. "Now go take a shower. You'll feel better once you're dressed." As Tonya headed out the door, she called after her, "I'll do your makeup so you look good for the cameras."

CHAPTER EIGHT

D ebbie gazed out across a white world pockmarked with dark blotches—the tracks of SAR team members. Hundreds of searchers were spread out along the entire route from Cortez to Dove Creek, and to the reservoir, and helicopters were conducting an aerial search. Lone said that although nobody was calling it a search-and-recovery operation yet, anyone with a clue knew they were looking for a body.

Debbie didn't want to believe that. She imagined happier scenarios—the child taken as a prank, then left safe and wrapped against the elements somewhere he would be found, or abandoned alive by kidnappers who had a change of heart. She kept waiting for that triumphant shout, the thrill of hearing a soft cry and seeing a little one held high in the air and rushed to open ground where one of the helicopters would swoop down to carry him to the hospital. She wanted to see the mother weeping on TV, thanking everyone who had braved the snow and freezing cold to bring her baby back.

That morning, as they'd assembled at the staging area in Cahone, the Montezuma County sheriff had announced that this was the most extensive search operation ever mounted in the Four Corners. Debbie warmed with pride to be a part of something bigger than herself. Most of the time, she never felt as if her life amounted to anything. Today was different. She was filled with energy and determination. She felt good about herself and not as shy around people as she normally did.

Although they were among strangers, everyone seemed to be a friend. It happened at times like this, when a community had to pull together. Barriers broke down and people understood that their shared humanity meant more than their differences. No one had given her and Lone a second glance, even when Lone took her hand to help her over difficult terrain.

An hour earlier, when an SAR leader noticed Lone's equipment and Lone mentioned her military experience, she and Debbie were reassigned to the crew searching upstream along a ten-mile shoreline of the Dolores River between Bradfield Bridge and Lone Dome. They were with three K-9 units from Dolores, German Shepherds and their handlers and navigators, plus fifty searchers including a Nordic rescue team on skis.

This part of the Dolores was one of those places you'd never find unless you knew exactly where to look. The River of Sorrows meandered through a remote canyon in the Mesa Verde country. Snow hung over the sandstone walls on either side of the river basin and clung to the spindly junipers that straggled along the riverbanks. The water's silent, sluggish progress was oddly hypnotic.

As she stared down at it, Debbie gulped in the dry Colorado air and tried not to picture a child's body drifting by. The mere fact that they were searching here meant this was a possibility. The police had to have suspicions. She probed the snow with her pole, this way and that, feeling for what lay beneath and placing her feet where the ground felt level. She had snowshoes in her backpack, but for now wore heavy snow boots and gaiters that kept her feet and legs dry.

Apart from her nose and cheeks, the only parts of her face not covered by her muffler and goggles, she was warm and damp with sweat. They were moving slowly, scouring every square foot, but it was still hard work, and with every hour that passed, a daunting inevitability clawed at her resolve. It was hard to sustain hope, yet the searchers did. That morning, as they waited at the staging area, Debbie had heard various stories of unbelievable survival. Just a few years earlier, a small boy had made it after forty-eight hours lost in this area, in winter conditions. It could happen.

"I'll take the bottom of this rise, at the river." Lone headed down a sharp incline. "Carry on and I'll join you when it levels out again."

"Okay. Be careful," Debbie called after her.

She stopped to pull up her gaiters after a few minutes and looked back when she heard the sound of panting. A Montezuma County deputy halted his bloodhound a few feet from her. The dog was wearing boots and a snow jacket. To Debbie's astonishment this garment was emblazoned on both sides with a Marlboro logo.

"How come your dog is advertising cigarettes?" she asked. "I thought tobacco sponsorship was illegal."

"No one else came up with the cash." The deputy, a young man with coal black hair flattened by his helmet, lifted his goggles. "The Marlboro people have been good to Smoke'm and me."

"Your dog's name is Smoke'm?" Debbie almost fell over. Literally.

The deputy caught her arm and helped her find her balance. His face was so handsome, she couldn't help but stare. Where was the justice in men getting the best eyelashes? This guy had the longest she had ever seen, and they framed eyes the rich golden brown of caramelized sugar.

He smiled at her with the sweet shyness of a girl, and Debbie thought if she'd been straight and impressionable, she'd have fallen at his feet. While she was trying to assemble some coherent words, Lone marched briskly back up the slope and introduced the both of them.

They all shook gloved paws and the deputy said, "I'm Virgil Tulley. I'm with the MCSO, based in Paradox Valley."

"In the old schoolhouse?" Debbie asked.

"Yes, ma'am. There's just the two of us. One detective and myself. It's a remote substation, you understand."

"My place is right down the road." Debbie smiled. "Small world, huh?"

"Sure is. It's real community-minded of you both coming down here, by the way." Tulley lifted his field glasses and signaled to a figure some way ahead of them.

Debbie was immediately embarrassed that she was distracting a K-9 handler from his duties, not to mention staring at a man, even though she'd never found one attractive. Lone had warned her about losing focus. It was easy to let her mind drift in the sprawling white expanse. The glare from the snow was strangely mesmerizing, and she was also tired. She glanced sideways at Lone and smiled at the thought. They'd had so little sleep the previous night, she was amazed either of them could stay upright.

Her heart jumped as she met Lone's eyes. A jolt of raw awareness passed between them, and Debbie's knees almost buckled. She might appreciate Deputy Tulley's looks the way she would admire any beautiful creature, but Lone aroused a completely different reaction. Debbie felt hot, stifled in her layers of cotton and wool. If they'd been by themselves here she would have torn off her clothes and rolled naked in the snow, just to wallow in sensation.

Thinking her feelings for Lone must be written all over her face for the whole world to see, she was grateful when Deputy Tulley moved a few paces ahead and urged his dog on. They exchanged a wave with the deputy as he hastened away and Debbie reached for Lone's hand, marveling all over again at her good fortune. Apart from making her feel incredibly sexy, Lone made her feel special. She did all those little things that people laughed at these days. She opened doors, helped Debbie into the truck, got things down from high places for her, unscrewed caps and lids, got rid of creepy crawlies.

"Take some water, Debbie doll." Lone handed her a bottle.

Dehydration was the enemy of alpine rescuers, and Lone had packed all the water they would both need in her own backpack so that Debbie would not be weighed down. They stopped where the contour of the riverbank rose sharply and Debbie drank. The water was so cold it hurt her teeth. She stared at the aqua-gray reservoir in the distance and out across the unforgiving plateau. Winter had vanquished the red and blue of the Four Corners landscape, bleeding the painted hues of all vibrancy until what remained was a mere negative of the summer glory, a colorless infinity with no discernable horizon.

For the first time since they'd started out that morning, Debbie felt a sick chill of apprehension as she gazed around. Lowering her eyes to the icy waters below, she burst into tears and mopped pointlessly at her face with her waterproof gloves.

Lone immediately gathered her close and reassured her, "Everything's okay, baby. You're perfectly safe. I'll never let anything, or anyone, hurt you."

"It's not that." She'd told Lone she found wide-open spaces scary these days.

"Then what?" Lone kissed her cheek. "You can tell me."

Shocked by her own sudden despair, Debbie whispered, "He's dead. I know it." She could just make out the sound of Lone's heart through her dense clothing.

Lone rocked her slowly, letting her take comfort. "I'm sorry, Debbie doll," she said eventually. "I know it hurts."

Debbie played the words over. In Lone's shoes, having insisted from the start that the little boy was dead, Meg would have said *I told you so.* Being right would have mattered more to her than being supportive.

Lone's reaction told Debbie something important. She knew how to love.

❖

"Thought I'd find you out here," a man's voice carried damply in the snow-burdened air.

Tulley peered back over his shoulder. "Hey, Bobby Lee."

This was a surprise. Bobby Lee Parker wasn't the type to hike voluntarily. He kept fit with Pilates for men. He said grunt exercise was for yesterday's insecure macho man.

Bobby Lee took some long strides to catch up. "How's it going?"

"Nothing so far." Tulley whistled Smoke'm to heel and checked the Velcro that secured his mush boots. "You been out long?"

"An hour, tops."

Which was about all he was dressed for, Tulley thought. Who else but Bobby Lee would show up for a big SAR operation wearing a black cowboy hat, jeans, and a fashionable snow vest over a wool plaid shirt. His only concession to the task at hand was gaiters, like that was all it took. Tulley knew what this was about. Bobby Lee was so vain he couldn't bring himself to be seen in goggles and a helmet. He'd rather look good than behave responsibly.

Not for the first time Tulley wondered what Jude saw in the self-satisfied cowboy. Admittedly he was a smooth talker who could charm a hog gone wild, and he had what one of the female deputies called bad boy pheromones. Agatha was always harping on about his James Dean charisma and how as Jude should count herself lucky he didn't mind her being taller than him. Tulley didn't see what the fuss was all about. He had a better six-pack than Bobby Lee, and he could shoot straight.

Only a few weeks back, Bobby Lee had got down on his knees and proposed to Jude in Nero's restaurant, while the staff was all standing around with champagne and one of those French desserts they set fire to. Tulley would have paid fifty bucks to see that. But Jude told Bobby Lee she needed time to think about the proposal, an answer that made everyone at the MCSO lose their minds once the story got around. No one had expected the relationship to last a week, let alone four months, and now there was a marriage offer. Tulley couldn't set foot in the Cortez stationhouse without everyone pestering him to spill.

People had trouble picturing Jude in a wedding dress and were always asking Tulley if she was going to get married in her uniform instead. That's if she went for the offer, which a lot of folks thought would be wise, since a woman like her probably didn't meet too many males who would overlook her job and her lack of feminine qualities. There was also talk that Jude wouldn't do it because she'd be marrying beneath her. She was a decorated detective and college educated, and Bobby Lee had a rap sheet and a pothead artist mother who went to that antiwar protest in Crawford, Texas.

But Tulley couldn't imagine those differences in background would factor in; Jude wasn't snooty. No, he thought the problem was something else besides that. Jude and Bobby Lee had been dating for the past four months, but they were the least affectionate couple Tulley had ever seen. He suspected the difficulty lay with Jude, since Bobby Lee was always bragging on his conquests and the special talent he had for pleasuring his ladyfolk. Maybe it was job-related. Maybe she was scarred. Before she took a step down to work in a two-bit sheriff's office, she was an FBI agent working in child protection. That had to leave its mark.

Any rate, she had intimacy issues. That's what Tulley had learned from reading magazines with sealed sections on relationships. He found these helpful because he had issues himself. After his last girlfriend, Alyssa Critch, decided to give him a black eye when he broke up with her, he thought it was time he got to the bottom of his bad luck with the ladies. Since then, he'd discovered how little he knew from his parents or his schooling. It had been quite a shock to find out he'd been lied to by the people he trusted. In the end, he wrote to The Answer Man for advice about his extreme nervousness around the female sex. His letter and the answer got featured on the Web site.

He showed this to Bobby Lee the night of the marriage proposal, after he arrived wanting to unload his hard-luck story over beer and pretzels. Bobby Lee agreed with The Answer Man that the only way for Tulley to get beyond these crippling social handicaps was to practice with women he would never see again. They were planning a trip to

Denver where Bobby Lee knew some nice ladies who would not talk about Tulley behind his back, ask embarrassing questions about the scars all over his torso, or make him do stuff unless he wanted to. Sure, they were paid for their services. But Bobby Lee said, sometimes a professional was exactly what the situation called for. Tulley had been saving for the trip.

They'd watched *Gladiator* that night, which was one of the two DVDs Bobby Lee ever picked out when he came by. The other was *Terminator 2*. This taste for action movies was, at least, one thing he had in common with Jude. Neither of them could watch *Dancing at Lughnasa* all the way through, and if they were visiting and Tulley wanted to get rid of them, he'd put on *The English Patient* and it was run, don't walk. They fidgeted with their popcorn so much during *The Hours* that Tulley and Agatha had to move to a different part of the theater so they wouldn't be humiliated. Later Jude said the movie was a downer and she wished they'd gone to *The Recruit* instead.

"Looks like he's caught a whiff of something." Bobby Lee indicated Smoke'm.

He had his head back and was taking in the faint southerly breeze so keenly his jowls were vibrating.

Tulley tightened the K-9 harness, a sign to Smoke'm that he was working. "Good boy," he praised. "Go to work."

Smoke'm needed no encouragement. He gave a short howl and set off swinging his head slightly from side to side like an elephant, velvet ears flapping.

"He's fanning the scent to his olfactory receptors," Tulley explained.

The area they were searching was a stretch of the Dolores local fly fishermen liked to keep secret. A couple of them involved with the search had already told Tulley they hadn't seen a brown in these waters for ten years and the cutthroats weren't worth the price of a lure. Smoke'm bayed and Tulley's mouth went dry with excitement. He scanned the snow ahead seeking a suspicious-looking mound or a stain that didn't belong.

"You think he can smell the kid?" Bobby Lee asked.

"Can't tell till he signals."

"Man, we'll be all over the news if we're the ones who find him."

"I hope he's alive."

"I'm not real optimistic about that," Bobby Lee said flatly. "You better prepare yourself, buddy."

Tulley glanced sideways and read the warning in Bobby Lee's sleepy blue eyes. He wanted to keep an open mind and stay positive, but he had no idea how he would react if they found a body. The only time he had ever seen a dead kid was when he attended a traffic accident once and a paramedic had carried a limp six-year-old from the wreckage.

Smoke'm screeched to a halt about thirty feet from the forest road, where it started cutting in toward the reservoir. Whining, he pawed a patch of snow and gazed at Tulley with mournful dignity, waiting for the next command.

Tulley gave him one of the treats he coveted most, half a knockwurst sausage, and said, "Dig." He took Bobby Lee's advice and prepared himself. He could hardly bear to look. If Smoke'm had to dig, the news was going to be bad.

Bobby Lee clapped him on the shoulder. "Whatever it is, think about this—at least we'll all know."

"Yep." Tulley's mind strayed to Jude's brother, the one that went missing when they were kids.

Jude had never said a word about him until the dust settled after the Darlene Huntsberger homicide the previous year. Then one day she just up and told him the whole story. How Ben was twelve, and one day he didn't come home from school. How close they were and how she'd spent most of her life trying to find out what happened to him, becoming an FBI agent so she could work in the Crimes Against Children Unit. The not knowing had done her head in.

She'd showed him a picture of the two of them dressed up in home-sewn pilot uniforms. Ben had blond waves, big gentle eyes, and a sweet smile. He looked more like a girl than she did.

Gone, Tulley thought, vanished without a trace. How did that happen? He could see how it affected Jude, even now. She had moved all the way out here so she could leave the past behind, but geography only changed the view from your truck window. He knew that himself.

He thought everything would change when he left Ohio. No one knew him in Colorado. He wasn't going to run into any of the guys who picked on him all through school. And what if he did? He was the one with the gun and the badge. He'd only been back to visit his ma once since he graduated from the police academy. That visit was for Thanksgiving a few months back, and he made sure to show up in town wearing his uniform. That wiped the grins from a few faces.

He felt like a million bucks the day he was at old man Gleeson's gas station filling up the truck and who should pull in behind him but Mr. Star Quarterback, Greg Helms. You'd think a guy who called you faggot all through high school and held you down in the john so he could put out his cigarettes on your chest would remember your name. But Helms walked right on by before he even recognized Tulley, then he turned around and his face went dark red.

He said, "Fuck, is that you...uh...uh..."

The guy was slightly shorter than Tulley, and his football jock muscles had been replaced with a big gut. Bobby Lee would have said he'd gone from fab to flab.

Tulley rested his hand on his gun and drawled in his deepest voice, "Yeah, it's me. Virgil Tulley."

Helms looked like he was about to spew. "Hey, pal. That shit back in school—I never meant nothing by it. Okay?"

Here was the moment he'd fantasized about most of his life. Face to face with one of the bullies who made his life hell, and the guy was shitting himself. Tulley had a feeling if he told Helms to kneel down and lick the oil stains off of the concrete, he'd do it.

Instead, he said, "That was a long time ago. What are you up to these days, Greg?"

Helms flicked sweat away from his nose with his chubby fingers. "Not much. Still bumming around here."

They talked for a few minutes more. Turned out he was a loser living in his mom's basement and bagging groceries part-time. He'd married a girl from his senior year, and she'd taken their kid and left him for another man. He was taking Zoloft.

They said good-bye and Tulley drove off slapping the steering wheel and singing "We Don't Need Another Hero" from that underrated masterpiece *Mad Max Beyond Thunderdome*. Not once had he stuttered during the encounter. Greg Helms couldn't even look him in the eye. Who was the tough guy now?

Tulley pumped a few muscles and reminded himself that he'd missed a day on the Bowflex thanks to the unfolding drama of Corban

Foley's disappearance. He called encouragement to Smoke'm, who had dug a hole so deep all you could see was snow spraying up over the edges.

Finally he gave a low whine and the snow stopped flying. Tulley and Bobby Lee moved to the edge of the hole and stared down. Smoke'm was on his haunches next to a plastic Safeway shopping bag knotted at the top.

"Want me to get it out?" Bobby Lee offered.

Tulley dropped his backpack and took a camera from the front pocket. "I have to photograph it first."

He wasn't entirely sure what to do after that, whether to open it or call the mobile command post and wait for them to send the right people. The procedure had been explained, but now that he wanted to remember he couldn't. The bag wasn't big enough to hold a child so there was no rush to look inside. Tulley took photos, including several of Smoke'm standing in his alert pose over the hole.

Then he phoned the powers that be and they told him to mark the site and carefully extract the bag, then open it. Tulley exchanged his Kevlar gloves for latex and extracted the bag. It weighed almost nothing.

Relieved he said, "At least it's not body parts."

Bobby Lee crouched down, watching closely as Tulley photographed, then loosened, the knot. They both peered into the bag.

"Kid's clothes," Bobby Lee said.

Tulley studied the dark stain around the neckline of a blue sweater. He pointed it out to Bobby Lee. "That's blood."

They looked at each other.

Bobby Lee said, "Jude'll want to hear about this. Like, now."

CHAPTER NINE

Tonya tugged at the hem of her black Lycra dress, trying to pull it down so it covered her legs better. All she succeeded in doing was lowering the neckline. She wished she'd spent more than two seconds looking in the mirror before she walked out onto the front door step and all the cameras started clicking and popping. The dress was Amberlee's idea. She said it was slimming, being black, and the color was appropriate since she was the grieving mother. Tonya was too exhausted to point out that Corban was missing, not dead.

Shivering with the cold, she fended off microphones and started to read the short statement she'd been practicing. But her throat tightened so much she had to stop. The cameras loomed like vultures. Everywhere she looked big black glass eyes gleamed at her and flashes popped.

Amberlee said loudly, "My sister will take a few questions," and shoved an elbow into her ribs.

A TV reporter shouted, "The police are still questioning your boyfriend, Wade Miller. Do you think he had something to do with your son's disappearance?"

"No." Tonya was angry that anyone would even suggest it. "Wade loves Corban. He loves little kids."

"Do you think Corban's alive?" a woman asked. Tonya recognized Suzette Kelly from Channel 8.

The reporter was everything Tonya would choose to be if she could dial a new life. Size 2 but with implants. A narrow face with a cute little nose. Perfect blond hair flicked softly back in a layered Jennifer Anniston style. The kind of pink designer suit you'd have to leave Cortez to buy. Normally Tonya thought pearl necklaces were ridiculous, but Suzette looked classy in hers. It was the expensive kind with the really big pearls. Over the top of her outfit, she had on a pale pink coat with a white fur collar that made her look like a fashion model. Tonya thought it probably cost more than Wade's truck.

She tried to answer Suzette's question. "I don't know. I—"

Before she could put her feelings into words, Amberlee cut in and said, "We're praying our little angel will come home soon, Suzette."

"And you are?"

"Mrs. Amberlee Foley, Tonya's big sister. Corban's my nephew."

"Corban is your ex-husband's son with your sister, the half brother of your daughter. Do I have that right?"

"Yes." Before Suzette had time to ask another awkward question, Amberlee pointed to a man with the whitest teeth Tonya had ever seen.

"Brendon Bailey, Channel Four," he announced. "Tonya, sources close to the inquiry have alleged that your boyfriend has a history of domestic violence, yet you left your baby with him. Weren't you concerned?"

Tonya floundered. The only domestic violence she knew about was Brittany Kemple giving Wade a nose bleed. She said, "Wade's really good with Corban." It sounded feeble. She started to frame a better response when Suzette Kelly cut in.

"You were in a bar celebrating your sister's birthday while this man was with your child. Do you blame yourself?"

Tonya gasped. She wanted to say something dignified, but all that came out was a soft grunting sound.

Amberlee said, "My sister's upset. That's all for now, folks. I'll be available for more comments later." She offered a big smile and placed her arm around Tonya's shoulder, leaning into her so their heads were level. In Tonya's ear, she whispered, "Make another plea."

Tonya prayed for the strength to pull herself together for Corban's sake. Her voice shook and she felt light-headed as she said, "I'd like to thank all of you for covering this story. I have a message for the person who took Corban. Please, bring him back. I miss my baby. Please. I just want to hold him."

Shouts erupted as Amberlee steered her back into the house, but only one of them penetrated the fog in her head. She turned at exactly the same time Amberlee did, and a fist connected with her face. Tonya reeled back against the door frame and lost her balance. As she fell in the center of the doorway, the scene around her turned instantly into chaos. It was like something from the Jerry Springer show. People shouting and grabbing one another. Amberlee screaming at the man who'd landed the punch, Dan Foley, Corban's dad. He was yelling back at her and trying to reach Tonya.

A group of reporters struggled to hold him back. He looked past them to Tonya and hollered, "Satisfied now? You gave my son to a fucking killer, you stupid, lazy bitch."

Tonya tried to block the words out, but they kept coming.

"Call yourself a mother? Fucking useless, that's what you are." He tore himself away from the reporters and lunged past Amberlee, who seemed frozen on the spot. Standing over Tonya, he screamed at her, "I'm going to destroy you. And I'm going to kill that animal for what he did."

Tonya huddled against the door frame, sobbing and begging him to stop. As she peered out from beneath the arm protecting her face, she was stunned by a strange sight. The crowds of reporters were hard at work shooting the whole incident, some of them standing in front of cameras talking nonstop. Amberlee was smoothing her hairstyle and talking to the reporter with the extra-white teeth. No one was coming to help her. They were all just watching like this was happening on TV, not in real life.

Dan swung his foot like he was going to kick her, but instead said, "You're not even worth it," and spat in her face.

The crowd parted as he walked through them, then they were running after him, hurling questions and crowding around his car. Suzette Kelly had stayed behind. She hurried up the steps with her crew.

Crouching next to Tonya, she said to the camera, "I'm with Corban's mom. She was just knocked to the ground by Corban's enraged dad. Tonya, are you okay?"

Fluff from a microphone tickled Tonya's mouth. Her face ached. She was freezing. All she could say was, "Yes."

"Your ex-husband said some terrible things to you just then. How do you feel?"

"I don't know," Tonya whispered. She was too shocked to cry. All she could think was this had to be a dream, the worst dream of her life. Silently, she prayed, "Please God, let me wake up now."

"It sounds like Corban's dad blames you for what happened."

Tonya stared at the spectacular white fur around Suzette's neck. "Is that fox?" she asked.

"No." Suzette looked affronted. "Channel Eight."

Tonya laughed, and as the sound rose, so did a loud wailing sob.

Suzette positioned a comforting arm around her and glanced up at her cameraman. "Are you getting this?"

❖

Jude marched into the interview room with Pete Koertig and placed a series of evidence bags on the table in front of Wade Miller. Each contained an item of baby clothing recovered by the searchers.

"Recognize these garments?"

Miller shrugged.

"Yes or no, Mr. Miller?"

"Corban might have had a top like that."

"You talk like he's dead," Jude said coldly.

Koertig taunted, "Something you want to share with us?"

Miller was silent.

Jude lifted one of the bags. "His mother says these are the clothes Corban was wearing when she left him in your care." She pointed to a stain around the neckline of the light blue sweatshirt. "This is Corban's blood. How did it get there?"

"I wouldn't know."

"Don't waste my time. Did his clothes get blood on them when he injured himself?"

"I didn't see any."

"This clothing was found on the banks of the Dolores not far from where your truck was sighted the night Corban disappeared. Can you explain that?"

"No, ma'am."

"We're combing that area right now with scent dogs," Jude continued. "One of them is a specialist cadaver hound that can detect a body, even in water."

Miller sipped from the can of Coke he was holding, apparently unmoved. "I appreciate everyone giving up their time. It's mighty generous."

He was one cool customer, Jude thought, an accomplished liar who cultivated a flaky, harmless demeanor because it suited him to be underestimated. If she was hoping to rattle him by producing hard evidence, she'd misjudged his nerve.

Looking for a way to get under his skin, she said, "Not everyone likes small children. It might surprise you how many people actually sympathize with a parent figure when an accident occurs. People know how easy it is to take your eyes off a kid at the wrong moment."

He absorbed this with an expression of patient incomprehension, then replied, "I guess you guys see that kind of thing all the time."

Jude gave Koertig a nod. Her colleague had already suggested that they consider aiming a shotgun at Miller's balls to make him give up where he'd dumped the body. She'd brought him into the interview to frighten Miller, if that was even possible. The more she saw of this suspect, the more convinced she was that he had not just caused a child's death accidentally and covered it up. He was a cold-blooded killer.

Koertig loosened his tie and rolled up his shirt sleeves to reveal muscular, bronzed forearms that were a perfect foil for his sky blue eyes and straight blond buzz cut. Sixty years ago, he would have been recruited by Goebbels for master-race propaganda.

"We see plenty," he responded to Miller's disingenuous remark. "Wanna know something about these lowlife chickenshits that hurt little kids? They're always the first to give it up in the pen. Real fucking sissies."

"You'd have to expect that." Jude directed her remark to Koertig. "It's a certain type of coward who hurts a child. I read somewhere a lot of them are impotent or they have other sexual performance problems."

Koertig sneered. "They can't satisfy a woman so they take it out on a kid?"

"That's one theory. Shrinks say they're basically immature, so they get jealous of their girlfriend's kids and bully them."

"You mean like sibling rivalry?"

"Pretty pathetic, huh? A grown man acting like he has to compete with a baby."

Koertig jerked a thumb at Miller. "Looks like our friend here can relate."

Miller's face didn't register a flicker of emotion, but Jude could hear a soft rapping beneath the table and knew the barbs had struck home. Miller was aggravated but concealing it well. She pushed a little harder.

"Your ex, Brittany Kemple, had some pretty unkind things to say about your bedroom skills."

Koertig started laughing, then made a show of smothering it. The table tapping grew louder and more erratic. Miller was on the brink of losing it and Jude wanted to see him go there, so they'd have something to show a jury. Miller wouldn't fool anyone in a courtroom with his laid-back halfwit act if they had video of him out of control.

Jude grinned up at Koertig. "Nothing like a disappointed woman to spill the beans."

"Oh, she was harsh. The size issue." Koertig's attempt at sympathy was undermined by the snicker he choked back. "That must be hard on you, pal."

"I don't know what lies that fucking little tramp told you." Miller's voice rose. "But I measure up okay and I can prove it."

"That won't be necessary." Jude smirked. "We believe you, Mr. Miller."

Koertig adopted a conciliatory tone. "Yeah, women make up stories to explain why they dump a guy. That stuff about not even feeling it...we thought that was pretty far-fetched. I mean even if it is just four inches and the girth is what she said...well she'd feel it. Probably." He looked at Jude as if seeking confirmation.

She shrugged. "I can't honestly say. I've never seen one that sm... of those dimensions."

Miller was red in the face. He'd stopped tapping. Jude guessed he had his fists clenched so he wouldn't throw a punch. "You think you're so fucking smart," he ground out. "I know what this is. Cop tricks to get me all riled up so I make myself look bad."

"I think we hurt his feelings," Koertig said.

Miller's eyes glittered with venom. "You got nothing on me."

It was not a response they heard too often from an innocent man. Watching him intently, Jude realized he was not going to reveal himself. They'd come close, but he was self-aware enough not to blow it. Miller had a temper, but self-preservation came first. Along the track, when they had more against him than his own constantly changing stories, she would find a way to take advantage of that.

She said, "We have a warrant to search your home, Mr. Miller."

"Be my guest."

"Is there anything you want to mention before we begin?"

"Such as?"

She wanted to backhand the arrogant half-grin off his face and yell *don't fuck with me, you murdering piece of shit.* Instead she delivered a routine answer. "The presence of illegal substances. Any bloodstains you might care to explain."

Miller shrugged. "No."

Cautioning herself again to keep her temper in check, Jude opened the case file she'd brought in and flipped through the typed sheets of notes. "Mr. Miller. In your last statement you described finding the goat's head on Ms. Perkins's front yard. According to the physical evidence in the house and the statement of the individual who confessed to the vandalism, the head was originally thrown into the living room. What can you tell us about that?"

Miller took a moment, then his face crumpled and he was suddenly outpouring, "It was dumb. I know that. You gotta understand something. She'd have gone hysterical on me. So I took it outside and made it look like a joke. I did it for her."

"So, you lied in your earlier statement?"

"Only about finding it in the yard. Everything else was true." He had the passionate self-righteousness of a man who believed his own fiction.

Unimpressed, Jude said, "It doesn't look good, Mr. Miller. The lies. The baby clothes we found exactly where you admitted you drove that night. Who knows what we'll discover when the divers start work in the reservoir. I think it's time we heard the whole story, don't you?"

Wade buried his head in his hands, the personality change complete. His shoulders shook convincingly. He said, "I fucked it all up. I should have told you, but I knew what she'd think."

"Of you?"

"What the fuck do you think? I was supposed to be looking after him, and there's bricks through the windows and blood everywhere and a fucking goat's head. And he's disappeared. Jesus."

"Is there anything else you'd like to change about your last statement?"

"I didn't go out to get diapers. The crying was making me nuts."

"Corban was awake and crying when you left to drive in the direction of Dove Creek?"

"Yeah. I couldn't shut him up. I gave him Jim Beam and then some pills I found, and then I went out."

"Pills." Jude repeated this new information. "What pills?"

"I dunno. I thought they were for her headaches or something."

"I see."

"I know what you're thinking, but you're wrong. He was there when I left, and the next time I looked he was gone."

"I'm still not clear how his clothes ended up in the middle of nowhere a few miles from where your truck was seen," Jude said.

Miller shrugged. "You're the detective, not me."

❖

In tourist literature Cortez was described as the "gateway to the Mesa Verde National Park." Visitors passing through thought the place looked like a quaint Southwestern backwater. Its olde worlde charm was enhanced by historic signage and the careful preservation of the original bank buildings and trading posts. People from back East tended to get excited when they saw horses tethered in the main street, so the city council offered incentives for this, and the local dude ranches routinely drove a few head of cattle along the roads out of town so their clients, in full cowboy getup, could add to the general vibe.

Wade Miller lived in a part of town no visitor saw unless they were dealing drugs. His was a low-rent mobile home, one of a cluster crammed on a small dusty lot. There wasn't a blade of grass to be seen. The area reverberated with nerve-shattering barking.

"He's got dogs," the supervisor noted. Speech barely budged the cigarette that hung off his lower lip. He seemed smug about unlocking Miller's door so the police could execute a search warrant. "Guy's a real fuckwad."

Pete Koertig engaged him in discussion about this observation while Jude escorted a couple of animal control officers in to remove the dogs while the search was conducted. Their water bowls still had puddles in the bottom. Wade Miller hadn't been home since early Sunday morning, when he'd arrived at the police station, but the dogs seemed fine so they must have been fed before he went to Tonya's on Saturday evening.

"When did you last see Mr. Miller?" Jude asked the smoke-shrouded super.

He scrunched his eyebrows and scratched his freckled head, destroying a glued-down comb-over. "Saturday night."

"At what time?"

"I wanna say twelve thirty midnight."

"Midnight," she repeated.

"Fucking dogs start carrying on soon as they hear his truck. I was awake anyways. Can't sleep more than five hours on account of my prostate."

Jude offered the appropriate sympathetic nod. Koertig was chafing his hands together behind his back, keeping a lid on the high-five impulse. Yet again, they'd caught Wade Miller out in a lie, and this one was important. He had come back to his apartment after his supposed diaper quest, a piece of information he hadn't volunteered. There had to be a reason he stopped by. He would cite the dogs, of course, and from all accounts he treated them better than his girlfriends. But Jude had a hard time believing that a guy who was only planning to be away for one night would have to check on his pets after only a few hours.

"Did you actually see Mr. Miller arrive?" she asked blandly.

"Oh, yeah." The super was rearranging his stringy hair. "I got a door scope. The deluxe model. That's a security measure. You can see who's coming and going in the parking lot."

Jude asked one of the detectives on the search team to accompany the guy to his trailer, photograph the door scope, and take a statement. Animal control had the three dogs on leashes, and Jude waited for them to be led out before motioning to the search team.

They didn't have a lot of area to cover. The trailer was your basic single man's sty, the kind that only saw a vacuum cleaner when female company was anticipated. They examined every square inch, progressively taking the place apart, looking for a hair, smudge of blood, a child's fingerprint. They got into the plumbing, lifted the carpets, emptied every cupboard. Eventually they reached Miller's bed and inspected it with the same methodical deliberation, collecting yet more trace.

So far, there was no murder weapon, no bloodstained clothing conveniently piled in the laundry basket, no sign of a methodical cleanup. If this place had ever seen bleach Jude would be surprised. She lifted the mattress, ignoring Koertig's half-hearted offer to do it for her.

"Anything?" She was about to lower it when she realized her companions were not silent because they hadn't heard her. They were staring at the box base, completely transfixed. She craned down. Wade Miller kept his money under his mattress. Laid out flat, in row after orderly row.

"There must be five hundred bucks here," Koertig said.

Jude handed the mattress on to him and took several photographs of the cash, then she picked up a twenty-dollar bill by one corner. There was something odd about the way it hung. She peeled a glove away with her teeth and cautiously felt the bill.

"It's wet."

Koertig moved the mattress away and propped it against the wall. They inspected Miller's cache more closely. Every bill was wet.

"It can't have been under the mattress for long," Jude said. "In this weather it could take three or four days to dry out, I guess."

"He's going to say his wallet fell in the toilet," Koertig said.

"And we're going to say every body of water has its own special diatom profile."

For the first time ever, Koertig stared at her like he was impressed. With a wry smirk, he said, "This is why they pay you the big bucks."

Jude grinned. "Nope. It's because I'm good-looking."

This raised howls of laughter from the entire search team, not exactly a vote of confidence for her feminine charms.

Feigning chagrin, she muttered, "You think I'm kidding."

"Not at all," Koertig gallantly announced. "What we think—and I hesitate to use the word 'think'—is that you are surrounded by dickbrains who are not fully evolved. Let me put that another way. We lack the sophistication to appreciate a woman of your Amazonian attributes."

"You're saying I could beat you at arm wrestling?"

Koertig's big pink face was doleful. "No comment."

❖

"What do you think?" Pratt asked as they headed for the meeting room.

"It's too soon to charge him."

"What if he tries to skip town?"

"We'll be waiting."

"Twenty-four-hour surveillance." Pratt was the picture of gloom. Jude could hear him calculating the resource commitment in his head.

She said, "We need to build a case against him. He's not going to confess, and everything we have right now is circumstantial."

Pratt paused at the door to cough into a Kleenex. Jude took a step back. A dose of the flu was all she needed. Pratt waved her on, and she left him in the hallway to wheeze in peace.

There were probably sixty people waiting for the afternoon meeting, all members of various agencies now involved in the case. Ten FBI agents had joined the investigation that morning, and additional detectives had been sent from each county as far up as Grand Junction. As Jude faced the room, she could feel the terse anticipation. There was none of the usual jocular chatter, the undercurrent of mumbling that typically provided background noise on these occasions.

The discovery of the bloodstained garments had cemented one hard fact. Corban Foley was dead. Their top priority now was to recover his body.

After getting the greetings and kudos out of the way, Jude kicked off her summary with the announcement everyone was anticipating. "This is now a criminal homicide investigation. Our primary suspect is Wade Miller, the boyfriend of Tonya Perkins, mother of the missing child."

She signaled one of the deputies and he dimmed the lights. Jude projected a photograph of Miller onto the screen for ID purposes.

"As yet, we do not have a confession from Mr. Miller. He has provided us with several statements, all of which are contradictory, and has routinely lied to police since the commencement of this inquiry. An examination of Mr. Miller's vehicle by Montezuma County's K-9 cadaver dog produced a positive alert for residual scent. It is our contention that Mr. Miller's truck was used to transport the body of Corban Foley to a site in the vicinity of the Dolores River and the McPhee reservoir, where evidence was disposed of and the body concealed."

She brought up the first of several pictures of the clothing just discovered. "These are Corban Foley's garments. The blood is human and male. We are awaiting DNA results to confirm if it belongs to the victim. Note the concentration around the neck area and the lower torso. A knife may be our murder weapon."

Jude switched to the next image, but was interrupted by the shrill of an alarm siren and Sheriff Pratt yelling from the back of the room, "Clear the doorway!"

He was on his radio, waving his arm for quiet. After a few seconds, he cursed and said, "Folks, we have a situation out front. Corban Foley's father is armed and in the building. He's taken a female deputy hostage. Juanita Perry."

The FBI agents looked like someone had just announced a lottery win for them. Almost in unison they unholstered their weapons and headed for the door. "We'll handle this, sir," the one in the lead informed Pratt.

They hadn't made it into the hallway when a voice yelled, "Get back or I'll shoot her."

The agents fell back and waved for everyone in the room to get down and take cover. Jude ducked past the clamor of cops turning tables on their sides and made it to the door. "Sir, get down," she told Pratt.

A few seconds later a man in his late twenties loomed into view dragging a terrified young deputy. He had a gun to her temple.

"Where's the sheriff," he bellowed.

"Drop your weapon, Mr. Foley," Jude yelled. "This isn't helping your son."

"My son is dead."

Jude signaled the FBI agent nearest her and gestured toward one of the side doors that expanded the meeting room. Out of Foley's view, several agents waved some deputies to join them and filed silently from the room.

"Sir, I'm asking you to release the deputy." Jude kept her voice calm.

"Not until I see the sheriff."

Pratt stepped out from his spot against the wall and moved into the hallway. "I'm Sheriff Pratt, son."

Jude glanced across to the agent waiting at the middle door. He signaled an affirmative. They had Foley covered from the rear.

"Where are you keeping him?" Foley demanded.

"We don't have Corban, sir."

"Not my son. That murdering filth, Miller. Where is he?"

"We can discuss Mr. Miller when you release the deputy."

"I have a better idea," Foley said. "I'll swap her for him."

Jude edged out into the hall to shield Pratt. "At least lower your gun, Mr. Foley. You're not a killer. If something goes wrong and you shoot Deputy Perry by accident, how will you live with yourself? She has a baby the same age as Corban. She's a good mom."

Foley's expression grew even more anguished, but he lowered the gun and instead pointed it at the deputy's back. "Don't try anything," he warned. "Bring him out. Now!"

Jude took a step closer, this time getting directly between Pratt and the gunman. Past Foley, she could see several FBI agents crouched at the far end of the hallway. They had a clean shot. She only had to signal and they would take it.

Behind her, Pratt whispered, "Don't."

Jude knew exactly what he was thinking. The distressed father of a missing child gets shot dead by police in a hostage incident. Tragic, yes. But also a public relations disaster.

She said, "I'm laying my weapon down, Mr. Foley. And I'm going to swap places with Deputy Perry." Slowly she lowered the Glock to the floor. "Now let her go."

When Foley hesitated, Jude rose and moved toward him, her arms in the air. Indecision flashed across his face, then he pushed his hostage forward and trained his gun on Jude.

As Pratt steered the dazed deputy into the meeting room, Jude took rapid stock of Foley. She had the height advantage, and he was stressed and emotional. The combination was dangerous because it made him unpredictable. Yet, from all she had read, Foley was a decent guy who had left Cortez so he could improve himself and build a better life. He was ambitious and loved his son. He'd applied for sole custody of Corban, claiming Tonya was unfit to be a full-time parent. He was not about to destroy everything he'd worked for. At least that's what she chose to gamble on.

"Mr. Foley, I'm the detective in charge of this case. I know where Mr. Miller is and I'm willing to take you to him, but I need you to put your weapon down first."

"I'm not stupid." Foley was pointing the gun half-heartedly now, wavering in his aim at her chest. He was plainly uncomfortable playing the vigilante. "I know you're going to arrest me as soon as I drop it."

"That's true. We will arrest you. But you could still walk out of here in one piece tonight. You haven't hurt anyone. You are in a state of emotional distress, and we understand that. If you put it down, you have my word I'll make sure you get to talk to Mr. Miller."

Foley was panting. His eyes swung to Pratt, then back to Jude. She could take him, she thought. But if he fired a shot, even accidentally, he would be a dead man. She didn't want to risk it.

"How do I know you're not lying," he demanded.

"You don't. But frankly, your options aren't looking too good." She indicated the rear of the hall. "That's the FBI back there, and you *know* they want to shoot you. And on my left, there's maybe fifty cops in that room. They'll make sure you're carried out of here on a stretcher if you fire that weapon. You can come see Mr. Miller with me now, or take your chances here. I'm walking away."

Jude turned her back on him. She hadn't taken two paces when the wind hissed out of him, the gun clattered onto the floor, and he choked out, "I'm sorry. I never meant for things to turn out this way. I just wanted to speak to someone."

Jude kicked the weapon back into the meeting room and took her handcuffs from her belt as officers swarmed from all directions to restrain him. "You're under arrest, Mr. Foley. Place your hands behind your back." As she cuffed him, she said, "I'm very sorry about your son. We all are."

"You know he did it, don't you?"

Jude said neutrally, "Mr. Miller is helping us with our inquiries."

"He's not helping, trust me. I know the guy. He's playing you."

She took Foley by the arm and started walking. Catching a look of consternation from Sheriff Pratt she said, "Stand everyone down, sir. I'll bring Mr. Foley to booking once we're done."

"I wasn't going to shoot you," Foley said as they walked. A couple of deputies followed them.

"I know. But plans can go wrong and people can get hurt."

"Have you arrested him?"

"Mr. Foley," Jude said patiently, "we haven't found Corban yet. We have no idea what really happened that night. We can't make an arrest unless we have hard evidence that Mr. Miller committed a crime. I know you don't want to hear this, but Wade Miller is probably going to walk out of here tonight."

"Jesus H. Christ."

"All I can promise you is that we are watching him. If he has something to hide, we are going to find out what it is. But we need time."

"He killed my son, and he's dumped him somewhere like trash. You want me to back off?"

"I'm asking you to let us do our job." Jude knew he felt helpless and wanted to give him a sense of purpose. "You could help us. Talk to Tonya. We need to know if she's telling us everything."

"I think I blew that already. I went round to Amberlee's place and they were out there talking to the reporters, dressed like hookers. I don't know what happened. I went crazy and hit her."

Great. The father beats up the mother in front of the whole world, then takes a deputy hostage at gunpoint, just in case anyone thought the only guy with a temper was Miller.

"She used to be nice," Foley said wistfully. "When she was a kid. Real sweet."

So nice, you had sex with her while you were married to her sister. Jude kept her thoughts to herself.

Foley stopped walking and turned bewildered eyes to her. "Why would she have left Corban with him? How could she trust that guy?"

Tempting the Fates? Had Tonya unconsciously placed her child at risk because on some level she wanted him gone? Did she want her life back the way it was before, but without the guilt of being a bad mother who gave her child up willingly to the father who thought she was unfit? She had to know there was a risk in leaving Corban with Wade. If he had been violent or even threatening with the child at any time when she was present, she could not pretend she thought her son would be safe.

"Mr. Foley, why apply for custody now?" Jude asked.

"I went to a lawyer the minute I heard she was with that jerk. I know stuff about Wade Miller—I went to school with him. I knew he'd hurt Corban."

"Has anyone said anything to you about how he treats your son?"

Foley gave a short, bitter laugh. "He's been on his best behavior.

They only got hooked up a couple of months ago. But there's something Amberlee said—"

"About Mr. Miller?"

"Yeah. He cut Corban's hair. Did it himself. But he shaved out the center so Corban was bald on the top of his head. Amberlee said it was like he meant to make Corban look ugly, just like him."

"This was just a few days ago?" And Tonya hadn't thought it was worth mentioning?

"Tuesday, I think."

Jude frowned. "We were hoping to get a statement from you before all...this."

With a pained grimace, Foley said, "I guess nothing I tell you guys is worth shit now."

"We'll still need to interview you. We have to clear you as a suspect in Corban's disappearance."

"About Miller...can we drop it?"

Jude was surprised. She'd never intended to do anything more than confront Wade Miller with the enraged Foley and threaten to leave them alone. But she was reluctant to take advantage of this man's desperation.

"Why?" she asked.

"I'd have to kill him and I'm in enough trouble. Why should I go to prison when he's the criminal."

"Smart thinking." Jude instructed the deputies, "Book Mr. Foley, and when you're done let me know."

"The hair." He looked ill. "That was weird, right?"

Jude met his eyes. "Very weird."

CHAPTER TEN

A unt Chastity! Come see!" Adeline stuck her head around the door of Chastity's office. "Guess who's on TV."

"Is it really important?" Chastity Young completed a column of figures before she turned to face her fourteen-year-old niece. It was time she hired someone to do her accounts for the business. Her home health care company was growing so quickly the administration, coupled with the nursing hours she put in, was becoming more than she could handle.

Adeline heaved a teenage sigh. "You've been stuck doing that boring stuff all night."

"Okay." Chastity allowed herself to be hauled out of her chair and down the hallway. "But only for five minutes."

"I'll wind it back." Adeline, a TiVo junkie, snatched up the remote and smugly returned the picture to "play."

Chastity stood behind an easy chair, wearily resting her elbows on the back. "Tell me it's not *MythBusters*," she mumbled.

To Chastity's surprise, they were watching CNN. The face on the screen was a little thinner than she remembered, and slightly drawn. But Detective Jude Devine did exactly what she did the very first time Chastity set eyes on her. She made her very uncomfortable.

"There's a little boy missing where Detective Devine lives," Adeline said. "It looks like he got kidnapped."

Jude was introduced as the detective leading the investigation. The camera zoomed in, and Chastity was struck anew by the languid gray-green beauty of her eyes. They seemed an odd fit with features that were almost severe. Her face was lean, her jaw sharply defined and squarish, the chin as stubborn as any Chastity had seen. She had the kind of classic Roman nose plastic surgeons across the nation bobbed into pert inanity. It lent her profile a granite authority few women possessed.

With her boyishly cut black-brown hair and her tall, powerful build, she had an androgynous quality Chastity found disconcerting. Yet there was a vulnerability to her as well.

Chastity had seen it that day in Rapture, after the shooting, when Jude walked Adeline across the desert toward her. On her trail bike, the injured child Daniel clinging to her, Chastity had rolled to a halt a few feet away from them. The moment was etched in her mind's eye, perpetually replaying itself even when she attempted to dwell on something else. She had tried to distance herself from what happened in various ways, rationalizing it in the context of extreme circumstances, determinedly referring to Jude as "Detective Devine"—which only made matters worse because that came out as "divine"—and dismissing her own behavior as unsurprising, given her relief to see Adeline alive and well.

She'd kicked her side-stand out, dismounted, and helped Daniel slide down from behind her. Adeline squealed his name, opened her arms out wide, and the two children ran into a frantic embrace. Chastity dropped her helmet on the seat and faced Jude. Automatically, they took a few tentative steps toward one another, but there was such naked grief in the detective's face, Chastity reached for her automatically. She was not even surprised that Jude stepped into her arms without hesitation. She was taller, stronger, harder. Yet Chastity sensed a need in her so intense she answered it the only way she knew how—by giving. By holding her and murmuring soothing words, stroking her hair, gentling her. She could remember wanting desperately to give her back the morning, changed. She wanted to evict from memory whatever had gouged away at the cool confidence that seemed so much a part of the detective the first time they met.

The strength of those feelings still startled her; that she could have them for a stranger startled her even more. She wasn't sure how long they'd stood there washing into one another, ignoring the constraints of unfamiliarity. She could still feel the weight of Jude's hands resting below the small of her back, the shape of her head, the press of her thighs. How strange it was, she'd thought since, that even naked she'd never felt so connected to another person. When finally they drew back to stare at each other, she knew Jude felt the same connection.

She took Chastity's face between her hands as if cupping a butterfly she was afraid to hurt, and Chastity found herself mesmerized.

Helplessly, she imprinted the dark-fringed eyes, the firm nose and straight but sensual mouth, on the canvas of her mind.

"You have no idea," Jude said. Then she lowered her head and brushed her lips across Chastity's.

The kiss was so swift, so cautious, Chastity had barely closed her eyes when she was released and suddenly Adeline was in her arms, weeping for the loss of her dead sister and begging to go home. When Chastity looked up from ministering to her a few minutes later, Jude had gone.

That day seemed like a long time ago, now, yet barely six months had passed. Chastity had meant to call Jude at least once to say how thankful she was. Instead she wrote a letter and had Adeline do the same. She sent them together. A few weeks later, Jude replied, also in writing. She invited them to drop by if they were ever in Paradox Valley.

"We could go down there and join the search," Adeline said.

"It's nice of you to think about that." Chastity couldn't stop her eyes from lingering once again on Jude's mouth as she spoke to the reporter.

What had happened in that moment out in the Utah desert belonged to the emotional terrain of that day only, she told herself. People did uncharacteristic things at such times. She understood the kiss as a recognition of the human frailty they shared and a thank you from Jude for the brief escape from horror witnessed. Likewise those mystifying words: *You have no idea.*

"How far is it to Cortez?" Adeline asked.

"About four hundred miles."

"Then it will only take us a day to get there." Adeline bounced in her seat. "Can we?"

"You have school."

Chastity knew how ineffectual that argument was. Adeline was easily two years ahead of her age group academically. Attempting to assess her learning needs, the school had just given her an SAT. Out of 2400, she'd scored an impressive 2300. In other words, her dean said, she would be able to pick her school when the time came. In fact, she could start college now if she wanted. But at fourteen, Adeline had led such a sheltered life she seemed very young for her age.

Her upbringing was responsible for that. Adeline was one of Chastity's older sister's many children. Vonda had married a man who, only a few years into their marriage, decided polygamy was the lifestyle he wanted. Tucker Fleming had offered Chastity the honor of becoming his second wife and, when she'd foolishly declined, packed up his family and moved south to the polygamist stronghold of Hildale/Colorado City. He'd since acquired a harem of three other "celestial wives," another ten children, and the sister Chastity loved and looked up to had all but vanished.

Adeline was brought up in this nightmare until she was eleven, at which time Tucker started planning her "sealing" to a friend of his, who thought marrying children was the Heavenly Father's plan for all right-thinking males of forty. Somehow Vonda had persuaded her husband that Adeline was not going to make a good enough wife for the chosen pedophile and that they should hand her over to Chastity. She was supposed to see to it that Adeline acquired the necessary feminine attributes to serve a husband appropriately in the future.

They'd returned for Adeline when she was fourteen, with Tucker hell-bent on marrying her to his brother Loudell, another convert to the child-bride fraternity. In the end, they were ordered by their "prophet" to give Adeline to Nathaniel Epperson, the seventy-something they'd pimped another of their daughters to. It was at the Epperson compound in Rapture that Chastity first encountered Jude Devine.

The detective was investigating the slaying of one of Epperson's wives and had just arrested Naoma Epperson, the head wife. This set off a chain of events Chastity had never fully pieced together. All she knew was that after the dust had settled, Adeline's older sister Summer was dead. And so was the baby she was giving birth to. Gunned down by the "family" they were part of as they tried to run to safety.

Chastity had legally adopted Adeline a few months later.

"School." Adeline snorted. "Like I'm going to learn anything. This is important. They said it's the biggest search they've ever had."

"By the time we get there they'll probably have found him already," Chastity warned lamely.

"Then we can go see the Anasazi ruins." Adeline had it all figured out. "And maybe do some climbing. We can take the snowmobile."

Chastity sighed. "I can't leave the business."

"What about Mrs. Smith? You said she was trained now so she can take over if anything happens." For good measure, she cranked up the emotional blackmail. "How are we ever going to climb to Everest Base

Camp next year if you can't leave this place for a day?"

"Okay, you can cease and desist." Chastity refocused her attention on the screen. Jude looked...bleak. "I'll phone Mrs. Smith. But we'll have to leave tomorrow morning if we're going to help."

Adeline's dark eyes flashed wayward delight. "Don't worry. I'm ready now." At Chastity's frown, she explained, "They ran this on CNN a few hours ago. I figured you'd be up for it since you feel indebted to Detective Devine. So I got packed. I've put your hiking gear in the car."

"Remind me..." Chastity muttered. "Why did I adopt you?"

❖

Jude parked just inside her driveway so she wouldn't have to shovel her way out of her garage the next morning. The lights were on thanks to an electronic timer. A motorist passing would assume someone was home, which was the general idea. Jude quickly swept a glance around the house and yard, then focused automatically on a small dark shape on her front porch, the one thing that was not as she'd left it that morning.

Unholstering her Glock, she took a circumspect path toward her front door, eyes sweeping the surrounding trees for any movement. Not that she could see anything but her yellow outdoor light bouncing off mounds of snow. She reached the house, flattened her back to the wall, sidled quickly to the corner, and peered around.

A small black cat lay inert on her doormat.

Jude mounted the steps uncertainly. Was this some kind of sick joke? A message from crazy Hank Thompson, maybe? Back to the wall, she darted constant looks around, alert to any shaft of light or crunch of snow or crack of a twig. She didn't feel as though she were being watched, but that could just be tiredness.

From the shadowed corner by the front door, she gazed down at the animal, then crouched, moving slowly so she didn't spook it if it was actually alive and just sheltering where it could find some scant protection from the elements. She was filled with pity when she saw how thin it was. Emaciated.

A perfect end to a perfect day. She gets home and has to bury a fellow creature robbed of its life by a quirk of fate that has one of its kind starve and the next dine daily on Fancy Feast. She'd read once that black cats were the least adoptable. Some shelters euthanized them automatically because they would never find homes.

"I'm so sorry," she said and ran her hand over the thin, dry fur.

The feline quickened and two huge gold green eyes gazed up at her from a pinched face. It could barely lift its head, but it offered a silent meow that cut Jude to the heart. The little cat was asking for its life.

"Don't move," she commanded.

She got up quickly, jammed her key into the lock, and shoved the front door open. The cat weighed nothing. She carried it indoors and laid it on the nearest soft chair, frantically wondering what she should do and whether there was enough time left to make it to a veterinarian. The nearest were in Montrose, but none would be open at this hour, and the emergency animal hospital in Grand Junction was over an hour away.

Jude ran upstairs to her linen closet and found a soft towel and a face cloth. She wet the cloth, swaddled the cat in the towel, picked up a sofa cushion, and headed out the door once more.

"I'll make a deal with you," she told her dying visitor as she carried it back down to the Dakota. "Hang on for an hour and thirty minutes, and you'll have a home for the rest of your life."

She slapped the cushion onto the passenger seat, punched a hollow in the center, and laid the cat there. Then she squeezed some water from the face cloth into the side of its mouth.

"You can do this," she said. "Don't give up."

The cat stared up at her for a beat, then seemed to relax. Jude pushed the door almost closed and hurried around to the driver's side. Once she was in her seat, she leaned over to pull the passenger door swiftly shut, talking soothing nonsense to the cat the whole time.

She headed north on Highway 50, her headlights bouncing off the snowbanks on either side of the road. The drive was more familiar than her own backyard, but in these conditions the road was iced over and so treacherous she could take no risks. Fresh snow was no longer coming down to provide something for her tires to grip.

When she came to a straight stretch that still had a powder snow surface, she phoned ahead to tell the vet who she was and that she was bringing in an animal that would probably die. The woman she spoke to told her to drive carefully so she didn't get herself killed trying to be a hero.

It felt like the longest drive of her life, and when she finally saw the Welcome to Grand Junction sign, she stopped the Dakota for a moment to slow her heart rate.

The roads around the town had been plowed, creating trenches wide enough for two vehicles. No one was out driving. Jude followed the directions to North Road and felt sick with relief when she finally spotted the veterinary emergency hospital. The cat was still alive and put up no resistance when she rushed it indoors bundled against her body, her overcoat wrapped around the two of them.

She was greeted by a wispy-haired brunette vet tech who looked slightly older than twelve and slightly taller than five feet. When she saw the cat, she hustled Jude directly into an examination room and ran through the Staff Only door yelling, "Dr. Gordon!"

Not a good sign, Jude thought.

The veterinarian entered the room a moment later and briefly examined the cat. He said, "I can euthanize her humanely or we can fight for her."

When Jude said, "Fight," he rushed the cat away.

The young vet tech came back and announced, "This is going to take a while. Would you like to wait or call us in the morning?"

Jude contemplated driving back to Montrose, exhausted, in extreme conditions and decided she'd like to stay alive. "I'll wait," she said. "Any chance of coffee?"

The vet tech, whose name badge said Courtney, smiled. "That sounds like a really good idea. Maybe I'll join you."

She showed Jude back to the waiting room and turned up shortly after with a pot of coffee and a real mug. "I know I should be giving you a plastic cup, but I thought you might like this better, Detective."

She sat with Jude for a short while, answering the phone occasionally. Between times, Jude tried to read magazines with pretty but vacuous-looking women on the covers. In the end she phoned Eddie House, one of the few people she was close to in the Four Corners. Eddie was an expert at rehabilitating sick and maimed creatures. He was pretty effective with injured people, too.

She said, "It's Jude. I'm sitting in the vet clinic in Grand Junction."

"You hit an animal with your truck?" Eddie asked.

"No. I found a stray cat on my doorstep when I got home. Starving. Almost dead." She didn't expand. With Eddie, she found herself cutting the excess from her conversation almost as much as he did. Right now, it was easier, too. She was exhausted.

As usual, Eddie's mind worked in different ways from hers. He asked gravely, "Have you named her?"

"Not yet. I thought I'd wait and see if she makes it first."

Eddie took his time answering, also the norm. "I name all my animals when they are sent to me."

"It's easy for you," Jude muttered. "But I don't have your hookup to the Great Spirit." These days she understood Eddie's sense of humor well enough to tease him sometimes. All the same, she was relieved when he laughed.

"What does this cat look like?"

"Small and black with big golden eyes. And it meows without making any sound."

Eddie said, "She will live. Or she would not have come to you."

"I don't know if it's a female."

He said, "I bet five dollars."

"Done." Jude laughed. "How's Zach?"

Zachariah Carter had been a key prosecution witness in the Huntsberger case. Another casualty of the FLDS polygamists, he'd been expelled by his community after a life of beatings and brainwashing. Jude had asked Eddie to take him in, and the kid was barely recognizable after six months of care and good food. He was now working toward his high school diploma and planning to become an army medic.

"He speaks of going back," Eddie surprised her by saying.

"To his family?"

"Only to shoot a man."

Jude rolled her eyes. "What did you tell him?"

"There are many paths."

"And?"

"A gun gives you the body, not the bird."

"Navajo wisdom?"

"No. Henry Thoreau."

"And what else?" Jude waited.

"Why go to jail for scum?"

"Thank you."

"He won't make that journey," Eddie said with conviction.

"And you know this how?"

"I have the car keys."

"Great. I feel confident."

"It could be worse," Eddie said.

"How? How could it be worse than him going back to the people who half-killed him?"

"I could be Apache. Then I would go with him."

Jude groaned. "I don't know why I called you expecting comfort and peace of mind."

"Me either."

"You're a big help," Jude said.

"You, too."

Jude laughed. "Does that mean you want me to come talk some white folks' sense into him?"

"Yes."

"Then why not say so in the first place?"

"Because I am letting you make the offer."

Jude wasn't going to rise to the bait. Eddie was always hinting about her being a control freak. She said, "I'll come by later in the week."

"Good." He hung up.

An hour went by, and just as Jude felt herself falling asleep sitting up, the vet came out and announced, "We managed to get an IV in. I need to tell you she may not make it."

Jude said, "Just do the best you can. I don't care how much it costs."

"You got it." Dr. Gordon hesitated. "I guess you're up to your neck down there with that kidnapping. Terrible thing. Taken from his bed." He shook his head, a bewildered bystander in a world gone mad.

Jude hadn't seen any television that evening. Obviously the media had chosen their angle; a child abducted from the safety of his bed was the scariest spin they could place on the story. "They are such asses," she said.

Dr. Gordon gave her an odd look. "There's a sofa out back. You ought to get some sleep." He led the way.

Mercy's house was only a mile from the clinic, Jude thought, but she was going to sleep on a ratty old sofa in a place that smelled of antiseptic and reverberated with the cries of frightened animals. What else was there to say about the nature of their relationship? Sure, she could call Mercy and be invited over and given the spare bedroom, free occupancy of the special hell that came with knowing her girlfriend was on the other side of the wall, sleeping with another woman. If she got really lucky, maybe she would hear them having sex. Yep, that was how she wanted to end the day.

Jude winced. What did it say about her that she'd invested the past six months trying to build a relationship with a woman who would never love her and never be there when she needed anything more than sex? Jude took the blanket Dr. Gordon offered, said good night, and lay down on the lumpy cushions. Shafts of light infiltrated the room through various portals, the perfect recipe for restlessness. Her mind drifted to something Mercy had said a couple of months back, after they were lolling, sated, against their pillows.

"It's going nowhere, but the going is really good."

She was always dismayed when Mercy talked like that, writing off all possibility of a future as though they had no choice in the matter. "Why is it going nowhere?" she'd demanded.

"Because love requires more than either of us can give. We both need other people for that."

"Are you saying we're inherently selfish?"

"That's a value judgment I wouldn't make." Mercy seemed genuinely thoughtful. "I'm saying we have to own up to who we are. I know my nature, and I think you know yours. But you keep making decisions as if you're a different kind of person."

"You're the one who tells me not to be a jealous Neanderthal," Jude said.

"Because if you make choices a jealous Neanderthal can't live with, you'll never be happy," Mercy pointed out reasonably. "Either *you* have to change, or your choices have to change."

Jude watched a pair of feet move past the door and heard Dr. Gordon's voice in the hallway. Maybe Mercy was right. Maybe she kept herself in situations that would doom her to dissatisfaction. Why? Was that how she avoided tying herself down? Was it easier to blame her flunk record in relationships on bad luck than self-sabotage? Did she want to be alone?

She rolled over and studied the wall. No, she didn't want to be alone. *Alone* was not all it was cracked up to be. But she had no idea how she was going to change that state of affairs.

Meantime, it was Mercy or nothing. And she'd just chosen nothing.

CHAPTER ELEVEN

Tonya stared at Wade across the kitchen table and said, "It's late. I think you should go."

"Go? Go where? The cops have torn my place apart."

"I don't know why you came here." Over and over, Tonya saw Corban's sweatshirt with the bloodstains around the neck. He was dead. The sheriff had said the case was now a homicide investigation and Wade was the main suspect.

Tonya had to sit there listening to that mean bitch detective telling her how Wade murdered Corban, and almost everything he'd said to her and the police was a lie. They'd found Corban's clothes where Wade's truck was seen by the state patrol. He even admitted he'd gone to Cahone when they said. According to the detective, that meant he was out getting rid of Corban's body when he'd told Tonya he was at home.

They said he'd tried to make it look like the goat's head boys took Corban. They'd thrown that goat's head into her living room, but Wade had moved it to the front yard and taken the rug out of her bedroom to hide the bloodstain. The detective, who Wade said must be a lesbo because look at her muscles, went on about a police dog that could smell where dead bodies had been and how dogs like that didn't make mistakes. She showed Tonya a video of the dog making its special signal in the backseat of Wade's pickup.

What Tonya couldn't stop thinking about was that Wade had brought her home to an empty house, but told her Corban was asleep in bed. And she hadn't looked. She would never know for sure what was true because she hadn't even thought about going into Corban's room to check. All the detectives said she'd given her baby to a killer. How could she live with that?

Now she had the chance to make up for it. She was wearing a tape recorder, and the police were listening in on her conversation. She was supposed to act natural and try to get Wade to confess. But how did you act natural with the person who'd killed your son?

They said start out reluctant. Make him do the work.

"This is so fucked up," she mumbled.

Sitting a few feet away, Amberlee gave Wade a dirty look and said, "This is my home and you're not welcome in it."

Tonya hadn't told Amberlee about the tape recorder, but one of the TV people had said it would look bad if they let Wade stay after he was let out. Amberlee didn't want to piss them off. She had an agent now and was going to do an exclusive interview on TV. She said they could make five times as much if Tonya used her brains and agreed to be on the show as well.

Wade said, "I got nowhere else to go."

"What about your buddies?" Tonya asked.

"Come on, babe." He reached for her hand, but Tonya snatched it away and covered her face.

"I saw the clothes. God, Wade. What did you do? He's just a baby."

"I didn't do anything. You have to believe me. I know how it looks, but I swear. I never touched a hair on his head."

Tonya lifted her head. "Why did you tell all those lies?"

"You gotta understand something. When he hurt himself, I got scared. Real scared." Sobs rattled their way from Wade's chest to his throat. "I thought you'd never marry me then, because I'd be a useless dad that let his kid get hurt."

"Marry you?" Even though she was feeling devastated, Tonya's heart gave a small joyful leap.

Wade had always had a lot of girlfriends, and he never stayed with any of them for more than a few months. She had no idea he was serious about her, and it changed something. She thought, what if they're wrong? The police made mistakes all the time. Men were in prison for crimes they never committed. Now that there was DNA testing, they were letting out innocent people all the time.

"I was going to ask you this weekend," he said hoarsely. "I've been looking for a job in Denver. I was going to get us a place of our own."

"You never said anything."

"It was gonna be a surprise. Now our whole life is ruined because they let Gums Thompson out on the streets and that fucking nutjob doesn't take his meds."

"The police say he didn't do it," Tonya said nervously.

"How do they know? You think he'd confess? He's a fucking psycho, and I'm your boyfriend that loves you. Who do you trust, me or him?"

When he put it like that, Tonya couldn't argue. She could see why he was upset. He had a job and was making plans for the future, then all this happened. Gums Thompson should be locked up. Tonya felt angry then, and realized the police had already made their minds up and they wanted her to help them send Wade to prison. She was being used.

She said, "I wish you'd just told the truth right from the start."

"Who would have believed me?"

"Don't you trust me?" Tonya felt hurt. She looked over at Amberlee, but she could tell she wasn't going to get any support there.

Amberlee glared at her and said, "What about the clothes?"

"Did it ever occur to you two silly bitches that I'm getting framed," Wade whined. "I'll tell you what really happened. Those guys were watching your house, and they waited till I went out, then one of them followed me. There was a car behind me the whole way out there. The reason I stopped in Cahone was to see who it was. But he drove away before I got a look at him. They knew I was in Cahone, and that's why they dumped the clothes out there."

"Did you tell the cops about that?"

"What's the point? They've been out to get me from the second we walked in the door. They always think the boyfriend did it."

"But you could clear your name," Tonya objected.

"I tried telling them about Gums." Wade looked like a dog someone had kicked. "They weren't interested. They want a scapegoat."

"Why should we believe you?" Amberlee ranted. "If you had nothing to hide, why all the bullshit? Why'd you make up that story about the hospital? It doesn't make any sense."

"Yeah, well you would say that." Wade sneered. "It pissed you off when I started going out with your sister. Did you tell her you were trying to get me in bed before that?"

Amberlee shook her head. "He's lying again," she told Tonya. "He thinks he can turn us against each other."

Wade stared into Tonya's eyes and said, "She told me she'd pay you back one day for taking Dan off her. Maybe you should be asking *her* where Corban is."

"Is that true?"

"Don't be stupid. You've known me your whole life and you believe *him*?"

Tonya stared down at her hands, miserably aware of the recording device inside her clothes. The police were hearing all this family bickering, and they'd probably take it the wrong way. She thought about the blood on Corban's clothes. Something awful had happened to him. Whoever took him had hurt him.

A sob rose inside of her and she said, "He's out there somewhere. I just want him found. I want to bury him properly, with his toys and everything."

It was hard to say that when she kept hoping it wasn't true and praying there would be a miracle. But she knew deep inside that it was too late for miracles. Her son was dead, and all she wanted was for this nightmare to end. She tried to see herself in a year's time, all of this behind her. But the only image she could make out in the fog of her thinking was one of her in a wedding dress. She was not going to wear white. It made her look fat.

Wade took her hand. "Listen to me, baby. If I was guilty do you think I'd have told the cops I was in Cahone? Do you think I'd have let them search my truck? Fuck no. I'd have got myself a lawyer and I'd be taking the fifth. Instead I cooperated. Big mistake."

He looked like a frantic puppy dog, just wanting her to pat him. He wasn't the perfect male, but he had a job and he wanted to marry her. Most of the guys she dated were losers. Tonya weighed things up for a few seconds and realized that if she didn't have Corban anymore, even though that was an unbelievable nightmare, she could move to Denver and start a whole new life. If she couldn't get a job in television, she would go to beauty school and learn makeup. Cortez sucked. She could hardly wait to leave.

Standing up, she reached a decision and said, "Gotta go potty."

Once she got inside the bathroom, she pulled the wires out and tore away the tape that hugged the device to her body. This had gone far enough. Until the police proved something, she owed Wade her support, and he was going to get it. She sat down on the toilet and peed.

These days she was going all the time. It had to be nerves. After she flushed and washed her hands, she went into the spare room and threw the tape recorder under the bed.

When she got back to the living room, Amberlee had one of her arms around Wade's shoulders, comforting him. Tonya knew it was innocent, but she felt jealous anyway, especially after the stuff Wade had said about Amberlee trying to seduce him. Tonya made a point of standing between the two of them so Amberlee had to back off.

"I've got an idea," she said, wiping the tears that kept popping from the corners of her eyes. "I'm going out there to show my support in public. I'm going to tell them my fiancé had nothing to do with it and if there's any more harassment by the police, we'll get a lawyer."

Wade's eyes glowed at her, soft with love. "Are you for real?"

"I love you, ding dong," Tonya choked.

"I love you too. You know I didn't do it, don't you, babe?"

"Yes," Tonya said softly. They were both crying.

"I think we should go out there as a family," Amberlee said. "All together, supporting each other."

Wade nodded enthusiastically. "Yeah. Get that on TV instead of the false allegations."

Amberlee grabbed Tonya's arm and pulled her into the master bedroom. She opened her top drawer and foraged in a trinket box. "Here. Put this on."

"What is it?" Tonya couldn't see what she was holding.

Amberlee opened her hand triumphantly. "Your engagement ring. Remember I took it for safekeeping when Matt was making all those threats."

Tonya didn't, but she'd been binging on Southern Comfort at the time, so she took Amberlee's word for it. She rubbed the ring against her skirt to shine it up and slid it onto her finger.

"I hope Wade's okay about it being another man's ring," she said as they stepped back into the living room.

Wade was on his feet. He looked happier than she'd ever seen him. "I'll buy you a new one soon as this blows over," he said, dismissing her worries. "With a bigger diamond."

Tonya slid her arm into his and they kissed just as Amberlee threw open the front door. The three of them stood together, Wade in the middle.

Feeling more confident than she had in two days, Tonya announced as loudly as she could, "There's a man with mental health problems that has a personal vendetta against my family. It's him the police should be talking to. My fiancé was released today, and as far as I am concerned, he had nothing to do with my son's kidnapping."

Someone shouted above the din, "Have the police ruled you out as a suspect, Mr. Miller?"

"I'm here, aren't I?" Wade said.

"Tonya referred to you as her fiancé. Is that official?"

Wade lifted Tonya's hand and showed off the ring. "I just asked her and she said yes."

Tonya could hear Suzette Kelly talking to the camera no more than a foot away. "This evening Tonya Perkins is standing by her man. The newly engaged couple have just appeared in front of Amberlee Foley's residence to make the announcement."

She pushed the microphone under Tonya's nose and asked, "Tonya, what made you say yes to a man the police have named as their primary suspect in the homicide of your son?"

"They don't know Wade like I do. I love him and…" Tonya hesitated, giving room finally to a suspicion that had hovered in the back of her mind over the past few days. "I'm carrying his baby."

This met with a loud gasp followed by the first hush Tonya could remember since everything began.

"You're pregnant?" Amberlee's voice sounded weak. She seemed as shocked as the reporters.

Tonya leaned into Wade's embrace and lowered her hand to rest on her belly. She caught his eye, and he gave her the hot, bad-boy grin that always made her heart beat faster.

Placing his hand over hers, he said proudly, "I fucking knew it. I'm gonna be a dad."

CHAPTER TWELVE

A pink pallor bloomed across the pewter sky. Shafts of light pierced the cliff tops, finding every fissure and carving out deep rivers of bright pink and gold. The sun floated higher until it could cast half an eye over the earth's body, painting each contour with the bright transient halo of dawn, the pledge of a newborn day.

The sight filled Jude with hope and foolish optimism. Yesterday was done. Today was hers; she'd earned it by waiting out the night with all its fears and gloom. She continued to watch the sun slowly climb above the mountains, assembling its fractured beams all at once into a perfect whole. Below, the world emerged from shapeless shadow to form and beauty. Snow sucked light until it glowed along the mesa ridges and ran like shimmering treacle down to the land below. There it massed in a heavy quilt unstirred by the body beneath, that of Mother Earth.

Still as a painting in morning repose, the canyon lands stretched out in an unclaimed wilderness as close to eternal as Jude could conceive. Could humanity ever sully this perfection beyond recognition? No, Mother Earth would fight back. She already was, and climate change could be her ultimate revenge, the retaking of her body from those who abused it.

"Detective Devine?" Footsteps intruded on her musings.

Jude turned reluctantly, almost certain the news would be bad. If so, she had done the best she could, and at least in its final moments, the cat had known kindness, perhaps the only kindness in its sad life.

But the young vet tech's face told a more hopeful story.

"How is she?" Jude dared.

"You won't believe it." Courtney clapped her hands together at her breast. "She's on her feet."

Astonished, Jude took off her gloves and followed the bearer of good tidings into a room at the back of the surgery center where several animals were housed in large recovery cages. The little black cat sat on a folded towel staring curiously through the wire. Her head lifted slightly as Jude approached, and her golden eyes widened. Jude poked a finger through one of the gaps and let the cat take her scent. She was greeted with a purr.

"Oh, wow," Courtney grinned. "I wasn't sure if we'd ever hear one of those from her."

"Do you think she's feral?" Jude asked.

"No. She was probably someone's pet once. She knows to use the litter box."

"Lost, I guess. Or abandoned."

"If you want to find a home for her, there's a shelter off D Road."

"No. I'm keeping her." So much for her no-pets rule. Jude had decided a few years earlier that it wasn't fair to have animals; she was never at home enough to pay attention to them.

"Well, we've done blood work and a dental, and checked everything out. She'll need another day or two on IV fluids, then you can take her home."

Jude stroked her new roommate's bony head. "Okay. Call me when she's ready to be picked up."

And what then? The cat was so weak she would need love and care for at least a week before she was completely well. Instead she was going to be left at home alone to fend for herself. Was that the right thing to do? Jude thought about the animal shelter option again. It wasn't as though she and the cat knew each other, or that the cat had understood Jude's promise of a home for life.

"I don't know how she pulled through," Courtney said. "The vet gave her a twenty percent chance."

"Quite a fighter."

"She would have died last night if you hadn't brought her in. She'll make a great companion for you."

Jude groaned inwardly. Emotional blackmail, just in case she thought she could back out of her pledge. "I hope I make a decent one for her."

"You saved her life and she knows it."

Jude met the cat's relentless stare and had the oddest sense that Courtney was right. "Yes, maybe she does."

Half an hour later, on the way back home, she called Eddie House again.

"Okay?" he asked, not a man of many words.

"The vet thought she didn't have a chance, but she fought. We both made it through the night."

"Ah." His satisfied sigh was audible. "Then her name is chosen for you. Yiska."

"Is that Navajo?"

"Yes. It means the night has passed."

❖

"Someone in your neck of the woods just took delivery of two hundred pounds of C-4, and it wasn't your man Hawke."

Jude raised her eyebrows. "Jesus. That's enough to blow Telluride off the map."

"Funny you should say that." Her FBI handler sounded strangely perky for a high-level intelligence officer. "There's some chatter about an attack on the next Telluride festival. Not from the C-4 buyer."

"The film festival?"

"Uh-huh. I guess the sweet-corn parade doesn't do it for them."

Jude thought the cachet-deficit was pretty similar for both events. Who cared if a bunch of pretentious slackers in dark glasses wanted to crawl up each other's asses for a week? There had to be more meaningful targets for domestic terrorism. What kind of point were they hoping to make by attacking a film festival: *Enough with the subtitles*?

She moved farther around the side of her Dakota, trying to shield herself against the icy winds. She could have taken the call inside the office, she supposed, but she liked to keep the two worlds she moved between separate when she could.

"I don't get it," she said. "Why would they waste their time?"

"Think about it, Devine. We're talking wall-to-wall celebrities. Saturation media coverage for any incident. That kind of publicity could tempt a wannabe group looking to make a name for themselves."

"Okay, you're scaring the crap out of me now." Jude could only imagine the hysteria among the local enforcement if they actually had a real problem to deal with at festival time instead of the usual cokehead-drives-his-Beamer-off-the-road incidents.

"The Telluride threat involves a C/B agent," Arbiter said.

Which changed everything. Chemical/biological agents weren't funny, and the people who trafficked in them weren't playing. Jude was still having trouble believing that any self-respecting terrorist would see Telluride as a high-value target, when there was Disneyland or even that ridiculous Holy Land park in Florida. Any place where you could pay to watch a faux Christ performing faux miracles had to be a fruitcake-bomber magnet.

"Do we have any specifics?" Jude asked.

"We've had a spike in communications between several individuals calling themselves the Aryan Sunrise Stormtroopers, and they've been mouthing off around some of the neo-nazi blogs. Seems they may have their hands on a supply of abrin or ricin."

"Aryan Sunrise…yeah, I know them."

The fledging white supremacist organization was on Jude's radar as well. A handful of disgruntled former members of the Christian Republic of Aryan Patriots, they'd set themselves up as a rival group soon after Republic leader, Harrison Hawke, ran his infamous "Aryan Defense Days" the previous November. Philosophical differences had blighted these unity rallies, and while the various different militias and national socialist groups quarreled with one another, the Sunrise faction had attempted to depose Hawke in an internal coup. He'd fought off the takeover bid and blamed the minor stroke he suffered in December on the stress of this power struggle.

Just before he abandoned his bunker in Black Dog Gulch to recuperate on vacation with friends in Buenos Aires, he'd expressed his dismay to Jude in one of their heart-to-heart conversations. The schisms in the Aryan movement were almost as big an enemy as the Zionist Occupied Government. How would progress for the white race ever be anything but tenuous unless there was unity? Some brothers and sisters had asked him if he would consider running for President in 2008. Hawke wanted to know what Jude thought about that idea.

As she did every time they spoke alone, she wondered if he had blown her cover and wanted to keep the enemy close, or if he had truly bought her story—the one-time FBI agent who traded a big career for life in the slow lane because she was disenchanted with the political climate. Whatever his reasons, he continued to seek out her company, a fact that thrilled her masters at the Bureau, who saw in the unappealing eugenicist the future leader of a united, reborn Aryan Nations—a vision Jude thought was as naive as it was depressing.

At their behest, she'd been building intelligence on Hawke ever since she'd moved into the Four Corners, and she'd struck up a rapport with him the previous fall. He seemed to have a thing for women in uniform, her in particular. In a touching parting gesture on his way to the airport he'd dropped by the Paradox Valley station house to entrust her with his latest writings on the role of white women in a "cleansed" America, headed up *Smart White Females Make Yesterday Thinkers Shape Up.*

On a Post-it note stuck to the front of the folder, he'd written extravagantly:

> *As yet you cannot know what an inspiration you are to me, Fraulein, but there will come a tomorrow when we will share the mantle of glory bestowed upon the few racially aware Aryans whose courage and race honor determine the fate of the many. Our White brothers and sisters are depending on us.*

This he signed off with one of his oft-quoted Nazi maxims:

> *"In the hand and in the nature of woman lies the preservation of our race."*

He concluded this note with the warm and fuzzy sentiment, "At your side, *Bruder* Hawke."

The Post-it was as close as he came to writing a love letter, and Jude had since received a couple of sneakily worded postcards from Argentina. Hawke was nothing if not paranoid, and firmly believed his every communication was inspected by the government. Jude hoped the Office of Homeland Security was that efficient, but she doubted it.

"Is it confirmed that these Aryan Sunrise individuals are in possession of the agent at this time?" she asked, wondering how in hell a few amateurs could lay their hands on toxins that were not exactly available over the drugstore counter.

"That's your job, Devine. Verify the status."

"And if they are?"

"Sayonara. They're a single-cell operation only."

Jude allowed a doubt to surface. The arrest of a group of domestic terrorists planning a biological attack would provide exactly the kind of political capital the Administration was looking for in the lead-up to the midterm elections.

"Tell me this is not just part of another bullshit Ministry for Propaganda scam," she said. "Because if I wanted to work for Karl Rove, I'd apply formally for one of those pathological liar positions. Remind me of the qualifications: no moral compass, will commit treason if it puts a buck in Halliburton's pocket—"

"It's for real," Arbiter said dryly.

The handler's word was good enough for her. And it made sense in a twisted race-hate-think kind of way, now that she'd had time to consider it. A film festival, in the minds of these white supremacists, was little more than a celebration of Jewish "control" of Hollywood and the media. Attacking one would not only net vast publicity for their group in a horrified mainstream media, it would also elevate them to warrior status among rank and file neo-nazis.

"So, you're saying the C-4 purchase is unrelated to the white power dipshits and the Telluride plot?"

"Different informant," Arbiter said. "The timing is pure coincidence."

"This place is kook central," Jude muttered. "Do you have an ID for the buyer?"

"The name is Debbie Basher. Age thirty-five. Part-time hairdresser. Registered Democrat. No known connections with dissident or terrorist organizations. She was intermittently active in a Denver gay rights organization between 1998 and 2004, then left the area and relocated to Paradox Valley. It appears the loss of a domestic partnership prompted the change of venue."

Jude had trouble absorbing what she was hearing. A lesbian hairdresser was purchasing plastic explosive on a big enough scale to attract Bureau attention? Something was wrong with that picture.

"Doesn't exactly mesh with the lone-operative profile," she said.

"We're assuming she's hooked up with someone. The ALF or ELF, maybe."

"Not all lesbians are radical vegetarians."

"No, but stats show overrepresentation among animal rights

extremists, and since there are no known gay domestic terrorism groups…" Arbiter paused. "Surprising, isn't it, all things considered?"

"I guess the homosexual agenda doesn't include telling everyone else how to live their lives and blowing up people who prefer to think for themselves," Jude remarked.

Arbiter murmured something noncommittal and kept focus. "The ELF is a priority target at this time."

"I thought we had an agent in there."

"He was blown after a failed chicken-farm operation."

Jude frowned. The FBI had successfully infiltrated PETA, Greenpeace, and most of the animal rights-lite crowd. But the Earth Liberation Front and Animal Liberation Front had dumped the Kumbaya mindset a while back. They were deeply paranoid and modeled their structure on that of terrorist organizations, operating as a network of anonymous cells. This made them tough to penetrate.

When Jude switched from Crimes Against Children to counterterrorism, she'd narrowly missed being sent on a long-term undercover gig in Portland, Oregon, a hub for ALF/ELF activists. Instead she'd received her present choice assignment, keeping tabs on the extreme right in the Four Corners region of Colorado.

"There must be a way in," Arbiter said. "She has a few financial problems."

"You want me to flip her?" Jude surmised.

"That would be ideal."

"I'll check her out."

"Call me as soon as you have something on the ASS."

"Roger that."

Jude couldn't help a small chuckle. In the heat of the moment, some genius had come up with "Aryan Sunrise Stormtroopers," and he and his *sieg heil* buddies were so swept up in the Third Reich imagery and potential for new arm patches that no one had stopped to consider the acronym.

"For people who take themselves pretty seriously, that's a strange handle to choose," Arbiter remarked.

"Yep. These guys don't call themselves the master race for nothing."

"Their leader. Pure West Virginia," Arbiter noted. "Couldn't drown a rat in that gene pool."

He signed off, and Jude stared up at the Marlboro Man. Even on a dull day he seemed to glow with rugged individualism, a free spirit sharing the open range with his horse and the setting sun. The emblem of a simpler time.

Or maybe not.

❖

Debbie Basher was a small, slender brunette woman with a shy demeanor and the apprehensive smile of someone who expected bad news when there was a knock at her door. She looked Jude up and down and blushed, her gaydar evidently functional.

Jude identified herself and asked, "May I come in?"

"Yes. Please do." She seemed a little tense. "I can't believe this weather."

"But there's no global warming. Yeah, right."

Debbie laughed. It was a polite, lukewarm laugh, the reaction of someone who strived to please others.

"You look like you're about to go out," Jude said. "Is this a convenient time to talk?"

"Sure." Debbie indicated the snow boots and orange gaiters standing by a backpack on the kitchen floor and explained, "I was just getting ready to join the search again."

"You've been out?" Jude could hear a shower running in a room along the short hallway. Someone had spent the night.

"A friend and I were at Lone Dome yesterday." She gave a rueful laugh. "We were so worn out—well, at least I was—we thought we'd start a bit later today."

"You earned it," Jude said. "Search and rescue is hard work."

"It was our team that found the evidence," Debbie said a little breathlessly.

"That was an important find."

Debbie blushed a deeper shade of ruby pink, clearly proud of herself. Jude tried to picture her running fuse to a detonator and a slab of plastic explosive and blowing up a building. She had a hard time believing Debbie Basher would even know what a detonator looked like.

"Oh. Wow. Duh! I just realized who you are." Debbie seemed wildly impressed. "You were on TV. You're the detective in charge of the whole case, aren't you?"

"Yes, I'm leading the sheriff's part of the investigation," Jude confirmed. The shower had stopped and she could hear someone moving around.

"I saw what happened, on the news. With the baby's father and the hostage. Oh, my God. That must have been so scary."

Empathy for others—not the most sought-after personal trait for terrorists. Jude said, "These things happen. It's an emotional situation."

"He must be desperate, the poor guy. I was shocked that they got engaged after you let the boyfriend go."

Jude raised her eyebrows but said nothing so she wouldn't sound startled. Wade and Tonya were engaged? It was a sorry state of affairs when you had to find out what was going on with your primary suspects by hearing secondhand television reports from the subject of an unrelated investigation.

"Here I am chattering away." Debbie hurried into the kitchen. "I just made fresh coffee. Would you like a cup, Detective."

Jude smiled. "You read my mind."

She took in the surroundings as Debbie added a third mug to the two standing on the counter. The cottage was compact and plainly furnished. Thin, dated carpets. Freshly painted walls and ceilings. Jude guessed Debbie had done the work herself to brighten the place up. It wasn't the home of a person who had prospered in life, yet it was welcoming and very clean. Two satisfied cats snoozed on cozy pet beds next to the gas heater, and the walls were lined with bookcases.

While Debbie bustled about in the kitchen, Jude scanned the contents. Photograph albums. Biographies. Assorted self-help books about relationship breakup and low self-esteem. No pretentiously titled novels. No animal liberation classics. No conspiracy literature. No *Anarchist's Cookbook*.

"Cream and sugar?" Debbie asked.

"No, thanks. Just black for me."

"I know I should feel sorry for her, you know…the mother," Debbie confided as she poured cream into two of the mugs. "And I do. But, I have to tell you, I think she's crazy getting engaged to him. I suppose she doesn't want to believe the worst and she's trying to make a statement."

"Yeah. It goes like this—*I'm so dumb I'll stand by my man even if he killed my kid.*"

The cynical remark came from a narrow hallway leading to the rear rooms of the dwelling. Jude felt the speaker's hard-eyed gaze before she looked at her directly. She was maybe five eight but held herself taller. Her bearing and presence announced her as military even more than the khaki fatigues she wore.

She walked into the room with an owner's casual authority and swept astoundingly blue eyes over Jude, then looked harder, subjecting her to the measuring scrutiny of a fighter sizing up an opponent. Her pupils dilated slightly. It was the only indication that something had registered with her.

"I'm Sandy Lane." No handshake. "Is this a social call or do you have business here, Detective?"

Jude noted the play of expressions on Debbie's face. Happiness. Lust. Startled dismay. She hastily picked up a mug and handed it to Jude. "I was just telling Detective Devine about us being on the search yesterday. She's in charge of the case."

Sandy continued with the authoritarian questioning. "Are you here in connection with the investigation?"

Her manner suggested she expected answers when she asked questions. An officer, Jude decided. Maybe a marine. If this woman didn't know what C-4 was and how to work with it, Jude would resign from intelligence work and begin a new career flipping burgers. She had a story concocted to explain her early morning visit and ran it by her dubious audience.

"It's probably a wild-goose chase, but a car matching the description of Ms. Basher's was seen on Highway 666 on Saturday evening, the evening Corban disappeared. We're trying to locate the driver."

"It wasn't me." Debbie sounded disappointed not to be a sought-after potential witness.

"Where were you that evening between ten p.m. and midnight?" Jude asked. "Just a routine question."

"At home. It was snowing too much to go out."

"Can anyone confirm that?"

Debbie shook her head. "I was by myself."

"Would you mind if I took a look inside your vehicle?"

"Sure. I'll get the keys."

Debbie's antisocial companion didn't share her eagerness. "Is that really necessary?"

"It's strictly routine," Jude replied with good humor. "And no one's going to impound the vehicle if Ms. Basher declines to cooperate."

Debbie giggled nervously. "I don't mind. I have nothing to hide." Hardly the response of a would-be domestic terrorist. "I hope I can find the damn keys. I was so tired I put them somewhere weird last night."

Jude finished her coffee and contemplated how she might strike up a friendly rapport with this couple—which they obviously were—given that the dominant half was totally unreceptive. She didn't buy for a second that Debbie Basher was in the market for serious explosives. But it was conceivable that her name had been used by the real purchaser. No prizes for guessing who that might be.

As Debbie roamed around the kitchen mumbling to herself about the keys, Jude opened her coat and made a show of finding her notepad and pen. All the while, she studied Sandy covertly. The woman was built; she probably worked out more in a week than Jude managed in a month, and Jude was no slouch. Every move she made was economic and deliberate, her physical self-awareness so innate it spoke of years of rigorous conditioning. She had nothing to prove and she knew it.

Jude recognized that hard-won confidence; she possessed it herself. Which was one reason Sandy's assessing stare unsettled her. Very few men, and no women, ever sized her up as if evaluating how to cut her throat if necessary. Jude's body prickled its primal awareness of menace, yet she had a sense that Sandy was taken aback by her as well. A cold respect had entered her expression.

In opening her coat, and all but removing it as she looked for her writing materials, Jude had intentionally displayed her physique. Even in a bulky shirt and wool pants it was obvious to anyone who undertook hard physical training that she was in peak condition. The point hadn't been lost on Sandy.

She caught Jude's eye and they stared at each other for several taut, calculating seconds.

"Here they are." Debbie waved the keys, and for the first time Jude glimpsed a softening in Sandy's expression.

An Achilles heel. Finally. Sandy Lane loved this woman and it appeared to be mutual. So why would she expose Debbie to risk by using her name during an explosives purchase, if indeed she had? Maybe she hadn't and this was a simple case of identity theft by a stranger.

Jude took the keys. "If you'd like to be present while I search, that's okay."

Sandy touched Debbie's arm. "Stay here. I'll take care of it."

Jude gave Debbie a smile. "I'm sorry to have interrupted you, Ms. Basher. We may be close to an arrest, so we're trying to build the strongest case we can. Thanks for the coffee."

"You're welcome. It was good to meet you." Debbie returned the smile with a trace of awe.

With ill-concealed irritation, Sandy asked Jude, "It's the boyfriend, right?"

"I'm not free to comment on that. But Mr. Miller is a person of interest."

As they stepped outside into a shock of frozen air, Sandy demanded, "What's this really about? Did her ex make a complaint?"

Jude kept her expression impassive, but she knew she'd just been given an opening. All she had to do was find a way to use it. "I can't discuss any details," she said vaguely and motioned toward a Subaru that had seen better days. "Is that the car?"

"Yes." Sandy folded her arms as Jude unlocked the rear door and took a long hard look at the neat interior. "That woman is a piece of work," she returned to her topic. "I finally talked Debbie into taking legal action to claim her half of their house, and the ex comes back with threats that she'll out Debbie to her boss and make a complaint that Debbie sexually abused a niece who used to stay with them."

Jude smiled inwardly. Sandy had just handed her the perfect means to befriend Debbie Basher. She took a few swabs and bagged them to be tested for explosive residue. Pensively, she said, "I don't think Ms. Basher has much to worry about. The burden of proof is high in cases like that, especially where money and property can motivate false allegations."

"That won't help her keep her job. I know *you* know what I am saying."

Jude conceded the observation with a yes-I'm-gay nod. "It's not San Francisco out here."

She had contemplated coming out to the people she worked with most closely, and if she had no other role than sheriff's detective, she would—at the very least in a don't-ask-don't-tell sense. But she didn't have that luxury. If Harrison Hawke or any other of her targets knew she was a lesbian, she could kiss her undercover assignment good-bye, not a risk she was willing to take after investing two years building a deep-cover identity. Instead she'd created a smoke screen.

Late the previous year she'd agreed to date Bobby Lee Parker, a compulsive flirt who wanted an excuse to chat up Virgil Tulley, the true object of his desires. A bisexual former gas-station robber, Bobby Lee had a reputation as a ladies' man and had left a trail of female conquests around the Four Corners, including a couple at the sheriff's office. Jude's and his unlikely coupling had ended growing speculation about her sexuality, replacing it with puzzled acceptance and relentless teasing.

Bobby Lee had recently come up with a plan to cement their deception, asking her to marry him in a spectacle so public no one would ever dream it could have been driven by anything but foolhardy passion. Jude's heartless non-answer had lent a poignancy to their situation that had captured the imaginations of locals who had nothing better to do than read the gossip pages in the *Cortez Journal*.

Bobby Lee thought they could let this soap opera run for most of the year before Jude would have to break his heart, by which time no one would care that she was tall and cut her hair too short for a woman. Instead they would be whispering behind her back that she was a callous ball-breaker who'd dumped the only half-decent male ever likely to propose to her.

Jude could live with that.

She closed the hatch and took a cursory look inside the front of Debbie's SUV. As she moved from the front seat to the back, she said, "If this ex is determined to play dirty, maybe Ms. Basher can come up with something she can use as emotional blackmail herself. Everyone has secrets. If she thinks about it, she probably knows a thing or two the ex would rather keep to herself."

"I'll work on it," Sandy said in a tone of grudging thanks.

Jude closed the driver's door. "I'm all done here."

Sandy accepted the keys from her. "I hope you nail that jerk."

"Finding Corban would help." Jude offered a professional smile. "By the way, thanks for getting involved in the search."

Sandy shrugged. "It's a good workout."

"You think you need one?"

The subtle compliment garnered a hint of satisfaction. With a faint grin, she murmured, "Old habits…"

"When were you discharged?" Jude put her best guess out there.

"That obvious, huh?" Sandy glanced down at herself in wry appraisal. "I was wounded during my second tour of duty in Iraq. I completed my tour, but after that I decided not to roll the dice anymore."

"Was it an IED?"

"Funny, that always sounds so clean."

Jude took that for a "yes."

"I wasn't in the vehicle that took the hit. We were back a ways, but there was a mortar exchange. We took the position out. Another day, another martyr." The comment was cold and bitter, and Jude could see in the stiffness of Sandy's mouth and the shuttered lowering of her gaze, the strain of holding back emotion.

Carefully—wanting to get an inside track with this woman—she said, "I never served. In my job there's the occasional shoot-out and you have to deal with dangerous situations, but you're not under constant random attack. I can't even imagine what it was like for you over there."

"Be thankful for that." Sandy's expression grew distant. Jude could feel her slipping out of reach, finding the place she went, mentally, to escape.

"Friends of my family lost a son in Iraq recently," she said, rebuttoning her coat against the cold. Her face felt numb, but she wanted to keep Sandy talking. "He was in Tikrit."

"4th Infantry Division?"

"Yes. First Lieutenant Carl Sandler."

"That's tough," Sandy said. "You never know who the bad guys are over there."

"Where else have you served?"

"Kosovo and Afghanistan." Sandy hesitated. "I was with the 82nd Airborne."

"The maroon berets?" Jude was intrigued. There weren't too many female paratroopers in the armed forces, and Sandy couldn't resist letting her know she was one of that elite. "I didn't realize we still had paratroopers in Iraq."

"The eighty-deuce is usually deployed for offensive combat operations. We were in Iraq for the start of Operation Iraqi Freedom. Later we redeployed on a support mission for the elections."

"No picnic, huh?"

Sandy fell silent, blinking rapidly. She shoved her hands into the pockets of her jacket and glanced back toward the house. Everything about her seemed strangely still, and Jude sensed she was exerting tremendous control. Something had welled inside, an inner rage that frayed at the edges of her control, making her eyes dark and fierce and her bottom jaw so tight, she had to have her teeth painfully clamped. Almost anything could push her over the edge, Jude decided, and she would explode.

Aware that this was a tricky moment, Jude weighed her options and suggested in an impulsive manner, "We should have a drink some time."

Sandy stared at her like she'd taken leave of her senses. During the long silence that followed, Jude had plenty of time to observe the paratrooper's train of thought as her tense expression shifted from surprise to puzzled incredulity, then stark paranoia.

"You're not my type, Detective," she responded eventually.

"You're not my type either." Jude offered a grin to lighten things up. "Good we got that out of the way."

Sandy gave herself a moment, perhaps to regroup, then said, "I'll take a rain check."

"Your girlfriend's invited too," Jude coaxed.

A pause. "Why? Is *she* your type?"

Jude took this for Sandy's version of humor and ran with it. "No. I prefer them fickle and high maintenance."

This self-effacing irony raised a faint grin. Her voice warming by a few degrees, Sandy commiserated, "Us simple types can't seem to leave the princesses alone."

They both shook their heads, sharing a moment of morose introspection. Then Jude said, "Okay, I'm out of here. Nice talking with you, Sandy. Thanks again for participating in the search."

"No sweat. Good luck."

Jude felt Sandy's eyes on her all the way to the Dakota. She couldn't help but wonder which one of them, in hand-to-hand combat, would walk away.

CHAPTER THIRTEEN

Heather Roache sat down at her desk in the tiny cubicle her boss liked to refer to as the Accounts and Administration department, dropped her purse next to her chair, and opened the *Durango Herald*, which she always read while she was drinking her morning coffee before work.

At the sight of the front page, she realized today was going to be a bad day. They should have sold the paper with a free barf bag like the ones they had on airplanes. The headline said MOM TO MARRY SUSPECT BOYFRIEND. Staring down at a photograph of Tonya Perkins and Wade Miller smooching for the camera, she almost threw up her low-carb snack bar.

Mr. McAllister crowded into the closet-sized space with her, donut box in one hand, two take-out caffè lattes in the other. These were from the Silver Bean, a small trailer that served the only good espresso in Cortez. Heather couldn't bring herself to set foot in a place where there were still Kerry/Edwards posters all over the walls from the last election and people mocked Vice-President Cheney over that quail-shooting accident.

The café was run by Wendy Mimiaga, the crazy chairwoman of the Montezuma County Green Party, so who could be surprised that it was always full of liberals and they showed Michael Moore movies over and over. If there was any other place that made good coffee, Heather would have insisted Mr. McAllister go there, but the Four Corners was not known for its high-class restaurants and European coffee, and Starbucks had recently passed Cortez by, instead opening its long-awaited franchise in Durango.

Desperate times called for desperate measures, and if there was one thing Heather couldn't stand, that was weak, lukewarm coffee with grounds floating around on a surface scum of flavored coffee creamer.

She sometimes wished she'd never accepted Mr. McAllister's offer of eight months at Covenant Bible College in Windsor. She'd gotten used to the cafés of Fort Collins with their espresso and foreign foods, and when she came back to Cortez she brought with her these newfound city tastes.

"I can't believe Orwell let that asshole go." Mr. McAllister planted a sticky finger on Wade Miller's face, leaving a blob of chocolate frosting behind when he resumed work on the donut he was munching.

Heather dabbed the spot clean with a paper towel. "I always knew Tonya Perkins was stupid about men, but this is incredible."

"You see what they're up to, don't you?" Mr. McAllister paused in his chewing. "Their theory is that we'll all be so distracted by the wedding and all, we won't notice they killed a kid."

Heather snorted softly. "They're assuming everyone else is as dumb as them."

"I don't think they're as dumb as they look." Mr. McAllister opened the donut box and extracted another, this time jelly, his favorite. "He did it. No doubt about it. Her…I'm not so sure."

Of course not, you're a man. Heather said, "She has to know something. But she's kidding herself. She wants to get married so she's going to believe what she wants to believe."

"Like O.J.'s kids."

"The difference being she's an adult and it's her baby that's gone missing."

"Look what it says here." Again the sticky finger, this time dusting the newspaper with powdered sugar. Mr. McAllister read aloud, "Montezuma County Sheriff, Orwell Pratt, on Monday told the *Durango Herald* that two members of the goat's head gang, Gums Thompson and Matthew Roache, are persons of interest to the authorities. So far Mr. Thompson and Mr. Roache have been interviewed by detectives and remain at large in the community."

"At large!" Heather gasped. "What are they saying? They're acting like Matt did something."

She read on. The article seemed strangely distorted. Tonya and Wade were called the "newly engaged couple," and the reporter said they were "understandably distressed over allegations about Mr. Miller's role in Corban's disappearance." The paper cautioned against "trying this young couple in the court of public opinion" and urged readers not to "destroy reputations before all the facts are available." The reporter wasn't half so considerate of Matt and Hank.

"This is unbelievable," Heather complained. "The sheriff told me Matt's an important witness. Now he gets treated like a criminal."

"Donut?" Mr. McAllister offered her the box.

Heather was so stressed she chose a bear claw and tore into it automatically. How much worse could this nightmare get? She'd just spent five years making the Roache name respectable in Cortez again, and now this had to happen.

"I don't know what to do," she hiccupped, tears collecting around her nose. She read a little further and gasped, "Oh, my God. She's pregnant."

It raised the matter of abortion, Heather thought. Maybe exceptions should be made in some cases.

Mr. McAllister put his non-sticky hand on her shoulder and said, "There, there. We'll think of something. Those fools at the *Herald* need a good talking to. Leave it to me."

Somehow that didn't inspire confidence. Her boss was shaped like a tree, tall and stout of trunk with spindly limbs. At first glance, he could be mistaken for a tough guy, but it was Heather who had to bully people into paying their accounts on time. Mr. McAllister was always promising to "tear them a new one," but she was the one who terrified the team leaders when they screwed up. He owned the company, but you'd never know it from his clothes or his attitude.

He'd stepped into his dad's boots six years earlier, after Randolph McAllister had a heart attack and fell off a roof. Ever since then, Heather and the building contracts manager had been in the business of making it seem like he fired off orders and had no time for fools, just like his old man. They'd been so effective he seemed to believe this propaganda himself.

Heather had no problem with that. Mr. McAllister and his wife had no kids, and they treated her almost like she was their own. They sent her to bible college, then they paid for her to study accounting part-time, and when she bought her house they helped her get it financed. She had the best health insurance money could buy, and any time she needed a day off, all she had to do was ask. She was lucky and she knew it.

If Matt was willing to put in a fair day's work he could walk into a well-paid job at McAllister's Roofing and Restoration. But Heather wasn't going to let him sign on unless he got his act together. She owed Mr. McAllister more than that.

Wiping her tears, she said, "My brother had nothing to do with the kidnapping, and I'm going to see to it that he doesn't get the blame."

"That's the spirit." Mr. McAllister gave her a fatherly squeeze and reached once more for the donuts, but Heather closed the box.

"Only two at a time. Remember what the doctor said."

"I should have known you were counting." He grinned. "Now just say the word if there's anything I can do to help you and your brother."

Heather hesitated. She had an idea, but she wasn't sure if it would just complicate matters. "Mr. McAllister, maybe there *is* something. That lawyer of your daddy's who made those weirdoes in Mancos pay their bill. Do you think we could get some advice from him?"

"Griffin Mahanes." Her boss pronounced with distaste. "A jackal, like the rest of them. But I'll call him."

"I can pay," Heather said. "I have savings."

"Keep your money in the bank. I'll take care of it."

Heather smiled awkwardly. Normally she would have said no, but she knew she couldn't afford pride at a time like this. "I just want Matt to get a chance to tell his side of the story," she said. "I don't want them to destroy his life over one stupid mistake."

"That's not going to happen." Mr. McAllister was already dialing the "jackal." Pointing at the donut box, he said, "I'll take a coconut cream. You know how I get, talking to city boys with Viagra in their pockets."

❖

Jude headed north, taking the long way out of Paradox Valley. The paved highway soon ran out, and she was bumping her way along the narrow gravel road that discouraged tourists and locals alike from making the climb up to Carpenter Ridge. From the top, the valley spread out 2500 feet below, offering a desirable-if-dangerous photo op. When it wasn't covered in snow and veiled by low clouds, you could look out across the red and ochre rock formations west to the La Sal Mountains in Utah.

Jude usually came up here on horseback in the summer, roaming the dusty paths over rainbow layers of sandstone and red rock, studded with fossils. Dried mudflats flaked in chunks, and pebbles spun like ball bearings beneath her horse's hooves. The temperatures got high, upwards of 110 degrees.

She loved the canyon. It felt holier than a church, infinitely closer to the divine, more ancient than life itself. A billion years old and bearing the footprints of species long extinct, clans of people long departed, wild horses, and warriors. Their spirits lingered in wind and echo, in the globs of light that bounced across the castellan walls as if the ancients were hurling snowballs.

Jude was trying to enjoy the moment without picturing her Dakota rolling down into the valley when her cell phone rang. She stared at the caller ID and vacillated. When she could not hold out any longer, she pulled over where the road widened and picked up.

Mercy's voice poured into her ear. "Hello? Is that you?"

"Well, I don't have a spare girlfriend who picks up the phone for me, so I guess it must be," Jude said pleasantly.

Mercy ignored the sarcasm. "I'm calling to apologize about bringing Elspeth to town the other day. You were right. I should have checked with you first."

"Apology accepted."

Jude waited. For what, she had no idea. It wasn't like Mercy would now announce that she'd been a fool and she was going to dump Elspeth and live with Jude forever in a secluded log cabin where they could have noisy sex all they wanted and no one would pound on the wall. It would be good-bye to seedy far-flung motels and hello to domestic bliss.

She edged the Dakota farther into the pull-off and killed the engine.

Mercy said, "I wanted to let you know...Elspeth and I have decided to get married. We're flying to New York for an exclusive interview with Paula Zahn next week."

"Married," Jude repeated flatly.

"Yes, we're going to Canada after the interview."

"You're coming out on TV?"

"Everyone's going to know in the end, anyway. We thought it would make sense to get in first."

"I don't know what to say."

"Congratulations?" Mercy suggested.

Jude's mouth refused to form the word. "I thought you weren't interested in long-term commitment."

"Things have changed. When Elspeth and I had that break from each other last year we both realized that everything works better when we're together."

"That break—you mean the one when you started sleeping with me?" Jude wondered why she was prolonging the conversation. She loosened the collar of her shirt. Her skin felt hot and damp.

"Yes." Impatience crept into Mercy's tone.

"Back then you said she was an ex."

"It's what I believed at the time. Jude, is this postmortem really necessary?"

"I guess I'm trying to understand why you picked her and not me." The words were out before Jude could come up with a more sophisticated way to express her bewilderment.

Mercy sighed. "How am I supposed to answer? I don't know why I love her and not you."

Well, she'd asked for that one. Jude flinched.

"Before you start reinventing everything, you might want to be honest with yourself for a change," Mercy said. "The fact is, it suits you not to share your life with a partner. You work all kinds of hours, you have weird phone calls on that spare cell phone of yours—I have *no* idea what that's about. And you don't like explaining yourself to anyone. You might think you want a full-time relationship, but trust me, you don't."

"Free therapy," Jude remarked dryly. "This is an unexpected bonus."

"Jude, I'm not the enemy."

"Then what is?"

"Loneliness." Softly, Mercy explained, "We got together because we were lonely."

"And sex starved," Jude recalled.

Mercy laughed. "Yes. That, too."

"It was good."

"Extremely good."

"I miss you," Jude said.

"You miss *someone*," Mercy replied after a long pause. "And for a while I've been your someone."

"Yes, you have."

"It's not enough. I'm Elspeth's everything."

Jude's mouth was as dry as dirt. She forced out a poorly formed, "Congratulations."

She wanted Mercy to be happy and maybe she would be, married to an actress who, Jude suspected, had never met a mirror she didn't like. Perhaps they understood one another well enough to make the compromises a long-term relationship demanded, the ones Mercy didn't think Jude was capable of.

"I know you won't want to come to the wedding," Mercy said in a strained voice. "But I hope you'll visit with us for dinner after we're back and the reporters have lost interest."

Jude would rather poke a stick in her eye, but she forced nonchalance. "Sure. I hope you'll be happy."

"Thank you." Mercy's soft breathing made Jude feel weak. And sad. "I care for you, Jude. You know that, don't you?"

Was this supposed to soften the blow? "I know. Take care of yourself, Mercy."

"I won't say good-bye. We'll still be working together."

Jude could hardly wait. "Sure. It's not good-bye. It's just see ya."

"Good luck with the search."

"Thanks. I'll try to have a body for you before you leave."

Jude closed her cell phone and stared out at the knee-shaking view of Paradox Valley. The Dolores River slithered like a silver-green ribbon along the canyon floor, cutting a path through a pristine postblizzard canvas. Clumps of snow fell from the branches of the few firs along the ridge. The vast sky was Colorado blue again, a deep intense lapis that made the snow so white it burned Jude's eyes. Copper ridges layered the valley in every shade from claret to rose gold, spilling in folds baked solid over millennia.

The sight purged Jude of her self-pity, supplanting it with a strange yearning to melt into the earth, to inherit its memories and lose her own. She felt hollow and directionless, stranded in a no-man's-land between hope and resignation, between living life or letting it slip by. She had no idea if everyone felt this way, or if it was some kind of existential angst she ignored most of the time, maybe even a pining for the certainty of a belief system. She'd never been religious. It was hard to accept that there was a loving God ordering events when you dwelled by necessity on the evil men do.

In Mercy, she'd taken sanctuary from thoughts like these. Now she was alone with them, and with all the doubts that galloped in their wake. She would henceforth be deprived of the transient solace of skin and flesh unless she found a stranger to sleep with. She'd never had a problem with that, yet the idea made her queasy right now. It was only natural, she supposed; she'd just broken up.

Jude draped her arms over the steering wheel and lowered her head to rest. In a few weeks, she'd take a drive to Denver and hook up with some eye candy for the weekend. She forced herself to imagine an unknown head on the pillow next to hers, a new body to explore. What was so bad about that?

She sat up straight and started the truck. The windshield blurred in front of her and she lifted her hands to her eyes, appalled to find tears. Worse still, she realized something. She didn't want to sleep with strangers anymore. Mercy was wrong. She didn't want someone, just anyone. She wanted her person. The one who would be her everything.

❖

"That body has to be in the reservoir," Jude told Orwell Pratt. "And we can't nail him without it."

The FBI agents attending the briefing agreed. One of them said, "The goat's head is the problem. We can make the case that he moved it, but it'll be a mental patient's word against his in the courtroom. We need more."

"That elf hat Matt Roache says was in the driveway. We found it inside the house in Corban's room," Jude said. "Either Miller or Perkins put it back in there. It seems odd they would have noticed it on the driveway when they returned from Ms. Foley's party."

Pratt coughed for a few seconds and mopped his forehead. "Who knows what goes on in the minds of pond scum? We've got the clothing and the wet cash. And we've got him lying every time he opens his mouth."

"But the amount of blood on the clothing indicates we don't have a murder scene," Jude pointed out. "All we have is the scene of an abduction and an act of vandalism. The two may or may not be related. We need to know where Corban was killed. And we need to search the homes of all the people closest to Miller in case he hid evidence elsewhere."

A Cortez PD detective observed, "The small amount of blood on Miller's clothing is inconsistent with the quantity on the baby's clothing."

"Correct," Jude said. "So if Miller is our guy he must have changed out of the clothing he was wearing, washed himself, and disposed of the garments. If we can find those, he's ours."

The FBI agents conferred for a moment, then one of them said, "We'll stay focused on the background check. We're running down everyone he's known since elementary school. If there's any dirt on him, we'll find it."

"What about motive?" Pete Koertig said. "If he just lost his temper with the kid, the DA might plead him down to manslaughter."

"Well, we now find out that Perkins is pregnant, and it seems as if he suspected she was." Jude responded. "Perhaps that factored into a rejection of Corban."

"Like a baby bird pushing another one out of the nest," Pratt remarked before sneezing into a tissue.

"More like rats," Jude said. "An adult male sometimes kills another male's young so he can sire a litter of his own. It happens in quite a few species actually. Maybe the urge exists in human beings, too."

In the midst of the general revulsion, Pete Koertig poked his head in the door and said, "Devine, you have visitors out in the waiting area."

"Who?" Jude asked.

Koertig shrugged. "The sergeant just asked me to pass it on. Want me to get rid of them?"

Jude shook her head and said dryly, "Maybe it's our lucky day. Five bucks says it's an eyewitness who saw Miller carry the body to his truck. Anyone?"

"Yeah, while we're placing bets, twenty says I'm running for President in 2008." Pratt checked his mustache for shreds of Kleenex.

"Let's reinterview every neighbor," Jude said as she got up. "Someone has to have seen something. Gums Thompson talked about a neighbor turning on lights. We need to find the guy."

She stalked down a labyrinth of hallways to the main entrance of the station house and caught her breath as she reached the final glass security door. Through it she could see the backs of two heads, one ash blond, the other burnished copper. As she entered the area the copper head turned and a small, perfectly formed oval face reacted to the sight of her with such naked joy, Jude felt shy.

Chastity Young seemed happy to see her.

"Hey, Detective Devine." Adeline leapt to her feet and bounded around the modular seating.

Jude gave her a hug. "If you get any taller, I'm going to feel inadequate." Looking past her to Chastity, she said, "This is a surprise."

"I should have called, but it was a spur-of-the-moment thing."

"We saw you on the news," Adeline said. "Have you guys found the baby yet?"

"Unfortunately not." Jude found herself remembering the feel of Chastity, her unexpected tenderness. She'd almost lost that moment in the daze that followed the Rapture shootout.

Adeline looked back toward her aunt. "See, I told you we'd get here in time."

"Adeline wanted to help with the search," Chastity explained. She looked a little embarrassed, hanging back, her expression hard to read. "I told her you'd probably stopped accepting volunteers by now."

"No," Jude said. "We'll take all the help we can get. Where are you staying?"

"I was hoping you'd be able to recommend something. I didn't have time to organize accommodations before we set off."

"I have a spare bedroom," Jude offered. "It's not the Holiday Inn, but you're very welcome. In fact, I insist on it."

"We won't be in the way?" Chastity began. "I mean, I'm sure you're just flat-out with—"

"I have an idea." Jude put an end to the protestations. "I'm starving and I bet you are after that drive. Let's go get dinner, then I'll take you back to my place. If you're joining the search you'll need to be at the command center before seven tomorrow morning, so we should all get an early night."

"No sweat." Adeline gazed around the room. With an air of disappointment, she said, "I thought there'd be wanted posters all over the walls."

"It's not the Wild West," Chastity said.

"As a matter of fact, we do have wanted posters. I'll show you." Jude walked Adeline over to the bulletin board and singled out the FBI Ten Most Wanted list. "Recognize anyone?"

"No way!" Adeline stabbed a finger into Warren Jeff's weasel face. "Aunt Chastity, look. It's the prophet."

Chastity picked up the down jacket beside her seat and strolled over, which gave Jude an excuse to appreciate her slender athleticism. She looked good in a dark green cardigan sweater and bone-colored chinos.

Staring at the mug shot, she said with prim disdain, "Not the kind of immortalization that asshole had in mind, I'm sure."

Adeline instantly burst into smothered laughter. "Straight to hell," she chortled, explaining to Jude, "We don't say asshole in our house."

Jude nodded sagely. "Well, we say it plenty in this place. So, when in Rome—"

"Oh please," Chastity protested. "Don't encourage her."

"Asshole. Asshole. Asshole," Adeline chanted maturely, then whipped out her cell phone and announced, "Daniel's texting me. Hang on."

As she moved away, Chastity lifted her unforgettable dark eyes to Jude and said, "It's good to see you."

Surprised to find her pulse accelerating, Jude said, "I'm really happy you came."

"How are you?" The way Chastity asked, it wasn't just a meaningless conversation starter. She looked at Jude like she really cared, like she could see past the face she showed the world. She'd done exactly the same thing in Rapture.

Disconcerted, Jude answered honestly. "I've had better weeks."

"I thought so." She searched Jude's eyes with such piercing intensity, Jude wasn't sure how to hide the feelings she wanted no one to glimpse. But Chastity didn't pry. Touching Jude's arm, she said, "Let's get out of here."

CHAPTER FOURTEEN

Lonewolf stared with satisfaction at the white blocks of C-4 plastic explosive arranged along her workbench. The quality was better than she'd hoped for. She picked a block up and squeezed it. The waxy, rubbery texture always amazed her. C-4 was happy to stick to any surface, it didn't care about temperature, it didn't explode in your face while you were trying to stuff it into a canister, it had a long shelf life, and it was fairly inexpensive. In fact, it was the perfect weapons-grade explosive in so many ways she wondered why people bothered with less stable alternatives.

She'd lucked out on the deal for this initial quantity. For the past year, since her lover Madeline's suicide, she'd been hanging around survivalist groups on the Internet until she struck pay dirt. A militia member in Texas who had a connection with William Krar was taking some heat and had decided to unload his arsenal. His son knew a methamphetamine dealer and had made an arrangement for his father that would conceal the money trail.

This suited Lone fine. If her Texan connection was picked up by the authorities, she didn't want anyone noticing a cash withdrawal from her bank account for the same amount received by the militia man and connecting the dots. She'd purchased the meth he wanted from a couple of lowlifes near the Mexican border and paid peanuts, which meant she was ahead of her financial target. The next few hundred pounds would be harder to come by, but she was patient and C-4 was easy to store.

She'd been accumulating cash by withdrawing small increments over time and hiding the money under a loose floorboard in her cabin. Within a couple more months she would be ready to buy again, and the operation would enter the next phase.

Lone glanced up at the wall above her workbench, where she had an official picture of Madeline's only son, Private First Class Brandon

Ewart. Next to this was a wooden plaque Lone had lettered herself with the quotation "Surrender is not in my creed." A Marine, Brandon had been deployed to Iraq straight out of training and was killed in Baghdad four months later. The usual story. Inadequate armor on the Humvee. Standard-issue helmet instead of the padded kind the army had switched to.

After their vehicle was blown up, Brandon, seriously injured, was captured by insurgents watching the explosion from a nearby building. They cut his throat later that day and left his mutilated body on the banks of the Tigris.

Madeline had always been high-strung and had been treated for depression in the past. Brandon's death put her in a tailspin, understandably, but Lone finished her tour of duty shortly after and took the honorable discharge she'd earned, so she could be at home to take care of family for a change. She had busted her ass and spent a pile of her savings to get Madeline the help she needed, to take her on vacations to Europe, to get her mind moving in new directions.

Just when she thought things were improving, Madeline pinned a note on the fridge one day, locked herself in the garage, and left the car engine running. Carbon monoxide killed her.

Her note said:

> *Lone,*
>
> *I can't go on. What did my son die for? They say freedom, but I don't believe that.*
>
> *Thank you for loving me. I wish I could feel something for you but I'm dead inside and I don't want to be here anymore.*
>
> *Madeline*

Lone made a solemn promise the day she watched them put Madeline in the ground. She was going to find out exactly what Brandon had really died for, and she was going to avenge him if she found he'd been sent into harm's way for any reason but the defense of his country.

What she'd discovered over the past year was that Brandon died a horrible death, and Madeline took her own life, because an evil alliance of men in government and industry had renamed their despicable ethos patriotism and marketed their indefensible acts to a gullible public as a noble fight against terrorism. It served their political and economic interests to keep Osama Bin Laden at large, so they made sure not to capture him. It was good news for them that the Middle East was unstable—it kept oil prices way up there and made them all a pile of money. Money that dripped with the blood of the fallen, the real heroes who made the real sacrifices.

Lately, Lone had begun to wonder if the evil alliance actually knew 9/11 was going to happen and chose to allow it. The loss of thousands of lives meant nothing to them. 9/11 had given them the ultimate propaganda tool, and they had profited from it every day since.

There was a time when contemplating ideas like these would have been unthinkable for her. She would have presented herself at the combat stress unit and obtained appropriate counseling from a division psychiatrist. She would have seen her refusal to accept official explanations as bordering on treason, conduct unbecoming. That was how successfully they'd brainwashed her.

Not anymore. She had joined the ranks of those who took the time to discover the facts, study the data, and draw intelligent conclusions. As a consequence, she knew what she had to do; she owed nothing less to her brothers and sisters in arms. Her mission was the elimination of the sniveling chicken hawks responsible for sending Brandon and thousands just like him to their deaths.

For starters, she was going to eliminate the Vice-President.

❖

"She's finally run out of juice," Chastity said.

They stood in the doorway of the spare room, looking in on the teenager asleep in one of the twin beds. Jude thought about the trauma of Adeline's experiences in Rapture. It was a relief to see her so lively and outgoing.

"How is she doing?" she asked on a serious note.

"Amazingly well. I found a good therapist for her. In fact, we've both been seeing the same woman." Chastity smiled. "Different issues, of course."

Jude couldn't imagine why a woman as together as Chastity seemed would need to spend time on a shrink's couch, but she supposed it couldn't have been easy helping Adeline come to terms with what had happened to her and her sister.

"I think one of the hardest things for Adeline was that she couldn't help Summer," Chastity reflected. "She blamed herself for not making Summer leave with her and Daniel when they escaped."

"Summer would never have gone," Jude said. "I met her before it went down. She was completely brainwashed."

"I know. They specialize in crushing the spirit." Chastity's tone flooded with bitterness. "My sister is a case in point. She used to be a person and now she's a robot. It hurts...I only understood recently—I've lost her. It's like I don't have a sister anymore." She flushed and broke off. "Forgive me. I forgot you're not Dr. Phil."

"Don't apologize. You can talk to me." Jude gestured toward the living room. "Can I get you a drink?"

Chastity walked with her and took the corner of the leather sofa nearest the gas fire. "I think I'd like that."

"Wine? Liqueur?"

"Surprise me."

Belatedly, Jude remembered Mormons didn't drink alcohol or anything with caffeine in it. Trying for host-of-the-year after the fact, she said, "I can make hot chocolate, if you'd prefer."

Chastity shook her head, sending a riot of copper curls bouncing around her shoulders. Her eyes gleamed warmly at Jude. On a teasing note, she said, "I'd rather be corrupted."

Jude dropped her gaze from the broad, full bow of Chastity's mouth directly to her breasts then looked away, about ready to kick herself. This was a straight woman sitting on her couch. A guest. A Mormon who had been brought up in Salt Lake City and had probably never heard of homosexuality, let alone contemplated experimenting with it.

Get a grip, Jude thought. This was rebound disease rearing its make-an-ass-of-yourself head. An attractive woman was in her home. Whoa! It was late in the evening, that lonely sad-sack time when desperate people flipped to adult cable and didn't crack up over hilariously named programs like *Lord of the G-Strings*. Celibacy was not working out for her, and she'd had her feelings hurt by a heartless sex-goddess.

Naturally she was afflicted with futile lust.

"You might like Frangelico," she suggested as casually as she could. "That's an Italian hazelnut liqueur."

Her next thought was how good it would taste on Chastity's lips, not that she would get an opportunity to explore that sensation unless she was shopping for a black eye. She couldn't resist another look at Chastity's mouth. It was really beautiful, sweetly turned up in each corner like a smile was always a mere breath away. Her small, straight nose and neat but strong chin were very feminine, but also hinted at the stubborn streak in her Jude had seen firsthand. She smiled, picturing her petite companion hitching her skirt and marching up to the FBI swat team that day in Rapture, so she could tell them exactly where to get off.

"Is something wrong?" Chastity asked.

Jude wanted not to blush, but it was too late. Embarrassed by her hot cheeks, she said, "No. I'll get that drink." She didn't even know if Chastity had said she wanted it.

Thankful to escape to the liquor cabinet, Jude spent an unnecessary amount of time pouring a shot of Frangelico, then sloshed some Talisker into a scotch glass with a dash of water. It was reprehensible to gulp a single malt down in one hit, but she gave in to her baser impulses, telling herself she would make up for it by sipping her second glass like the aficionado she was.

The scotch roared down her throat with a medicinal fire that made her temples burn and restored her thinking to that of a responsible adult. As she caught her breath and composed herself, she saw on Chastity's face the kind of wholesome smile that spelled out *Don't even think about it.*

"Can I ask you something?" Chastity inquired softly as she extended a hand for the Frangelico.

Jude passed the glass over and invited, "Shoot."

"Do you think there's such a thing as soul mates?"

A philosophical question; she could almost feel the headache sprouting. Jude quipped, "If there is, I'm in real trouble. I've never found one."

"Me either. I had a husband but that was a train wreck. We tried marriage rejuvenation and so on. But that was never going to work.

Then he started hitting me, and that was all she wrote." Chastity sipped her drink, slowly licked her lips. "This is yummy. Thank you."

"My pleasure." Jude didn't want to think about Chastity with a husband. She preferred the self-torture of wanting to help lick away the Frangelico.

"I keep wondering why I never meet anyone," Chastity said. "My friends try to fix me up but it's a waste of time."

Jude wanted to say *Why are we having this conversation?* But she figured they'd built up to it over dinner. Chastity and Adeline had asked all kinds of questions about Jude's family and how she became a detective, and she'd answered fairly frankly. Chastity was probably the kind of person who thought it was only right to engage in turnabout disclosures. Hence the personal stuff now.

Jude took a slow sip of her Talisker, normally a religious experience with that fine malt's memorable peat-and-salt-air character. But tonight she was having a hard time settling back in her chair to cherish the lingering notes of oak and pepper. Her mouth felt unpleasantly dry and she was weary. Talking was an effort.

Suppressing a yawn, she said, "My friends gave up on me a long time ago. My job makes it hard to have a long-term relationship, anyway."

"Because work comes first?"

"Yes."

"Same here. I run my own business. It's not like you can just take a day off whenever you feel like it. I don't think partners understand that very well."

"Are you happy alone?" Jude asked.

Chastity frowned as if entangled by this thought. "I'm not unhappy. I suppose the word is…disappointed. I pictured myself settling down. Being with someone."

"We all get sucked into thinking we're failures if we don't have that," Jude said. "I don't try anymore. If it happens, it happens."

"I'd settle for a few really close friends," Chastity said, compounding Jude's discouragement. "I had a lot of friends when I was still going to the temple, but when I got divorced we kind of…lost touch."

Jude detected unmistakable hurt in her tone and instantly wanted to hold her and tell her the world was full of assholes and not to take things so personally. She said, "People get threatened when someone leaves the fold. It happened to me when I left D.C. A lot of my old colleagues acted like I'd abandoned them. I get treated like an outsider these days."

It was true. Even though her friends in the CACU knew she'd taken an undercover assignment in counterterrorism, a bunker mentality tended to prevail in the different divisions of the Bureau. When an agent moved sideways, some saw it as jumping ship.

Chastity sipped some more of her Frangelico and said, "I suppose you think I'm weird, being brought up Mormon."

"Why should I?" Among the whackjob religions and cults Jude had examined, regular Mormons weren't exactly vying for pole position. "You seem pretty normal."

Chastity smiled. "Other than being unversed in cocktails."

"I like your innocence." The words were out before Jude had time to think about them. That's what two glasses of Talisker did for a person.

Chastity's cheeks went rosy and she concentrated on her drink. "I like your worldliness," she said after a moment.

Jude wasn't sure if it was a compliment, but she was happy Chastity could find something to like about her other than the fact that she'd shot the dirty old man who planned to "marry" Adeline. "More Frangelico?" she offered.

"I don't think so. It's making me a little light-headed." Chastity set her glass aside. Tucking her feet beneath her, she sank farther into the deep cushions and regarded Jude with a dark, languid gaze. "I'm curious about something. What's a woman like you doing working in a one-horse town like this? It can't be for the career opportunities."

"I wanted to get out of the city for a while," Jude said. There was truth in her answer. She had needed a break from the life she was leading. "Living in a place like D.C. can wear you down. The traffic. The crime. The intensity. I suppose I was looking for a change of pace."

"You picked the opposite extreme."

"That was the general idea."

"Were you a detective in Washington?"

"I was with the FBI, in the Crimes Against Children Unit."

Chastity's expression altered from friendly interest to dismay. "I can't imagine how people do a job like that—how you stay sane. What made you go into that field?"

Jude hesitated. A plausible half-truth presented itself, as they did when the chitchat got personal. "An opening came up and I thought it would be a good career move."

Chastity tilted her head to one side and slid a hand behind her head, an action that tightened her cardigan sweater across her breasts and made her neck look unfairly kissable. Jude forced her gaze elsewhere so she wouldn't come across the way she felt—like a dog eyeballing a hamburger. She felt too hot in her clothes.

"A good career move," Chastity repeated, plainly skeptical. "Why do I get the feeling that's not the whole story."

"Because it's not?" Jude suggested.

"We're strangers," Chastity said. "It won't leave these four walls."

"Why do you want to know?"

"Why is it so hard for you to answer?"

"I hate that," Jude grumbled.

"Answering a question with a question?"

"Yes."

Chastity looked her in the eye. "Here's what I think. You're not going to let me know you past a certain point. You've already decided we'll have pleasant, meaningless conversation tonight, and I am going to leave in a day or two, and then we won't talk again until the next time I bring Adeline back here for some hiking."

"You have a problem with that?" Jude asked.

"It may sound strange, but yes. I think you came into my life and I came into yours in extraordinary circumstances. I believe that means something—I just don't know what."

Unsettled because she'd entertained the same thought herself, Jude allowed herself a long look at her companion. Chastity stared right back. They sat motionless, intent on one another. Something passed between them, just as it had once before. The memory of that moment crowded Jude's head—herself, like a raw thing bereft of its skin. Chastity, soothing her. Shielding her. No one ever did that.

"What are you thinking?" Chastity asked, adding as Jude groped for a socially acceptable answer, "The truth. Please."

"The unvarnished truth?" Jude sighed. End of a beautiful friendship. "I'd like to sleep with you."

The dark in Chastity's eyes blossomed. Emotion played across her features. Faint shock. Happiness. Confusion.

Jude said dryly, "You asked."

"So I did." A small frown tugged her neatly shaped eyebrows together. She looked like a child struggling to fathom the rules of an adult game. "I'm trying to understand what you mean."

Here it was: the chance to finesse this rebound-driven lapse in judgment with observations about loneliness and a craving for company once the lights were out. Grown-up sleepover. Platonic pillow talk. Naturally Jude bypassed the sensible escape option to plunge straight down the rat hole.

"I'm saying I'd like to make love to you." She almost winced. By all means scare the bejesus out of a straight woman who probably thought homosexuality could be caught off toilet seats.

Chastity's hand slipped from behind her head to mesh with its counterpart in front of her body. Color careened up her neck and stained her face hot pink. Something else happened, too. Beneath her sweater her chest rose and fell at double time, and her nipples made themselves known. This unexpected development struck Jude as promising.

"We're strangers."

"Not really," Jude said.

"You're a woman."

Jude nodded. "Yep."

"We're both women." Another stunning disclosure, and articulated with such breathless incomprehension Jude couldn't help but smile.

"Is that a no I'm hearing?"

Chastity took a long time answering and managed to confound Jude when she said, "Not exactly."

Jude waited, sensing there was more.

"I'd like to kiss you." Mouth softly parted, she drew a nervous breath.

She would change her mind by the time they got there, Jude thought. All the same, she got up and went over to the couch and, taking Chastity's hands, pulled her to her feet.

"Are you sure?" she asked her guest. It was always good to avoid the face slap straight women needed to deliver at times like this to prove they weren't as curious as they might have seemed.

Chastity stepped into her arms and with a fetching shyness that made Jude want to carry her across the nearest threshold, she whispered, "Just a kiss."

Jude didn't spoil the moment by making an uncouth grab for her. Delicately she brushed her lips across Chastity's, tasting sweet hazelnut and scary temptation. Releasing Chastity's small, firm hands, she drew her into a lover's embrace and kissed her again. This time it wasn't delicate.

And this time Chastity kissed back.

❖

Lone finished storing the C-4 in the underground bunker she'd built during the previous summer. She kept an assortment of provisions down here. It had crossed her mind to be prepared for trouble if necessary, so she'd stockpiled enough food and water to survive for three months. She also had body armor and a sensible collection of weaponry—an AK-47, an M-4, several spare .50 caliber assault rifles, an array of 12 gauges, and about ten thousand rounds of ammunition. It bothered her that some of her weapons were illegal, but she was a responsible gun owner and made sure her arsenal was secure. No child would ever find a way into her bunker and be able to do harm to himself or others.

She bolted the trapdoor and activated the shed alarm system, then carefully reviewed the tapes of her security cameras before returning to the cabin. When you undertook a mission like hers, you could not take any chances. The men who ran the evil alliance were smart. They had co-opted the major law enforcement agencies throughout the nation, systematically ridding them of independent thinkers and replacing competent leadership with yes-men.

Homeland Security. Lone almost choked over that oxymoron. The evil alliance didn't want the homeland to be secure. They wanted fear and confusion so they could expand their powers without a nervous public noticing until it was too late. There was no question that they would come after her if they knew what she was planning, so Lone took no chances.

When she traveled to Texas to collect her purchase, she'd checked into the motel using Debbie's name and paid for everything in cash. If anyone tried to trace her, the trail would lead to someone so obviously innocent the agents on the case would have egg on their faces and assume their information was flawed. She felt bad about doing that without Debbie's permission, but keeping her in the dark was the best way Lone could think of to protect her. If Debbie knew absolutely nothing and had never been on Lone's property, she could not be seen as an accessory.

Knowing Debbie as she did, knowing how pure of heart she was, and how honorable, Lone felt one hundred percent confident she would understand why this mission was essential once the time came to tell her. Debbie was very naive about politics but she had an open mind.

Lone locked the shed and strode across the walkway to her cabin, casting a quick glance around the strip of land that separated the two. This was fenced off because it was booby-trapped and she didn't want someone innocently triggering a device. She made sure nobody ever came up here, but there was always the chance that a motorist would get lost on the back roads around this part of the valley and stumble on the cabin, seeking directions.

Collateral damage was an acceptable consequence if it were completely unavoidable and occurred in the execution of an operation. But Lone could control this environment to avoid needless risk to civilians. There was no excuse for laziness or behaving like a hothead, even when national security was under direct threat. She didn't fool herself that she would be able to arrest the decline single-handed. But Operation Houseclean would be an important first step.

She went to her room, stripped off her clothes, and hung them in the closet. Her hand brushed the plastic storage bag that held Madeline's favorite blue silk robe, and Lone lifted it down from its hanger. Unzipping it a few inches, she parted the plastic and lowered her face to the fabric, inhaling deeply.

She could still smell Madeline, and the sense memory triggered a rush of sorrow, mixed with guilt. That was about the recent changes. Lone hadn't planned on becoming Debbie's lover, even though she'd desired her nonstop almost since the day she saw her smacking that mountain lion over the head with a bike. However, she had a feeling Madeline would understand. It was hard to do what she was doing without a hand to hold in the dark, without the sound of another heart and the feel of a body accepting hers.

It wasn't wrong to love Debbie just because she'd loved Madeline so deeply all of the years they were together. "I still love you," she said as she zipped the bag closed on the scent of her past.

She owed Madeline so much for all she'd sacrificed: her marriage and financial security, the family and friends who'd disowned her when she divorced her husband for a woman, the life she'd left behind to live in foreign places so she could be near Lone.

Yet, in the most fundamental way, Lone had failed her. Madeline had not trusted her with the truth about how she felt, and Lone had not read between the lines. She should have known. She should have added the countless tiny clues together and seen the whole picture. But she'd seen what she wanted to see, just as America did. She'd kept her blinders on rather than be challenged by the truth.

Well, it was now time to resign from the ranks of the lemmings and confront the truth. The only way she could serve Madeline and truly serve her country was to take the fight to the enemy. A patriot was not silent in the face of power run amok; she was not complicit in the slow but sure erosion of everything her beloved land stood for at the hands of men who served only their own interests.

She refused to allow the death of Brandon Ewart to count for nothing. She refused to let her lover's suffering and suicide go unanswered. She would complete her mission or die trying. There was no alternative.

CHAPTER FIFTEEN

Anasazi legend tells of a Spirit Horse that appears in dreams. Like a flashing beacon, it gallops ahead of the dreamer, then slows down, but not enough to be caught. The horse will stop only for a rider as untamed and honorable as he, so they can journey together through the unfathomable world of the unconscious.

Jude awoke with a thud, convinced she had shared her dreams with this elusive creature. She felt exhausted, almost stunned. Eyes closed against the remorseless tread of the sun, she rolled onto her side and let her mind slide back down toward the watery unconscious once more.

The rules of dreaming defied explanation. Wingless flight for humans was unremarkable. A fall from a great height broke no bones, but usually ejected the dreamer from her magical realm and she would find herself awake and staring at the dull walls of her bedroom, thankful for her survival but strangely disappointed. Jude often woke that way, wondering what she was chasing and why she leapt from buildings and cliffs.

She took a deep breath and sank below the surface. Sleep, seductive as a sea anemone, waited to enchant and paralyze her. Jude almost let go, but her eyelids were tickled open by the light dawning beneath them. She tried to remember her dream more fully, but only fragments remained—the faint drumming of hooves and the rush of wind in her face.

Just as she resigned herself to another half-formed memory, there was something else. A shimmer in the trees, a slender, pale-haired boy who waved as she went by. The dream took form as she called it to mind. She and the spirit horse had slowed and wheeled around. Then they went back for him.

"Ben," she whispered with a jolt of knowing.

She lay there while the sun threw small patches of light on her wall until it resembled a page from a collector's album, littered with gaps where postage stamps belonged. She'd seen the same pattern play over Mercy's body on the rare mornings she stayed over, but Jude didn't want to think about that now. She focused on the pillow next to hers. She could make out the impression of a head. Sliding her hand over the sheet, she detected warmth.

It wasn't her imagination. Chastity had slept in her bed last night. With an odd shock of guilt, she threw the bedclothes off and padded to the window, raising the blind that carved the morning light into tiny sections to match its latticed border. The day was sunny and the surface of the snow glistened as it began to melt. The divers would go in again this morning, and the sunshine would help.

Jude had a feeling about today. The dream was an omen, she decided, the kind of dream Eddie House would consider significant. A tapping sound permeated her consciousness, and she crossed her room to crack the door. The smell of cooking assailed her, and she retreated and found a robe. Guilt prodded her again. There was no reason for it. So what if she and Chastity had fallen asleep in one another's arms? They didn't make love.

All they did was kiss. For quite a long time. Then, when the intensity had them both breathing hard, Jude moved Chastity onto her back and set about getting rid of the nightshirt. And it was over, just like that. She felt a telltale stiffening in the compact body beneath hers. A hand pressed against her chest.

"I can't," Chastity whispered in her ear. She was shaking. It wasn't a tease. She was upset.

"What's wrong? Tell me," Jude whispered back.

For a long time Chastity didn't answer and Jude could feel her fighting sobs. Her face was wet. Eventually she said despondently, "I think I'm like this because my husband used to rape me. I'm sorry. I thought it might be…different, with you."

"You have nothing to apologize for." Jude stroked her hair and kissed her forehead. "I'm sorry you went through that. I hate that what we did made you think of him. Even for a second."

"He didn't mean it abusively," Chastity said in a sad little voice. "He was doing what was expected of him by the church. But it seems to have left me…messed up."

"That can change. I promise you. Past experience doesn't have to ruin intimacy."

"It just did." Chastity moved back a little and turned on her side to face Jude. Caressing Jude's cheek, she said, "I liked kissing you."

"I had a feeling about that." Jude made her tone playful, wanting to reassure Chastity that everything was all right.

"I guess it's a start. Thank you for not being angry with me."

Saddened by the comment, Jude drew Chastity into her arms and bent to kiss the soft curls that tickled her cheek. The fact that Chastity, who was so confident and assertive on the outside, actually expected to be treated badly at a time like this was very telling. She was in her thirties, yet she had never been loved as she deserved; she had no idea what good sex was. And it sounded like she'd decided to experiment with Jude because she thought a female partner might not take her to that unhappy place. Jude could understand that, but she was not a sex therapist. Chastity needed help.

After that, they'd fallen asleep and Jude didn't even hear Chastity slip out of bed. Pondering on the twist of fate that had seen Chastity arrive just as Mercy was making an exit, she leaned against her bedroom door, briefly enjoying the unexpected but delicious breakfast aroma, then retreated to her shower.

As she turned on the jets and adjusted the temperature, she felt pessimistic all of a sudden. How did this happen? All she wanted was for something to be simple. There was chemistry between her and Chastity; she wasn't imagining that. Her body still felt tender from unrequited arousal, and every time she touched her clit as she washed, she wanted to come. Common sense had prevailed the night before, and she'd refrained from getting herself off while Chastity slept in her arms.

She supposed their odd sense of connection might be nothing more than the attraction of two hardworking women who were lonely and seeking a friend. Before they could consider the possibility of anything more than that, they needed to know whether Chastity was a lesbian. She kissed like one. But, given her issues, that could mean anything.

The soap bar shot from Jude's fingers and slithered around the shower floor as she tried haplessly to pick it up. Her fumbling, she decided, came down to the edginess of her unfulfilled state. Maybe she would take care of herself before she got out of the shower. That way she would be able to spend all day in her jeans without whimpering over seam pressure.

"Do you need help?"

Jude jumped guiltily and resisted the urge to gasp, *Yes.*

Chastity stood on the other side of the glass door regarding her with placid good humor. In one hand she had a mug of coffee, in the other a towel.

"I knocked," she said, blithely unaware, "but I guess you didn't hear."

Jude decided she had two choices: turn her back like an affronted nun and stick her hand through a gap on the shower door for the towel, or act like this was a locker room and she didn't give a rat's ass who saw her stark naked. She had a good body. More pertinently, a juvenile part of her wanted Chastity to see exactly how good a body. Maybe if she saw what she was missing out on, she would go home with something to think about. If she noticed.

"You work out," Chastity said, rewarding Jude's nonchalant exit from the shower with a candid interest that was encouraging, to say the least.

Jude took her time wrapping herself in the towel. She had a feeling from the dark gleam in Chastity's eyes that every inch of her body had been recorded for later review. The thought converted her arousal to a hot longing she knew she couldn't hide. She stared at Chastity and caught her breath sharply, stunned that she could be so turned on by a woman whose lack of experience was second only to a virgin's.

Not her usual type at all.

"I'm sorry to intrude on your privacy." Chastity handed Jude the coffee and started edging toward the door.

Jude said, "There's no need to rush off now that I'm decent. Sleep well?"

"Very happily. You?"

"I overslept. That's unusual for me."

"You probably needed it." Chastity toyed with the door handle. "Oh, there was a phone message for you. From the animal hospital in Grand Junction. Your cat is ready to be picked up."

"Great." Jude set the coffee down next to the wash basin and finished toweling off.

Chastity didn't seem in any hurry to leave, now.

"Is Adeline up yet?" Jude wondered what the teenager was thinking, having awakened to an empty bed where her aunt should have been sleeping.

"Amazingly, she's cooking breakfast. I think she's trying to impress you."

Jude laughed. "She said she wants to come out to the reservoir with me this morning to watch the divers." They'd spoken about that, driving home the previous night. Adeline had insisted on riding with her, while Chastity followed.

"I'm not so sure about that." Chastity frowned with adorable concentration.

She wasn't beautiful, Jude decided; she was captivating. Neatly muscled. Physically confident. Petite and not especially curvaceous. She could have been dainty, but her grace and agility were underpinned by a sinewy strength that made her seem more solid than she was. She carried herself with the straight back and squared shoulders of a dancer. Basically, Jude felt like a big lug next to her.

"I suppose if she really wants to, there's no reason why she shouldn't." Chastity finally resolved the parental dilemma. "It was her idea to come here."

"You know, you don't have to come with us," Jude said. "It's cold and not very exciting."

"I'll come." Chastity's chin lifted just enough to suggest she thought Jude might be implying she was a wimp.

Jude gave an it's-your-funeral shrug and said, "We'll go get my cat before we head out."

"What was the problem?"

"Starvation and who knows what else. She was a stray. Arrived on the doorstep a couple of nights ago."

"And you took her in. That's so sweet."

"Her name's Yiska," Jude said. "It's Navajo for getting through the night."

"I like that." Chastity stared at Jude as if she wanted to say something, then gave a small awkward laugh and seemed to change her mind. "Well, I better go help Adeline. Scrambling eggs is not one of her gifts."

"Wait," Jude took a couple of steps toward her. "We don't have to behave like strangers, you know."

Chastity searched her face quizzically. "What are we, exactly?"

"Do we have to decide that today?"

Chastity gave a shy smile. "I'd rather not."

"Good. Then let's take a rain check and see what happens."

A short while later, watching Chastity and Adeline at the table laughing and chatting and passing food around, Jude felt intensely aware of her solitary state. An odd yearning hit her hard in the belly. She missed family.

❖

"There's only one Sandy Lane and he's male," Arbiter said. "Honorably discharged from the First Infantry Division six months ago."

"So we have a false name," Jude concluded. "Or she's making it up about the 82nd Airborne."

"Do you think she's the real deal?" he asked.

"If not, she could be with the Company." It had crossed Jude's mind that if she had to guess Sandy's day job, CIA operative would be next in line after the military.

"We'll go back three years and profile every female discharged," her handler replied.

"She says she was in Kosovo and Afghanistan, and served two tours of duty in Iraq. That should narrow it down."

"Are you inside her place yet?"

"I haven't been able to locate it, sir. She's flying below the radar. We could fit a GPS device to her vehicle but this is a paranoid subject. She'd find it, and I don't want her spooked."

"Low tech, then?"

"I'm afraid so." Jude hoped she wouldn't have to resort to dumpster diving, but even though the war on terrorism was conducted largely according to a high tech/low legality model, the average domestic terrorist used low-tech methods. Sometimes you had to beat them using their own game, so it made no sense to rule these methods out for intelligence gathering.

"Anything on the Stormtroopers?"

"Not as yet. The target dwelling is pretty well snowed in."

"Just say when. We can have a SWAT team in there in two hours."

"Roger that." Jude glanced toward the veterinary clinic. She'd told Chastity and Adeline to wait in there where it was warm, while she made the call.

"How's the kidnapping investigation coming?"

"We're still a body short of a capital case." Jude was surprised Arbiter had taken an interest. He saw her MCSO work as a necessary evil and seldom showed an interest in the cases she worked.

"Obviously it's the boyfriend."

"Obviously." Was this a new national pastime?—guess which loser killed Corban Foley.

"Quite a creep show you've got going on," Arbiter remarked. "You need that kook with the false teeth locked up before he muddies the waters any more."

"You've lost me, sir."

"Last night's interview. Him and the village idiot, plus several of the dumbest hominids walking upright, trying to clear their names." He actually let loose a laugh. "You better hope they never take the stand."

"That bad, huh?"

"Put it this way—their lawyer's the type who files his canines."

Jude cursed and kicked some snow off the Dakota's tires. Gums Thompson and Matt Roache had hired a lawyer. She knew that had to be coming, but she'd hoped for a slower response time from a pair of lost souls who weren't exactly the local intelligentsia. She wanted to take another run at Thompson. He knew more than his mind was freeing up; she was convinced of that.

By now, Miller and Perkins would have lawyered up, too. Pratt could hardly contain himself over their engagement and Tonya's baby announcement. Jude had needed to hold the phone several inches from her ear when they'd touched base before she set out for Grand Junction. *People* magazine was set to run Tonya's triumph-over-tragedy cover story as soon as Corban's body turned up. They were planning a big photo shoot at the funeral.

Pratt had been caught off guard when they phoned him to get a few comments on the record. He'd wanted to tell them to take a walk, he informed Jude, but instead he talked his way into his own insert with a head shot. She could tell he was feeling plugged-in.

Before he hung up, he warned her that reporters were hanging around the reservoir like maggots on roadkill. Everyone was expecting that body.

❖

The reservoir was the biggest show in town, and Lonewolf had a front-row seat. One individual's insular act of violence had served up the latest in a long line of real-life soap operas that would obsess the nation until a satisfactory climax was served up, preferably a death sentence.

Today's juicy installment, the breathlessly anticipated discovery of a battered child's body, was exactly the kind of spectacle that would send old-hat news stories packing. Who would want to know about Iraq, Katrina, or Dafur when they could wring their hands over an event that had everything going for it: no wider social consequences, no important lessons to teach, and no meaningful impact on anyone but the few players involved.

The Corban Foley Tragedy would occupy a thousand percent more airtime than the not-civil war in Iraq. After all, who gave a damn if Islamic fundamentalists would probably end up controlling the untapped Iraqi oil reserves that were earmarked to become America's filling station in the coming oil crunch—the 2010 oil crunch the public wasn't meant to hear about.

More to the point, who would buy advertising if news shows were reduced to discussing serious issues that involved numbers and politics and other such channel-surfing prompts? It would be the end of news broadcasting, and all those overpaid anchors would have to become reality-TV producers, which was, after all, what their skill sets equipped them for.

Lone didn't have a problem with that idea. No one would know any less about the convergence of events that would soon send the American economy into free fall—a disaster wasn't news until after it happened. Ask anyone if they knew how much of the world's fast-diminishing oil reserves the Iraqis were sitting on. They had no idea and were usually amazed when Lone told them most of Iraq's oil was still in the ground.

Of course, that didn't mean anything unless you knew Iraqi oil represented fifty years of production and five trillion dollars in company profits. Annually, that was more than the biggest five oil companies made right now, combined. A motivation for invasion? Not according to evil-alliance propaganda.

Lone thought invasion priorities had to be fairly obvious when troops weren't dispatched to the National Museum to secure the priceless artifacts of the cradle of civilization. Hell, the first building U.S. soldiers occupied was the Iraqi Oil Ministry, the place with the thousands of seismic maps that showed where Iraq's oil was. It made perfect sense when you understood that the war had nothing to do with freedom or WMDs. Given that only twenty percent of Iraq's oil wells had been drilled at all, and the big oil men had already agreed on how the concessions were going to be carved up between them, it was kind of important that they knew where the undrilled eighty percent were at—duh.

Lone sometimes thought everything would have been so much better if the evil alliance had simply told the truth. She, and most every soldier she knew, would still have followed orders from their commander in chief. If her superiors had said the mission in Iraq was to convert the nation into an American military base sitting on top of the world's biggest oil reserves, she would have seen the sense in that.

She might have had a come-to-Jesus over whether it was worth dying so that a few oil billionaires could get richer, but orders were orders. She would have done her duty. But she knew Brandon Ewart would not have joined up for that. Brandon wanted to fight a noble fight that was about freedom for oppressed people and candy for grateful children. He was willing to die for his high ideals, and he was betrayed by men who had no ideals at all.

Once Madeline had realized that, she couldn't live with it.

Lone jumped slightly as a hand touched her cheek.

"You look so sad," Debbie said.

Lone focused on a diver emerging from the freezing water. They had to limit their immersion times so they weren't exposed to hypothermia. Organizing her thoughts, she said, "I wish the world was a better place."

Debbie's small, trusting face lifted to hers, sweetly framed with chestnut brown waves. "You make my world a better place." Her voice was husky with emotion.

"That's what I'm here for." Lone smiled tenderly at her and rearranged the muffler that protected her throat.

"I wonder if they'll find him." Debbie consulted the heavens. "It's warming up and the snow is melting. That should make it easier."

"Tell me something," Lone allowed herself the question that had bugged her ever since they'd embarked on the search, "why do you care?"

Debbie's bright hazel eyes widened with shock, then she frowned as if she'd been asked a trick question. Finally a sunny contentment settled on her features. "Because I'm part of the human race, and we're all in this together."

Lone thought about that as another diver went in, risking his health, and possibly his life, to search for the body of a child he didn't know. She stared around at the crowds, not the media but the people. Deputies. FBI agents. Police. SAR teams. Volunteers who'd now spent three days combing a vast area, enduring extreme conditions, on the slim chance of finding this child.

They must all feel that way, she thought. Why didn't she?

Gazing into Debbie's eyes, she lost herself for a moment in the tranquil forest hues, then asked, "Do you hate anybody, Debbie? Really hate them?"

Debbie considered the question with obvious unease. "No. I guess I don't hate anyone that much. Do you?"

Lone wanted to answer truthfully, but she knew Debbie would find the honest answer disturbing. She really did hate some people, so much that she wanted to watch them die. And she felt completely neutral about everyone else except Debbie. She wished others no ill, but she did not share Debbie's sense of connection to strangers. She had once, but that seemed so long ago she could no longer recapture the emotion. Even if she could, it had no place to reside.

Noticing her lover had started to shiver, Lone drew her close, holding her from behind. Debbie rested back against her with a happy murmur.

In her ear, Lone said, "I love you, Debbie doll."

Debbie wriggled so she could look up at her. "I love you, too,"

Lone could not resist stealing a quick, daring kiss. She needn't have worried about anyone noticing this reckless public lesbianism. At the very moment her lips found Debbie's, the crowd surged forward and shouts went up. Like a huge, self-cloning, armored centipede, the media crawled all over the banks of the reservoir, sunlight gleaming off cameras and tripods.

Everyone stared, transfixed, as a tow truck slowly hoisted a mesh basket from the murky water. Lone could make out a sledgehammer peeping through the webbing and what might be a black trash bag. A bloodhound standing on the bank emitted a long, low howl and lay down on its haunches next to its handler.

Debbie said, "That's the dog we met, remember."

How could Lone forget? Debbie had seemed enchanted by the K-9 handler, making Lone worry briefly that she'd fallen for a woman with bisexual tendencies. After a while, she understood that Debbie had seen something feminine in the deputy, and that's what she'd reacted to. The man was ridiculously good-looking and oozed an innocent country-boy charm that made him impossible to dislike.

But that night as soon as she held Debbie in her arms once more, Lone knew she had nothing to worry about in that department. She'd found the perfect woman. Sweet and gentle, kind, honest, passionate, and loyal.

Once she'd completed her mission, she planned to take Debbie somewhere far away and build them a house where they would live happily ever after. She owned a hundred acres on a lake in Canada and had a large trailer on the property. No one would come looking for her there.

"It must be him," Debbie said as the police herded the crowd back behind the barricades erected earlier, and an elegant blond woman was ushered through. Debbie seemed excited to see her, announcing, "That's Dr. Mercy Westmoreland from *Court TV*."

Sheriff Pratt then climbed onto a portable platform and read a statement he'd obviously prepared in advance, thanking the searchers and law enforcement professionals and asking everyone to go home. "I can confirm that we have located the body of a child," he said. "But until formal identification is carried out, that's all I can say, folks."

Lone released Debbie as people started moving around them. "It's over," she said. "Let's leave the experts to do their job."

"Okay." Debbie fell in step next to her and they started the long walk back to the parking area.

After a few minutes of silence, Lone asked, "Are you okay, baby?"

Debbie turned her head just enough so that Lone could see tears pouring down her face. "Why do people do these things?" she sobbed. "I don't understand."

"Of course, you don't. How could you?" Lone reached for her and rocked her in a tight embrace.

Waiting for the weeping to subside, she thought about Canada some more. There was extra planning to do now that she had Debbie to take care of. Lone had already set up a second false identity for herself and even had a bank account in Toronto. She would need to do the same for Debbie. It was probably wise to take her across the border ahead of time.

Lone wondered how she was going to explain all that without disclosing sensitive information. It wasn't as if Debbie would be leaving anything important behind. She wasn't close with her family and she was in a go-nowhere job. They would pack up the cats and Debbie's personal effects, and Lone would rent a van. If everything went according to plan, this time next year, they would be sitting on a patio overlooking a pristine wilderness and the FBI Director would be appearing in front of Congress to explain how come no one saw the assassination coming.

CHAPTER SIXTEEN

The death of children made no sense. Accidents happened. Lives were snuffed out as if the Fates demanded daily sacrifices and spun a roulette wheel to determine who would make them. Parents paid a terrible price for a moment's carelessness or distraction, dooming themselves to an eternity of self-blame if they lost their child as a consequence.

Murder was something else. To kill a child was to steal so much future, to destroy so many dreams and hopes, to end innocence in the cruelest way. Every child's body she saw filled Jude with despair, and the bodies of murdered children corroded her spirit in ways she could not fully comprehend. To weep for them was never enough; she had discovered that a long time ago. Revenge, the capturing of their killers, brought an end of sorts, yet no resolution. Justice was never done.

Jude knew survivors who had gone to executions believing the gnawing at their souls would end once they saw the death grimace of a man who'd killed their loved one. But they still awoke each day to a world haunted by the person their child could have been, by the unborn grandchildren they might have had, of infinite possibilities extinguished. Jude supposed she understood their pain better than most because of Ben.

Her brother had vanished when he was twelve. One day he was there and everything was normal; the next day he was gone and she was evicted from her world, never to return. From that day on, she'd occupied a new and different normality. Over the years, especially when she saw the remains of a child, Jude longed for Ben's body to be found. At least with the finality of death came the legitimacy of formal grieving. A funeral. A place to go and leave flowers. A name inscribed on stone to wear over time, as she would.

Jude wanted bones to touch. She wanted to see eyes closed forever to this world and tell herself they were open to another, the better place people talked about. The problem with dead children was the utter senselessness of a life given, only to be taken before it could bear fruit.

She lifted the evidence sheet that covered the body of Corban Foley. There was no point fighting it, so she allowed her tears to fall. Soon, anger would come and displace this helplessness. Once more she would focus on the mechanics of the investigation, the goal of seeing a man in handcuffs awaiting the verdict of his peers, as if a child killer had peers among ordinary citizens who led ordinary, honorable lives. But in this moment all she could think about was how cold and alone Corban Foley was. Neatly arranged on the steel gurney, wrapped in the sheet, he looked like a forlorn gray doll.

Strangely, she could almost feel him in her arms, alive and warm, heavy with sleep and trust. She could smell freshly washed hair, milk, and baby skin. These were the earliest smells she could remember, the scent of her baby brother on their mother's lap. She could still feel the curl of his tiny fingers and see his dark startled eyes, gray-blue like a storm on a lake.

Ben had been small for his age and Jude was tall. The last time she'd held him, she was ten and he'd fallen off his bike. She picked him up and carried him to the nearest patch of grass. It was weird—she'd thought then that it would be the last time she ever carried him, and she was right. His increasing size and boyish dignity meant he never let her baby him again after that day. Then he was gone.

Jude refastened the robe she was wearing and stretched latex gloves over her hands. She lifted a strand of hair from Corban's right cheek and stared down at the wound it had clung to. There was blotchy bruising and loss of skin below the eye across the cheekbone. Someone had struck the child.

"Ready, Detective?"

Jude heard the swinging doors open, but she didn't turn around. She had hoped the Montezuma County coroner would assign a pathologist from Durango to conduct the autopsy, but he'd been out at the site of a small plane crash when Corban's body was discovered, and Sheriff Pratt had called the Grand Junction M.E.'s office for help. They could have sent someone whose voice would not make Jude's heart beat faster, but instead they sent Mercy.

"Not in Canada yet?" Jude remarked. She had no idea why she said it. Mercy had told her she wasn't going right away.

"I said I'd wait for that body." As usual, Mercy could make scrubs and rubber gloves look sexy. "Besides, we're not in any rush."

"You seemed to be the last time we spoke." Jude wanted the remark to sound flippant and good-humored. Instead her voice shook just enough for Mercy to direct a long, hard look at her.

"I wanted to tell you before you heard it from anyone else, that's all," she said. "I think I owed you that."

Jude didn't answer. All she could see of Mercy's expression was an untroubled brow and a pair of arresting blue eyes gazing at her without a trace of languid sensuality. In the worst way, she wanted to drag Mercy out of the room and shake her. Kisses. She wanted those, and Mercy's sounds and smells and reckless full-tilt surrender. Where had she gone?

The woman a few feet from her was not her lover; she was a stranger. It was as if they'd never touched, as if they knew little more than each other's names. Was this how it would be? Jude suppressed the urge to yell *Look at me! Remember how it was.*

Didn't Mercy miss her at all? She hunted for a sign, a softening of that cool gaze, a hint of the throaty tone that spoke desire, the subtle unnecessary brush of her body. Nothing.

Mercy glanced past her toward the *diener*, a lanky African-American man who worked in expressionless silence. He wheeled the gurney closer, drew the sheet back, and removed the bags from Corban's hands. Mercy gave Jude a look of resignation and slowly paced around the body taking photographs.

Corban wore a pair of pajamas. His killer had put him into a black trash bag and dumped it in the reservoir weighed down with a sledgehammer.

Mercy glanced up at Jude and said, "Someone dressed him in the pajamas postmortem."

She removed the garments, taking close-ups as she went. The *diener* bagged and tagged these and placed them on a nearby table. He then assisted Mercy as she took hair and nail samples, and they continued the painstaking collection of external evidence under an ultraviolet light. All the while Mercy spoke crisply into her voice recorder.

As they hovered like birds intent over their young, Jude stared up at the Latin inscription on the plaque above the door. *Taceant colloquia. Effugiat risus. Hic locus est ubi mors gaudet succurrere vitae.* Let idle talk cease. Let laughter depart. This is the place where death delights to help the living. The same maxim, or part of it, was to be found in almost every autopsy room she'd ever seen.

Eventually Corban's body was x-rayed, weighed, measured, washed, and transferred to the autopsy table. Only then did Jude see that his right arm was splinted and bandaged from wrist to elbow and his body was covered with bruises. Corban Foley's life had ended painfully and violently.

"It wasn't a knife," she noted flatly.

"No." Mercy lifted his head a little and turned it away from Jude. The base of his skull seemed to have a hole in it. "It's too soon to determine cause of death conclusively, but this is a fatal head injury. Fracture of the right occipital bone, extending medially into the foramen magnum."

"That's where the spinal cord goes?"

"Yes." Mercy repositioned the body. "From the X-rays, it looks like he was beaten severely. The right arm is fractured in a couple of places, likewise several ribs. No callus formation. There's extensive bruising to the trunk. In a child that age, there would have been internal bleeding. The skull fracture would have been associated with significant brain injury."

Mercy's attempt to put into laymen's terms the nature of Corban's injuries somehow failed to capture their true horror. Wanting to confirm her initial observations, Jude asked, "How would he have sustained injuries like these? An adult couldn't do this with his bare hands, could he?"

"No. The nature and site of the head injury could only be caused by a direct blow. Probably a blunt instrument. I'll be able to make some suggestions once we're done here."

"He suffered, then?"

Mercy stiffened as if the question jarred her from her clinical detachment. After a short pause, her brow was smooth once more and her voice even. "The bones of his forearm would have moved against each other and caused extreme pain. The splinting was the work of an amateur. Completely pointless for such a fracture."

"A doctor didn't do it?"

"Certainly not."

Jude met her eyes. "I have to nail this monster. Do you understand?"

"You'll have my report on your desk tonight. Allow a few days for toxicology, fiber, and DNA, as usual."

Mercy picked up her scalpel, and the *diener* placed a small rubber body block beneath Corban's back. His fragile chest lifted and his arms and head fell limply away from his body, as if an invisible thread had just tightened high above him, connected directly to his heart. In a moment he would be opened out like a book, for the story of his death to be read in his flesh.

Jude left the room before the Y-cut was made. She wanted to remember him exactly like that, like an angel had just plucked his soul from his body and would not let go until they reached the sweet hereafter.

❖

People magazine paid for Corban's funeral. In exchange for a premium burial package and impressive stone-angel monument, they had received exclusive print-media rights and a reserved area at the front of the church and next to the graveside so they could capture every compelling moment.

They'd also paid for the new outfits Tonya and her sister wore, and both women had received a makeover so they would look their best in the close shots. This had transformed the color of Tonya's hair to albino white, and she was wearing it shorter and dead straight. Amberlee had gone with a radiant strawberry blond, in the same straight, layered style.

"CNN is in on the deal, too," Dan Foley told Jude. He was out on bail and seeing a psychiatrist as a condition of his release. "They've got something going with *People*."

"You're not planning to do anything unwise, are you?"

"So long as I'm there when you guys put the handcuffs on that scum-sucker, I can behave myself. Just promise me you're gonna wipe that shit-eating grin right off his face if you can't shoot his balls off. While you're at it, see if you can break every bone in his body."

Jude said mildly, "I'm the law, not the Terminator."

They both looked toward the doors of the Montezuma Valley Presbyterian Church where Wade Miller, in a rented suit, was accepting condolences like a grieving parent. Next to him, Tonya stood with her head down and a gold-embossed white prayer book clutched in her hands. The dress wasn't what Jude would have chosen for a funeral. Close fitting, it was midthigh length and had a plunging V-neckline. Her sister had gone with a scoop necked, long-sleeved Gothic style velvet gown. She had tiny white rosebuds in her hair.

These were a theme.

For the viewing, Corban's casket had lain several inches deep in them. As funeral service attendees filed in to the church, each was handed one to pin on a lapel. Corban's face was printed on the ribbon that was used to fasten them. Tonya had her rosebuds artfully arranged around the wide-brimmed hat she was wearing. A filmy black veil hung from this, which seemed to annoy her. She couldn't stop lifting it and glancing at herself in the huge polished brass urn on a pedestal by the door.

"Amberlee says they're going to be in a TV movie about the case," Dan said. "Can you believe it?"

"What else is she saying?"

Jude had sent Dan in to check out the lay of the land with Tonya's sister, who seemed less than happy that she was not the center of attention in this media circus. Rekindling the tender feelings he and Amberlee had once shared, he'd proven very useful. Hearsay wouldn't be much help in a trial, but it was good to know exactly what was going on in Tonya's private life, and Jude needed to keep track of Wade Miller's ever-changing versions of events.

"They hired the same lawyer Gums Thompson's using."

"Who's paying for that?" Jude asked.

"Old man McAllister from the building depot. Heather Roache got him to hire the guy to clear Matt's name."

"Seems like there's a conflict of interest."

"Not any more. After Matt and Gums went on TV he got them another lawyer. He's not charging Tonya and Wade a dime."

Jude wasn't surprised. Griffin Mahanes was a big-time criminal defense attorney from Denver. He would have arranged the *People* magazine deal and taken a piece of the action. No doubt he was content to wait and see what happened, poised to claim center stage if Miller ended up in a media-event trial.

"The funeral home did a good job fixing up Corban's face," Dan said.

He'd identified the body to spare Tonya. The first time she saw her dead son was at the viewing where he looked like a sleeping cherub, thanks to the embalmer's art. Pratt hadn't been happy about that decision, but he'd accepted that it was bad public relations to haul a weeping mother into the morgue to see firsthand how her child had died.

"You better get in there," Jude said.

She was thankful Dan wasn't going to be sharing a pew with Miller. He'd arranged to sit with Amberlee in the front row on the opposite side of the aisle, along with *People* and CNN.

Jude followed him into the small church to the strains of that infant-funeral standard, "Tears in Heaven." She sat down in the back pew next to Pete Koertig and the sheriff.

Koertig leaned over and said, "Thanks."

"My pleasure."

"It means a lot."

"You earned it." Jude said.

Koertig wasn't done. He got poetic. "You bust your chops and someone else always gets the glory. I don't resent it. But when it's a big-deal situation like this, you gotta know there's some pride involved."

"Damn straight," Jude agreed.

"Guess what I'm saying is it was big of you." He got choked up. "My wife and I want to invite you to our home for dinner."

Jude kept the wince off her face. "That's really thoughtful."

"How's next Sunday? She's got a half-marathon on Saturday."

"Sunday is good for me." Jude wondered what she was going to talk about over a meal with two of the squarest people she'd ever met.

"Your fiancé is also welcome," Koertig said awkwardly.

"We're not engaged," Jude said. "But I'll certainly see if he can make it. Thanks, Pete."

He nodded. "Fiancé—that was out of politeness. I know you haven't said yes. Hell, the whole town knows."

Because he obviously thought he'd been cute, Jude produced a small chuckle and tried for a coy shrug. "It's a big decision," she confided, knowing every word would be reported verbatim to the entire MCSO staff. She could tell from Pratt's body language that he was listening in, too. She gave them something to think about. "Strictly between the two of us, I have a fertility issue. As you can imagine, that's a concern."

To her shock, Koertig shuffled his burly body around in the cramped space of the pew to face her earnestly, then seized hold of her hand. "I hope you don't think I'm being forward." His head went scarlet through the sparse blond of his buzz cut, and he lowered his voice to a fraught whisper. "But you can't let that stand in the way of your happiness. My wife and I..." The whisper got even lower. "We're similarly afflicted."

Nothing if not resourceful in a crisis of deep-cover credibility, Jude said, "Then you understand my position. Bobby Lee wants children."

"You haven't told him?" Koertig let go of her hand so he could bite his nails, a habit he tried to temper with Control-It! Jude had noticed bottles of the nasty-tasting formula on his desk and in his truck.

"No," she confessed. "Somehow, there never seems to be a good time."

"Well, that's getting off on the wrong foot." Sheriff Pratt pushed Koertig back so that he could render his opinion. "Give the guy a chance. You don't know how he's going to react."

"You're right, sir." Jude offered him the words he seldom got to hear from her. "I guess I've been putting it off."

"If you want to talk to an understanding woman about this, my wife is a school counselor. Just part-time. She makes sure to be home for the girls."

"That's a very nice offer. I appreciate it."

"Funny..." He shook his head in wonderment. "You can get it all wrong about people. I had you picked for one of those women who'd never have kids by choice."

"It's my height." Jude said seriously.

"And the physique," Pratt observed. "You're not built like a... motherly type."

This man was in politics.

Even Koertig looked embarrassed. "My wife is not voluptuous either, but she loves kids. She's heartbroken thanks to our problem."

Pratt gnawed on his mustache. "And then you see bozos like that, breeding by accident. Makes you sick. Is it my imagination or do those two women have different hair every time we see them?"

"It's for the cameras." Jude tried to shine a less judgmental light on the young women. They were two twenty-somethings swept up in a maelstrom they had lost control over. She couldn't blame them for trying to look more sophisticated than they were. "I'm sure they must feel exposed having so much attention on them during this difficult time."

Pratt snorted. "They're sucking it up."

"She won't be posing like that after I drag her boyfriend away in handcuffs," Koertig noted darkly. "While I think about it, are we all set for the cemetery?"

"I think it's the best option," Jude said. "If he makes a run for it, then we won't have these crowds to deal with.

"If you want, we could work the arrest together," Koertig said, clearly feeling the burden of his arresting-officer role. "I could restrain him while you cuff him."

However it went down, it was Jude's call. She was entitled to the glory-hog role if she wanted it. But the fact that she'd taken a pass in favor of her subordinate made Koertig walk tall. It sent the signal that he'd played a major role in putting the case together and was now getting the respect he'd earned.

Sure, Jude would have liked to shove Miller against a car and make the arrest painfully memorable for him, but they had national media rolling footage, so it had to be tidy. She didn't feel bad. This wasn't the only case she would ever see, but small town law enforcement officers didn't get a big slice of the fame pie, and she wanted the whole team to bask in the moment.

"I'll stay on the outer perimeter," she said. "If he runs, I'll take him."

Someone in the pew in front of them craned around and said, "Shush."

It was standing room only in the church, and the music got loud as the minister approached the pulpit.

"Don't forget about dinner," Koertig said.

Jude shook her head. "I can see we'll have a lot to talk about." That's if she didn't shoot herself first.

❖

After the funeral service, close family departed in a fleet of black limousines the funeral director had brought in from Grand Junction and Durango. Jude and Koertig bypassed the funeral procession so they could get out to the Cortez Cemetery before they took retirement.

Corban's final resting place was a premium plot surrounded by neatly manicured grass and softly waving trees. Media without the exclusive deals had the place staked out well ahead of time, forming a caravan of trucks with satellite dishes and cameras mounted on their roofs. Jude and Koertig picked their way across a snarl of cables past a set of makeshift platforms and squeezed between various crews. Spotting Tulley, Jude waved and he jogged over.

"Detective Koertig is going to make the arrest," she said. "I want you close by to provide backup with several of the other deputies. Go talk to Belle Simmons. She was at the briefing you missed."

Jude had assigned Tulley to take Chastity and Adeline sledding in the hills while the funeral service was underway. They were now back at her place, where Adeline was taking care of Yiska. The cat had assumed immediate ownership of Jude's house from the moment they walked in the door three days earlier, and insisted on sleeping right on top of Jude every night.

Her presence brought with it another unexpected bonus. Chastity and Adeline had been so touched by her brush with death, they offered to extend their visit so they could care for her while Jude completed the vital stages of the homicide investigation. She had enough on her hands, Chastity said; this was one small thing they could do to help her bring Corban's killer to justice.

Having them in her home was surprisingly comfortable. Jude had always had trouble sharing her living space with another person. In many ways she was happy in her solitary state, and she had the living habits to show for it. An empty refrigerator. Mismatched sets of cooking utensils. An oven that was never used and had a spider living in it.

Chastity had said very little about any of this. But when Jude arrived home after midnight, the day of Corban's autopsy, there was hot homemade soup waiting for her. Afterwards, Chastity poured her a glass of scotch and sat with her in companionable silence, reading a book while Jude unwound. They didn't sleep together that night, but had cuddled for a while in Jude's bed until her frenetic exhaustion gave way to drowsiness.

The next day, Jude pulled an all-nighter with most of the team, collating and evaluating all the evidence and making the decision to arrest Wade Miller. Chastity and Adeline had happily occupied themselves exploring the Mesa Verde and spending time with Tulley, who showed them everything they would ever need to know about cadaver dog training.

Jude called Chastity periodically to make sure they were doing fine. She felt bad about neglecting her guests, and she also wanted to spend more time alone with Chastity, but it was impossible while they were putting the case against Wade Miller together. She'd napped for a few hours at the MDSO that night, not going home at all until the next morning.

When she got in, Chastity ran a hot bath for her and gave her a massage. This was a skill she'd acquired in her overseas travels, she told Jude, and she'd attended a couple of classes in Salt Lake City. She had good hands, firm and unhesitant.

"You could make money at this," Jude said.

"Then I'd have to massage people I don't care for."

That made sense, and Jude had to admit, she wasn't wild about the idea of Chastity touching the naked flesh of strangers. This jealous thought immediately triggered alarms. They weren't even lovers and she was already getting possessive. The Neanderthal gene wasn't going anywhere.

Later that morning, before Jude returned to work, they'd discussed Chastity and Adeline's departure. They were planning to leave the day after the funeral. Yiska was doing well, Chastity needed to get back to her business, and Adeline thought it was time she made an appearance at school.

"Will you come visit?" Chastity asked.

"Would you like me to?"

"Yes." As if she had to rush the words out before she changed her mind, Chastity said, "Jude...I'm going to see someone. I have a therapist, but we've never talked about my...problem."

Jude marveled that she was paying a shrink to listen to her avoid her main issue. They probably had clients who did that all the time. Would she, herself, tell a guy in a white coat about her sexual-performance problems if she had any? Forget it. She frowned as it crossed her mind that Chastity might be doing this for some screwed-up reason like wanting to please her.

Apparently able to read her like a book, Chastity said, "I'm doing this for me. It's time."

"I hope it works out." Jude felt she should say something more touchy-feely, but there was only so far down that track you could go without sounding like you belonged in California.

"I haven't had a relationship since my divorce." Chastity gave an ironic little smile. "Things can only get better."

Jude watched the corners of her mouth quirk into tiny dimpled hollows. She had a feeling Chastity knew she was finding the conversation awkward. Struggling with squeamishness, she lurched into the deep and meaningful. "I'm happy you're doing this. You matter to me, and I'd hate to see you cheated of a part of life that has so much joy to offer."

"You're saying I might like sex once I get beyond this?" Chastity interpreted.

Jude certainly hoped so. "You're a sensual woman."

"I was turned on when we were kissing."

"That's a start."

"I think we should try again," Chastity said.

"You mean, now?" Jude had been known to amend her priorities on carnal grounds, but it was out of the question today.

Chastity laughed softly. "No. A quickie on your sofa wasn't what I had in mind."

"Care to explain."

"Let's sleep together tonight and you can show me second base."

"That won't be onerous."

Chastity grew serious. "I don't know if I'm homosexual."

"We can work on finding out." Having had her ability to concentrate obliterated, Jude said, "I have to go."

Chastity walked her to the garage door and kissed her cheek. "Good luck."

Feeling like a husband sent off to work by the little woman, Jude replied, "Call me if you need anything."

There were worse things than coming home to someone, she reflected. Today, after they had Wade Miller locked in a cell, she would head up a long, winding mountain road to a house that had the lights on because people were in it. She would eat a nice meal, tell Adeline a colorful version of the arrest, then take Chastity to bed and second base.

Which was not something she could afford to dwell on at this time. She focused on her surroundings as a steady line of black limos with tinted windows glided along the inner road to the parking area. The media had roused themselves from their coffee-drinking, casting disposable cups in all directions and talking into their headsets. Tulley and his team maintained a somber vigil about twenty feet from the grave, as if entirely as a gesture of respect. Around the wider perimeter, officers from the MCSO and Cortez PD kept order among over-eager reporters and defused incidents between competing television crews.

The minister proceeded slowly to the head of the grave, escorting Tonya. The coffin bearers followed, just two: Dan Foley and an older man Jude took to be his father. Everyone else gathered around in a semicircle. There were probably fifteen people, all dressed in black. As the minister read verses from the scriptures, Tonya stood with her head bent and her shoulders shaking. A few feet away, Amberlee constantly scanned the media crews to see if she was on camera.

They sang a hymn as the small coffin was lowered. It was, Dan had told Jude, the best children's casket money could buy. He had expected to pay for it, but *People* picked up the tab. This was the moment. Ashes to ashes. Dust to dust. Jude signaled Koertig, who moved around the back of the mourners to a spot just a couple of feet behind Wade Miller.

A terrible sob tore from Tonya as the minister uttered his final blessing. She began to sway, crying, "Oh, my God. What did I do?"

Someone yelled, "She's fainting."

The media swarmed, but before she could hit the deck, Amberlee released a shrill cry and took a dramatic dive after the coffin. In hog heaven, media anchors swept the mourners aside and nabbed key positions around the grave, yelling for their crews to capture the money shots of the day.

Behind the fray, the minister and several shocked family members dragged Tonya under a tree and set about reviving her. No one was filming her. On what was surely the worst day of her life, and the pinnacle of her fifteen minutes of fame, she had been upstaged by her sister.

CHAPTER SEVENTEEN

Predictably, Wade Miller did not respond well to being arrested at the funeral. With the media already in a state of bliss over the coffin dive, he made sure they took home the added bonus of a grief-stricken, falsely accused man struggling with brutal police thugs.

Pete Koertig had done everything exactly to plan. He took Miller's arm and told him he was under arrest and to behave like a man and avoid making a scene. At that time, the cameras were still trained on Amberlee, as she writhed on a casket too small to prop up 250 pounds of woman. This unhappy situation meant that her arms and legs were covered in earth by the time she was extracted from the grave.

Chagrined, she yelled at Tonya, "I hope you're happy now."

Tonya, equally distraught, responded, "You've spoiled everything. This was meant to be beautiful."

Handcuffed, Miller broke away from Koertig and rushed to console her, hollering at Koertig, "You've arrested the wrong guy, you fucknut faggot."

Koertig took Miller's arm once more and said, "Please come with me, Mr. Miller. Your fiancée will be taken care of."

"I didn't do it," Miller wailed, falling to his knees instead of walking.

Koertig tried to drag him upright without using undue force, but Miller let fly a volley of profanities and hunched into a fetal position. Koertig waved to Tulley and the other deputies, and they hurried over. The recent snowmelt had rendered the winter-brown grass wet and slippery, and by the time Jude reached them, the struggle looked like a hog-wrestling event.

Slathered in mud, Miller was yanked to his feet and dragged toward a police car, screaming about his innocence, protesting damage to his suit, and claiming police brutality. Jude didn't even try to intervene. She figured Sheriff Pratt would seize the moment.

Tulley told her later that Miller cussed them out using words he'd never heard of all the way to the detention cells. He was now talking to his lawyer, who had been present at the funeral but had allowed events to take their course, doing nothing to advise his client. Jude had seen the guy, standing a few feet away in his shiny Italian suit and dark glasses, watching the unfolding events with reptilian anticipation. She figured he was hoping the police would rough Miller up.

The district attorney was planning a sit-down with Griffin Mahanes later in the day. He had assembled the primary investigators in a meeting room at the MCSO for a general debriefing in anticipation. They'd just watched the goat's head gang, as they were now described by the media, proclaiming their innocence in the TV interview they gave in the preceding week.

The DA, Carl Schrott, said, "What you're seeing here is a classic setup. Mahanes was hired to clear Matthew Roache's name. He did so by having Hank "Gums" Thompson implicate himself. We can be certain this tape will be produced at trial."

"It's going to be obvious to the jury that Thompson is an unreliable witness," Jude said. "Both the tape and his statements to police will be called into question, so I don't see how this is a problem."

"It wouldn't be, normally," Schrott replied. "But Griffin Mahanes makes his living distorting facts and selling juries. Trust me, he's going to work this angle."

"Are you saying we don't have a death-penalty case?"

"Our first offer to the defense will be life without parole. We can ask for the death penalty, but there isn't a judge in Colorado who'll buy it. There's no indication that the murder was premeditated." Schrott fingered his modest gray tie while he waited for the unrest to die down.

He wasn't a good-looking man, and his wavy brown hair was cut in a style straight out of a fifties high school yearbook, but he came across well to juries in the Four Corners. Locals tended to be suspicious of slick defense attorneys from far-flung cities, and Jude hoped this would buy them something at the Miller trial. One look at Griffin Mahanes and you knew Satan wouldn't want his soul if he offered to sell it.

"I know how you all feel," Schrott continued. "We'd have more to work with if there was evidence of long-term abuse, but the autopsy makes it pretty clear that the attack was not part of a pattern."

Jude glanced around the eight lawmen present, detecting a mixture of anger and resignation. The DA was making sense, but everyone had read the autopsy report. Emotion was inevitable.

"I'll be interviewing Mr. Thompson again today," she said, wondering if it was even worth the risk of adding another bizarre statement to the mounting proof of his insanity. "Can I see that video again. The part where he's talking about the hat."

They all watched in moribund silence as Suzette Kelly asked in her whispery, sorority-girl voice, "Did you ever see Corban Foley, Mr. Thompson?"

"Only when it happened."

"When what happened?"

"When I took the hat."

"Which hat?"

Thompson became agitated. "I forget."

"When did you see the hat?" Suzette pressed him, but his attention was wandering, and she had to swat his hand away when he reached for her pearl necklace.

At that point, Matt Roache interrupted, announcing, "That engagement ring she's wearing—that's the one I gave her. What does *that* tell you?"

Thompson picked up on the rhetorical question with a display of righteous disgust. "She's a whore, and God doesn't forget those who transgress."

Suzette immediately jumped in, like the prime-time heavy hitter she was. "Have you transgressed, Mr. Thompson?"

"Yes." He seemed to shrink in his chair. "And I was punished."

"What did you do?" Suzette asked softly.

"I can't speak of my wickedness without the elixir."

The interview continued along these lines for several more minutes before Suzette seemed to realize she was never going to get the hoped-for murder confession from a man who seemed to be missing his frontal lobe.

Schrott turned off the recording and remarked laconically, "It's almost worth getting the guy to confess so that we can prove why he couldn't have done it and clear the air before Miller faces trial."

"That seems like a desperate strategy," Sheriff Pratt said.

"I wasn't serious, sir."

"Okay," Pratt conceded, "but assuming you were, for the sake of a hypothetical discussion, would it work?"

"Let's not go there. The people have a good case against Miller. We don't need to play games."

"I don't suppose we can keep Thompson off the stand," Jude said morosely.

"Not when Mahanes wants him for a star witness."

"Perfect. We get a statement that proves Wade Miller is a liar and staged the crime scene, and they get a witness who makes Miller seem credible."

"Yep. It sucks." Schrott got to his feet. "I'll keep you posted."

Pratt waited until the DA had closed the door then muttered, "That sonofabitch Mahanes thinks he can laugh at us. Get out there and find us a star witness we can put on the stand. Make that sucker wish he'd never been born."

❖

Jude's interview with Gums Thompson started out like a waste of time. He reacted with bewilderment to the "hat" questions and marveled when Jude showed him the relevant parts of the Suzette Kelly interview.

He didn't remember talking to the emaciated anchor and wondered out loud if she had special arrangements with Satan by which men were rendered impotent if they touched her pearl necklace. Lately he'd noticed a malfunction in his member that made self-gratification impossible.

Jude offered a suggestion. "When you appear in court, you don't need to mention that to the jury."

"Am I guilty?" he asked, eyes darting to the door.

"No." Jude said calmly. "Wade Miller has been charged with murder. You are going to be asked some questions at his trial."

Comprehension dawned, and he ran his big pink tongue over his spaghetti-thin lips. "Because of the baby."

"Yes."

"I didn't take him."

"I know that, Hank."

A flash of lucidity froze his wandering gaze. "He wasn't there."

Jude's heart jolted. "What do you mean?"

"When I went back for the hat, he wasn't there."

Jude was almost afraid to ask another question in case she sent his train of thought careening away from its temporary stopover in sanity-ville. Cautiously, kindly, she echoed, "He wasn't there?"

Thompson's brow collapsed into tight furrows. "I took the hat then."

Jude waved the deputy at the door over and instructed him to go get the two hats they had in evidence. She had shown Thompson the photographs previously and drawn blank looks.

While she was waiting, she said, "Stay with me, Hank. You're doing fine. Just a few more questions."

The deputy returned with the two bagged hats, and Jude placed them in front of Thompson. He snatched up the ball cap the goat had been wearing and cried, "You found it."

"Yes."

"He wanted to keep it to remember that goat by," Thompson blurted. "But I had already cast it in. Now, Heather won't talk to me." He clutched the evidence bag to his chest. "Can I take it to her so she knows of my service?"

"I can give you a photograph of the cap, if you want. Heather likes photographs."

Mollified, he set the cap back on the table and proceeded to poke around inside his mouth, extracting food from his false teeth.

Piecing his ramblings together, Jude asked, "Is that why you went back? You wanted to get the goat's cap for Matt because he was angry at you?"

Thompson nodded weepily. "He threw my elixir out the window. He said I was undeserving."

"What a wicked thing to do." Jude humored him without mockery. "Is that when you went back?"

"No. He wanted to go home."

"I see."

"He wouldn't let me in. He said, no hat, no Heather."

"What did you do?"

"I tried to find the elixir, then I went back to the she-devil's house to seek the minion's hat."

Jude ran the timeline. Miller and Thompson vandalized the house at around 11:30 p.m. then drove back to Heather Roache's home, about twenty minutes away. Thompson then spent time looking for the discarded tequila. By her estimates he must have been back at Tonya's place at around 12:30 a.m.

"What happened at the she-devil's house?" she asked.

"I went inside."

"Did you climb in a window?"

He shook his head and confided, "I found the magic rock that conceals the keys."

"So you opened the door with a key?"

"I was fearful, but I asked the Big Guy to shine his light upon me and the house was filled with radiance."

Jude recalled that the hall lights came on automatically when the front door was opened. "Where did you go then?"

"To the bathroom. I couldn't hold it any longer."

Jude pictured the befuddled Thompson relieving himself, then wandering directly across the hallway. To Corban's bedroom. Did she really want to put him in there on the record, by his own admission? "And after that?"

"I looked in the first room. It wasn't there."

"Can you tell me about that room?"

"It had a small bed and," he wiggled his fingers above his head, "music from the angels."

The baby mobile that hung from Corban's ceiling. "Did you see who was in the bed, Hank?"

With a quick nod, he said, "Nobody. I was going to lie down on it, but that's when he came back."

"Who did?"

"Wade Miller, the jerkoff. I heard his truck, so I ran." He pointed at the elf hat on the table next to the cap. "This was on the ground, and I wanted to have it so I could show Heather. But he stole it from me and reviled me with his demon's tongue."

Jude thought she followed his twisted reasoning. He was trying to get the ball cap back for Matt because Matt was threatening him with limited access to Heather if he didn't. Then, having failed, he thought the elf hat he stumbled on in the driveway would at least serve as a souvenir of his brave entry into the she-devil's home. He imagined the adored Heather would be impressed by this.

"What did you do then?"

"I went far away and cleansed myself of his unclean touch."

"Smart move." Jude rested back in her chair and studied her star witness, the man who could testify that Corban was not in his bed when Miller claimed he'd left him there. The man who made it impossible to believe that Wade hadn't seen the vandalism until much later that night.

He'd chased Thompson from the property. He must have seen the damage at the time. But he'd said nothing about encountering Thompson. Jude found that puzzling. He was bound to have told Griffin Mahanes, and now Gums Thompson had put himself in Corban's room.

Her heart sank. This was going to come down to the word of a mental patient against the word of a violent loser. She knew who she believed. But by the time Mahanes was done making Thompson twist in the wind, she had no idea what a jury would think.

❖

Tulley removed his gum and was about to stick it in the ashtray on his desk when Miss Benham waved her forefinger at him. Meekly, he wrapped it in a shred of paper and flipped it into the trash. Hugging the phone against his shoulder to free his hands, he set about cleaning his sticky fingers with a Wet Wipe.

At the other end of the phone, his ma said, "I was thinking, if I had one of them vacuum machines I could package up our bacon with a fancy label and sell it at the farmers' market."

"Ma Tulley's home cured," Tulley mused. "Your own brand. That's smart thinking."

"Since your brother had his accident last year, we gotta come up with something. That missing testicle's ruining his marriage."

Tulley wasn't sure what the branded bacon had to do with his brother's marriage, but he figured his ma would get to that. "What's the problem?"

"Well, turns out it didn't take when they sewed it back on, and now they've had one of them prosthetic ones made specially. But Marybeth says it's too hard and she don't care for it in the act of love."

"Can't he take it off when they're going at it?" Tulley gave Miss Benham an apologetic look.

"It's an implant. Damn fool I brought up for a son."

"Tell him I'm real sorry."

Miss Benham tapped her watch.

Tulley said, "Ma, I gotta go."

But as usual, she was planning to hang up in her own good time. "Think they're gonna hang that baby killer?"

"Not so far as I heard. For a killing to be a hanging offense there has to be premeditation."

"An eye for an eye, a tooth for a tooth, and that's all I'm gonna say about it."

Tulley thought, praise the Lord.

She said, "You getting out here again some time before the Second Coming?"

It was the first time his ma had invited him home so warmly. Amazed, Tulley said, "I got some vacation owing to me. I can come if you want."

"Don't do me any favors."

Something in her tone made Tulley forget himself and ask, "You okay, Ma?"

"What the heck are you implying?"

"Nothing. Just asking."

"Never been better," she sniffed.

"Alrighty then." Tulley wanted to ask her if she'd been to the doctor recently for a checkup. At her age it seemed like a good idea. But he knew what she'd have to say about that.

"Well, what are you waiting for?" she said. "Get on back to work."

"Yes, ma'am."

The dial tone hummed before he could say good-bye, and Miss Benham asked, "How is she doing?"

"Okay, I think." Tulley put a harness on Smoke'm and fed him a couple of liver treats. "My brother and his wife are having marriage troubles, and that's got her all worked up."

Miss Benham handed him his hat and coat. "You'd best get going. You know the detective doesn't care to be kept waiting."

Tulley could immediately feel Jude's sleepy greenish eyes boring holes in him. Even after two years of working with her, he could never tell exactly what she was thinking. She kept a straight face most of the time, and she didn't smile much. These days he didn't get nervous around her like he used to, but he saw the effect she had on others. He hoped she wouldn't be in a pissy mood this afternoon. He was still feeling stoked after grabbing hold of Wade Miller's ankles so he couldn't go anywhere, during the arrest.

With a grin, Tulley headed for his Durango and loaded Smoke'm into the back. Happy to have another assignment so soon after they made the front page during the Corban Foley search, he said, "Okay, boy. Let's go kick some felon butt."

❖

"You're ten minutes late," Jude said when her subordinate finally rolled up. "And we don't have much time. The snow's melted and someone's going to find our evidence. Probably Griffin Mahanes."

Tulley bailed out of his vehicle, looking like he was in a daydream. It had gone to his head to have a television producer come up to him after the brawl with Wade Miller in the cemetery. The guy told Tulley how pretty he looked on camera, and asked him if he wanted to audition for an exciting new series.

Jude said, "I hope you're not planning to call that producer. He's just trying to get into your pants." It was time Tulley learned how the world worked.

He slid his hand over his coal black cowlick and stared at her blankly. "What producer?"

"Forget it." Jude stared past the police tape to Tonya Perkins's house, aware that she was aggravated and taking it out on him. She softened her tone. "You're looking for two things. A key and a bottle of tequila. Mr. Thompson believes he may have discarded both of these items somewhere in the immediate vicinity."

She handed him a piece of Gums Thompson's shirt, which he'd helpfully agreed she could cut off. Tulley promptly sniffed it.

"You might want to try that out on him," Jude suggested dryly, motioning toward Smoke'm. As usual, the hound looked like he'd been rudely awakened from the sleeping state he preferred.

Snickering, Tulley tightened the harness and let Smoke'm take the scent. "Chastity and Adeline still visiting with you?" he asked.

"They're leaving tomorrow," Jude said without inflection.

"That's a shame." He looked thoughtful. "Chastity's real nice."

"Yes."

"If she was staying longer, I was going to ask her out on a date. We've got some things in common."

Jude kept a straight face. Tulley was always talking about dating some woman or another, and then did nothing about it. Bobby Lee, who had all but given up on the idea of seducing the deputy himself, called him a disgrace to handsome men.

"Things in common," she repeated. "I'm afraid to ask."

Tulley looked a little huffy. "She loves dogs."

"That's it?"

With a noisy sigh, Tulley gave Smoke'm another hit of eau de Gums Thompson and said, "You expect a lot from people, ma'am."

She clapped him on the shoulder. "Tulley?" She did her best to reproduce Arnold Schwarzenegger's accent, "Talk to the hand."

CHAPTER EIGHTEEN

D etective Devine, what a surprise." Debbie Basher opened her door wide and invited warmly, "Please come in."

Jude smiled. "I was on my way back to work and I thought I'd drop by and say hello, since we're almost neighbors."

"Well, that's nice of you." Debbie clasped her hands together at her chest like a happy child. "Congratulations on the arrest. We thought he was the one, at least Lone did. Right from the start." Observing Jude's slight incomprehension, she said, "Sorry, that's Sandy's nickname. Lonewolf. Lone, for short."

Lonewolf. Jude could almost hear Arbiter's mind working. The nickname was a favorite of extremists all over the country.

Debbie gestured toward the sofa. "Have a seat. Can I get you something? Coffee?"

"Just what I was hoping you'd say." Jude gave her a look of warm appreciation. "Sandy not here today?"

"No, she had some work to do. The blizzard brought a tree down on her property."

"I thought she lived here." Jude made as if she were surprised. "Easy mistake. You two seem so much at home with one another."

Debbie blushed. "So, you know...I mean, you're..."

"Uh-huh," Jude admitted. "But in my line of work, in this part of the country, I don't advertise it."

"Me, either." Debbie moved into the kitchen and started making their coffee. "I'd lose my job, for sure. My boss is a nice lady, but you know how it goes—gay is an abomination."

"Yeah, there's plenty of that attitude round here. Good folk, but knee-deep in fear and ignorance."

"It's funny, at the search, people were so nice to us." Debbie sounded wistful. "I started thinking maybe I'm being too careful. But then I realized—it was because everyone thought Lone was a man."

Jude could see how that might happen. Lone would get called "sir" wearing a dress. She said, "Well, I'm sorry she's not here right now. I was hoping to talk with her about something we were discussing the other day."

Debbie brightened. "I have an idea. Why don't you come have dinner with us one night? I'll cook up a storm, and you and Lone can talk about whatever butches talk about when you're by yourselves with an unlimited amount of beer."

Jude laughed with genuine pleasure. It made a nice change not to have to be guarded about her sexuality. She wished she could get to know a few more lesbians around the area, but showing up at the local chapter of GLAD would attract more attention than she needed, and in this close-knit community, gossip traveled like wildfire. She wasn't willing to jeopardize her FBI assignment by being outed.

"Dinner sounds like a great idea," she said. "Want to pick a night now?"

"Sure." Debbie poured their coffee. "I'll call Lone and see when she's free."

Jude got to her feet and offered, "I'll take those." She made a point of looking Debbie up and down, just enough to communicate a sensual awareness of her.

Debbie got flustered and dropped her cell phone. Jude picked it up and stood just close enough so that Debbie would be aware of her height and strength, but not so close she would come across as disrespectful. Reaching past her, she picked up the coffee mugs.

Debbie gave a nervous laugh like a hiccup and focused on her phone once more, but instead of retreating politely while she dialed Lonewolf, Jude took a sip of coffee like she couldn't wait. Then she put one of the mugs back on the counter and distractedly patted her pockets as if her pager was going off.

With an apologetic smile, she produced her cell phone and mouthed in an undertone, "Excuse me a moment. I need to pick up a couple of messages."

As she moved away, she entered the number she had just observed Debbie dial and hit "save." Then she went through the motions of clearing her messages while Debbie spoke to her paranoid partner.

Sure enough, Debbie's tone started out animated, then she sounded a little startled and said, "She's right here, having coffee."

Jude put her cell phone away and said, "Want me to talk to her?"

Debbie hesitated, but she was the kind of woman who respected authority figures so she caved right away, blurting chirpily, "She wants to say hello, honey." She quickly passed the phone to Jude.

"Sandy. Hey," Jude said. "How are you doing?"

"Good." Sandy wasn't giving much away. "I saw you arrested the boyfriend."

"If you could call it that."

Sandy thawed slightly. "Don't you want to smack guys like him in the mouth?"

"In the worst way. I guess you've seen your share of them, too."

"It's one thing when they don't speak the language and get themselves confused. But your baby butcher was working it."

"Wall-to-wall TV reporters," Jude remarked. "I'll tell you all the details next week. Your lady is mighty persuasive, by the way."

Sandy was trapped and she knew it. "Yes. She said something about dinner." She couldn't have sounded less enthusiastic.

"I don't get home cooking very often," Jude continued, acting oblivious. "So it'll be a real pleasure to share a meal with you folks. Thanks for the invitation."

Try getting out of that one. She waited for Sandy to find an excuse not to break bread with her, but after a beat, their subject said, "How's next Friday?"

"I'll be here."

They said perfunctory good-byes, and Jude returned the phone to Debbie. "We're on for next Friday."

"That's great." Debbie beamed.

She was one of those women who glowed from inside, Jude thought. She wasn't good-looking in an obvious way, but she had the same appeal as a baby animal, all sweetness and vulnerability. She would never be able to hide her fear or guilt if she was involved in something illegal or if she knew her lover was. In either scenario, she would not have invited a cop to dinner.

Jude felt angry with Sandy, then. What was she thinking placing this woman at risk? Foraging in the recesses of her mind, she tried to come up with alternative explanations for the C-4 purchase. It could be entirely innocent. The woman had property. Maybe she was planning to blast an unwanted building or part of a hillside. Maybe she was simply a survivalist with a thing for weaponry.

Whatever she was up to, Jude was determined to be certain of her facts before she made a move. She wasn't going to jump to conclusions just because Sandy Lane was an intense individual with the kind of profile that could fit a domestic terrorist—ex-military, a loner, paranoid, antisocial. She had more pressing priorities, like finding out if the ASS was ninety percent hot air and wishful thinking, or if they posed a serious threat.

Now that the snows were melting and March was moving toward April, it would be viable to access the remote location their operations had been traced to. Jude anticipated a rundown shack complete with a stockpile of anti-Semitic literature, Nazi memorabilia, and unsophisticated half-built bombs.

Meanwhile, she would take her time getting to know Sandy and Debbie. She would build trust and gain access to the lives of these two women so that she could observe patterns. That way she could detect the tell-tale signs that signaled a plan underway. Now that she had a cell phone number for Sandy, she would be able to track her location and conduct some basic surveillance.

Sandy didn't strike her as a woman who rushed into anything, so Jude felt time was on her side. This mattered, because if the couple was involved in something stupid, she wanted the chance to change their minds. Maybe she could steer Sandy in a different direction before she could destroy what they had with each other.

❖

Quietly, Chastity closed the door to the guest room. "She's asleep."

Jude glanced at the suitcases next to the garage door, a gluey sensation in her stomach. Tomorrow she would be by herself again, and she was kidding herself if she thought it was going to feel good to watch Chastity and Adeline drive away. Yet part of her was relieved.

She had so much to think about in preparing for Miller's trial, she would be lousy company. Even Yiska would probably abandon her bed in disgust.

"It feels strange to be leaving," Chastity said as she moved across the living room toward Jude.

"Come back any time you want," Jude invited. "Next week is open."

Smiling, Chastity reached up and pulled the bands from her hair, allowing her copper curls to tumble down around her face. "Has it really been okay?"

"It's been better than okay." Jude allowed herself an eyeful of Chastity's breasts. The thought that she would soon get to caress them made her breathless. In fact, the thought of touching Chastity anywhere made her feel like a high school kid fantasizing about the class hottie she would never have.

"So, it's just us, now." Chastity advanced on Jude. Her dark eyes gleamed and her expression was playful. "Feeling the pressure?"

Jude hooted with laughter, then forced a solemn tone. "Well, I'm aware there's a lot riding on my performance. If it all goes south you could be scarred for life, and I'll spend yet another horny night feeling sorry for myself. No pressure."

"I've been worrying that I set my sights too low," Chastity confided. "Second base. It's not very adventurous, is it?"

Jude couldn't resist. "Well, that depends on who you're playing with."

Chastity's small gasp made her mouth part deliciously. "Come here and say that."

Jude grinned. Chastity was right in front of her, so close that her jeans were brushing against Jude's legs. All Jude had to do was reach out and she could unbutton her neat dove gray shirt. While she was contemplating that possibility, Chastity pushed her firmly into the sofa cushions, slung one leg over Jude's, and lowered herself to sit astride her.

"I can see that you've given this some thought," Jude said, impressed by the seductive move.

"Only all day." Chastity brushed her fingertips slowly past Jude's lips. "I did some reading."

"Really?"

"You have some very informative books."

"You checked out my bedroom bookshelves?"

Jude tried not to be horrified. Somehow, the thought of Chastity flicking through lesbian erotica was far more disturbing than it should have been. She wondered why. Chastity was not a child. If she was alarmed by something she read, she could close the book.

"You sound shocked."

"No. Just surprised." Jude was aware of an increasing ache in her groin and the tantalizing pressure of Chastity's weight. Huskily, she inquired, "Is this your norm? You don't do things by halves?" A compelling thought, on many levels.

"I was a late starter," Chastity murmured, her breath dampening Jude's cheek, "So I have this thing about making up for lost time."

Jude placed her hands around Chastity's waist and drew her firmly down, spreading her legs a little wider. The stifled gasp she heard made her ache even more, and she slid a hand between them, easing it beneath Chastity's crotch. Slowly she worked the knuckles back and forth.

"Does that feel good?"

Chastity's night-dark eyes met hers. She whispered, "Kiss me."

They moved together, their mouths caressing, gently teasing, not really going there. Jude had no idea how long she could keep this up. Holding herself in check was going to make her crazy. She thought maybe two more minutes would be a safe bet, then she would have to take a cold shower or she would totally blow it.

She kissed Chastity with a little more intensity and moved her hands down over her hips and around to her great little ass, exactly the kind she liked to spank occasionally. Trying not to go *there* she continued the gentle caresses, waiting for a cue from Chastity that she wanted more.

But slow, subtle buildup didn't seem to be working as it should. Chastity was returning her kisses and she seemed aroused, yet Jude had the impression she'd be happy if they made out on the sofa for the rest of the evening.

Experimentally, she parted Chastity's mouth with her tongue and lifted a hand to one of her breasts, taking its modest weight in her palm and squeezing. Chastity responded by kissing her more urgently and bucking slightly against Jude, and in that moment the second base plan was off the menu entirely. Months without sex had made gradual exploration torture instead of the erotic fun it was meant to be. All Jude could think about was standing up with Chastity's legs wrapped around her, finding the nearest wall, and fucking her senseless. What happened to finesse?

Jude's legs felt weak, but she stood up anyway, holding Chastity close until her feet hit the floor. She was promptly flooded with uncertainty instead of arousal. If she made love to Chastity now, in this state, she would scare her.

"What is it?" Chastity touched her face. "Did I do something wrong?"

"No." Jude took a step back. "I think we're going too fast."

Chastity's hand slipped into hers and she tugged Jude toward the bedroom. "We can slow down."

They made it inside the door. Chastity reached for the waistband of Jude's pants and unbuckled her belt. Jude cursed the tiny buttons that kept the gray shirt closed. She couldn't believe she was fumbling, trying to squeeze them through the holes. Chastity saved her the trouble, pulling the shirt up and over her head in a single fluid motion.

They stared at each other, both breathing hard.

Jude said, "I can't do the second-base thing."

"I don't care," Chastity was so close Jude felt her shiver. "I just want you."

They systematically discarded their clothes until they stood naked before one another. Chastity placed a fingertip on the hollow at the base of Jude's throat and tentatively stroked. Then she drew Jude's head down to hers and they kissed again, this time with greedy intensity.

As she lost herself in Chastity's mouth, Jude walked her to the edge of the bed and lowered her onto the pale sheets. "You're beautiful," she said. "And I have to make love to you. Please don't say no."

Chastity gazed up at her and opened her arms. "Come here."

CHAPTER NINETEEN

W e should be selling tickets to this," Sheriff Pratt grumbled as he and Jude fought their way through a swarm of reporters to the relative haven of the Montezuma County Courthouse.

Wade Miller's trial had now occupied the court for two weeks, which was a long time by local standards. Jury members were complaining about the heat and the food. The judge had thrown various people out of the courtroom: friends of the accused who tried to slip him a bottle of beer, outraged citizens calling for a hanging, and vocal supporters of the goat's head gang who kept leaping to their feet with placards that announced Gums Is Innocent. Jude thought Griffin Mahanes had probably hired these groupies.

Mahanes held court with the media on a daily basis, making the usual accusations: that police had a vendetta against his client and had ignored witnesses who might have implicated other potential killers; his client had been framed by planted evidence; and no one knew where Corban had been murdered.

Which was, as far as Jude was concerned, the biggest weakness in the people's case. They hadn't located the crime scene or clothing that would conclusively tie Miller to the killing. They also had no murder weapon. The sledgehammer used to weigh Corban's body down was not the weapon, and its owner was unidentified.

To get a conviction, they had to win the jury because they were relying on a combination of circumstantial evidence and the obvious guilt of the defendant. If the jury believed Miller, they would not convict. If they believed Gums Thompson, they would. And today was the day Jude and the sheriff would know. Thompson was taking the stand, the star witness for the prosecution. They hadn't found the key or the tequila bottle that would support his story, and Jude hoped this would not prove too costly.

Jude had heard that Mahanes was planning to put Miller on the stand when the defense presented their case, a decision that surprised her. She'd been fairly certain he wouldn't risk exposing his client to a probing cross-examination that was bound to expose him as lying through his teeth. But she figured he would want the jury to compare both men. Miller would be coached extensively, of course. He already looked like a blind date most women wouldn't hide from. The mullet was gone and so was the black hair dye. Mahanes had dressed him like a schoolteacher.

Jude cast a sideways glance at Pratt and found him looking distinctly ill at ease. "You were right," he said. "We should have waited."

Jude didn't comment. She was still seething over the rush to trial. Pratt had used all his considerable political muscle to obtain an early court date so they could get a guilty verdict in time for his re-election. Griffin Mahanes had played ball, falling over himself to make it easy for them. Jude would have done the same in his shoes. Why give the prosecution time to build a stronger case?

Throughout the trial, she and every other detective working the case had continued to chase every lead that could lead them to a murder site. This meant investigating the tips of half the crazies in the region, interviewing everyone they could track down who had ever had a beer with Miller, and canvassing door to door through most of the streets in Cortez. They had found more dead dogs and sorted through more bags of discarded clothing than she wanted to think about.

It confounded her that in a small town environment like this one, where every member of the public was obsessed with the case, a child could have been murdered bloodily and no one heard or saw a thing. She supposed there were a million places Wade Miller could have gone to do it. The Four Corners was a wilderness. One day, in years to come, hikers would probably find the rusted crowbar Mercy had flagged as the most likely murder weapon, and they would get the proof they needed long after the fat lady had sung.

Pratt mumbled something and stared past her toward a small crowd of people sweeping through the foyer. At their center was Griffin Mahanes, a man who dyed his light brown hair silver for added *gravitas* when he was appearing in the courtroom. This morning he was wearing a high quality but unpretentious navy blue suit and a conservative, almost dated, striped tie. He'd swapped his usual black cowboy boots for a pair of brown ones that had seen better days.

"His own family couldn't trust him to play Santa on Christmas Eve," Pratt commented in disgust.

Jude said, "I hope to Christ Gums can remember what he's supposed to say." Her cell phone was vibrating and she excused herself to take the call.

"I called to wish you luck." It was Chastity, sounding calm and happy.

"Hey, how are you?"

"We're doing fine. Adeline wants a tattoo."

Jude laughed. "Welcome to fifteen."

"You're still coming, aren't you?"

"Of course. Just as soon as this fiasco is over."

Despite their best intentions, they hadn't seen each other since the visit in March. Four months felt like a long time. They spoke often, and Jude felt they were building a real friendship, but she had no idea where it was headed. And on some level, it hurt that Chastity hadn't come back to the Four Corners to see her.

She knew it was impossible for Jude to get away. The investigation had consumed her, and she'd been preoccupied with her ongoing investigation into Sandy Lane. Arbiter was also on her tail about the ASS. So far, she had covertly entered two properties owned by the men in question, and the only biological agent she'd uncovered was a few sacks of chicken shit. With the Telluride film festival only six weeks away, they were no closer to confirming the credibility of the threat, and Arbiter had just ordered a bunch of agents into the area to focus on the case.

To be fair, Chastity had planned to make the trip several times, but something always came up. Jude wanted to believe that they were simply trapped by difficult circumstances and these would change once the Miller trial was over. She had promised to make the trip to Salt Lake City, and they had agreed to behave like adults in the meantime.

But Jude couldn't shake the lingering suspicion that Chastity had backed off the moment their connection became sexual. She was trying to be patient, reasoning that any woman who had been brought up the way Chastity was and had spent her whole life assuming she was straight could not suddenly discover her true sexuality and adjust overnight. There would have to be a period of doubt and self-questioning like the one Jude had experienced when she was thirteen and fell in love with her softball coach. She had tormented herself for an entire week. It was bound to be worse for a woman of thirty-three.

Her other unhappy suspicion centered on their lovemaking. After a promising start, it hadn't exactly gone to plan. There was no happy, mutually orgasmic conclusion. Chastity had become self-conscious all of a sudden, and they couldn't recapture the erotic connection that had driven them to the bedroom in the first place. Jude then got anxious about hurting her, or making her feel uncomfortable, and Chastity expressed some strange feelings about "leading you on, then disappointing you." All in all, it was a memorable sexual encounter, but for the wrong reasons. Jude wasn't surprised Chastity wasn't breaking down any doors to repeat it.

She felt a queasy uncertainty about the Salt Lake City visit. In her experience, you could only have disastrous sex so many times with someone before a pattern of negative expectations was established. If it didn't work early on, Jude had learned it probably never would. She had feelings for Chastity, and a sense of possibility with her that she seldom felt with anyone. She really liked the woman, and that mattered. But was it enough? If they were doomed never to have sex, or only to have careful sex, the kind where Jude could never be who she was, what was the point?

Gloomily, she tuned into Chastity's happy chatter about Adeline and the surfing holiday she'd just had with friends. God, she missed Mercy. Seeing her in court was wrenching. Knowing she had married Elspeth made her physically sick. They spoke to each other like two professionals, but Jude was incapable of neutral feelings. Some days she hated her. Other days she felt consumed with anger and betrayal. Then there were days like today, when all she could think about was her skin, her scent, her lithe elegant femininity. Their perfect sexual accord.

That was it, she thought. In Mercy her erotic self found a home, and she knew it was exactly the same for Mercy. They were so alike. They shared the same sexual vocabulary. There was no need for translation or interpretation. When they made love, it was as if they were two bodies within a single skin.

Did Mercy have that with Elspeth? Jude knew the answer; she'd read it in her eyes on the rare occasions when Mercy let her guard slip.

"Jude? Are you there?" Chastity sounded confused.

"I'm sorry. The reception is lousy in here," Jude disgusted herself by prevaricating.

"I was just saying my therapy is going pretty well."

"That's good. I'm proud of you."

Was she insane? Jude thought. How could she stand here with Mercy Westmoreland on the brain when she had an adorable, real, honorable woman at the other end of the phone. A woman who genuinely cared about her.

"They're going in now," she said. "I'll talk to you later."

"I'll be thinking of you," Chastity replied warmly.

Jude truly wished that did it for her.

❖

Griffin Mahanes knew how to make the most of a crazy witness. He didn't offend the jurors' sense of fair play by making fun of Gums Thompson or browbeating him. He was solicitous and respectful throughout the cross-examination, ensuring that by the end of Thompson's testimony, the entire courtroom would be sickened that the prosecution had placed this pitiful basket case on the stand.

When it came time to discuss Thompson's presence in Tonya's house, Mahanes said, "Mr. Thompson, you told the court you stood inside Corban Foley's bedroom. Did you speak?"

"I talked to the Big Guy."

"What did you say?"

"I asked for guidance so Heather would be pleased with my service."

"Heather Roache?"

"Yes."

"You are fond of Heather, are you not, Mr. Thompson?"

"She is radiant among women."

"What is your relationship to her?"

"I am not worthy to eat the worms she treads on."

When the snickering in the courtroom had desisted, Mahanes continued, "Does Heather like children?"

"Yes, sir. She loves children."

"What else does she like?"

Gums warmed to the topic. "Small white dogs, espresso coffee from the Silver Bean, Bush's maple baked beans, Matt, Beautiful by Estee Lauder, pictures of Jesus—"

"Yes, thank you. Mr. Thompson, you were arrested for shoplifting in December, weren't you? You had stolen a gift box of products from the 'Beautiful' range. Who was this for?"

"Heather."

"Is it true that in August 2004, you were charged with the theft of a Maltese terrier?" Mahanes asked.

"I gave it back," Gums protested.

Directing a meaningful stare at the jurors, Mahanes asked, "You stole that small white dog from inside its owner's home, did you not?"

"It was scratching at the window."

"How did you get into the house?"

"I found the keys under a magic stone."

"So you knew God meant for you to go inside?"

DA Schrott rose immediately. "Objection. He's leading the witness, Your Honor."

The judge agreed. "Sustained. Get to the point, Mr. Mahanes."

Mahanes nodded, apparently lost in earnest reflection. "Why did you try to steal the Maltese?"

"To offer it to Heather."

"Of course. Because Ms. Roache loves small white dogs. And 'Beautiful' perfume. Have you taken other items to offer Heather?"

"Yes."

"You mentioned Ms. Roache loves children. If you had a child, would you offer it to her?"

Gums looked at Mahanes like he was a loser if he even needed to ask the question. "Yes."

Mahanes took a couple of steps closer to him. "Have you ever stolen a child to offer to Heather Roache?" When Gums hesitated, Mahanes wheedled with a sucrose smile, "Please tell the court. You've promised God you would be truthful."

Gums's eyes darted back and forth until they landed on Jude. Her heart sank.

He mumbled, "Yes."

"That was a yes, my friends." Mahanes paced before the jury, letting this answer sink in. "When did you do that?"

"I don't know."

The courtroom erupted into avid speculation. The judge demanded order.

Mahanes lifted his mellifluous voice above the din. "You stole a child, but you don't know when?"

Shamefaced, Gums said, "I transgressed and God punished me."

"What happened to the child you stole?"

"I buried it."

Heather Roache fainted.

Jude said, "Oh, Christ."

Pratt was ashen.

Their case was over. It was that simple.

❖

No one was entirely sure how Mahanes had managed to decode Gums's ramblings, but everyone agreed that the next time they committed a class-one felony, he was their guy.

Gums took the police to a sad little grave in the Mesa Verde, and they found the body of a child who had disappeared from an Arizona trailer park three years earlier. Cause of death was choking. Gums had left the child eating a hamburger in his truck, at a rest stop on the way back to Cortez, and had panicked when he returned to find him dead.

Jude spent a long, discouraging week in Cortez finalizing the police reports on the Arizona child. On her last day, she was heading for her truck when she heard footsteps approaching. Somehow, Miller had managed to give his dwindling media entourage the slip and found his way into the MCSO parking garage. She was amazed by the nerve of the guy, but she supposed getting away with murder made a person feel invincible.

With soft menace he taunted, "You forgot to congratulate me, Detective."

The seductive weight of the gun at her hip drew Jude's hand. "Get out of here before I blow your brains out," she advised.

"You're not gonna do that." Miller drew closer, tempting her. His pupils were tiny black holes that seemed to suck the life from his pallid blue eyes.

Jude glanced around the parking garage, making automatic calculations. How would it play out? He threatened her. Assaulted her. She defended herself. He grabbed her gun from its holster. She disarmed him. The gun went off. No one would buy it. She would lose her badge and do time. Over this amoeba.

"You're right, I'm not," she said dismissively. She didn't want to give Miller the satisfaction of seeing how incensed she was. "I wouldn't waste a bullet on you."

As she moved toward the driver's door, he taunted in a voice so low she had to strain to hear, "What if I tell you right now, I killed the little shit and there's nothing you can do about it?"

"Is that what you *are* telling me, Mr. Miller. Or are you playing games again?"

He got cocky and pulled a comb from his top pocket. As he slid it through his lank tendrils, he said, "I'll give you a big fat clue, since you geniuses couldn't even figure out where it happened."

"I'm all ears."

"There's a buddy of mine with a boat parked out back of his place in Cahone. That was his cousin, Howie, on the jury."

Three seconds, Jude thought. That's all it would take. Point-blank. Straight between the eyes. She slid her balled fist into her pocket and met his gaze levelly. "So you took Corban out there after you'd broken his arm and used him as a punching bag?"

"Hey, I tried to fix up his arm. But he wouldn't shut up."

"I'm thinking I should break yours the same way, so you can understand why that was," Jude said.

"Yeah, right. That's gonna happen."

"So you took him onto the boat." Jude wanted the rest of the story. Several cars had come and gone while they were standing there, and it was only a matter of time before someone stopped to ask if there was a problem.

Apparently, Miller wanted to get it off his chest. He said, "I sleep out there sometimes, since my buddy is away most all the time. The plan was, I put the kid there and tell him when he shuts up I'll take him home. But he's not listening, is he? Fucking Mommy's boy."

"So you smashed his head in?"

"It was just a knock. Most people would have got up and walked away. But he's just lying there and there's blood all over the fucking place."

"Where was your buddy while this was taking place?"

"Last I heard, he was driving trucks for Halliburton in Iraq. Big bucks if you want your fucking head cut off."

"Not a risk you would take, being the coward you are," Jude noted.

His eyes glittered. "You think you're such a smart fucking bitch, but you weren't that smart this time, were you?"

Jude stepped right up, in his face, challenging him to take his best shot. "Go ahead." She tapped her chin in invitation. "Make my day."

"I saw that movie," Miller blustered. "And you aren't even close."

"Ouch, that hurt." She sneered at him, wanting to push his buttons.

If she couldn't put him inside for the crime he'd committed, a consolation prize was better than nothing. First-degree assault of a law enforcement officer was a felony that carried a ten to thirty-two-year prison term in the state of Colorado. Add obstruction and resisting arrest, and with any luck, Miller would serve most of his worthless life. Even second-degree assault would see him inside for a fourteen-year stretch.

"It must make you proud," she said. "Knowing you killed a child that was thirty-two inches tall and weighed twenty-seven pounds. What a hero."

He sidled edgily around her. "You can't prove anything."

"I already did. No one believes you're innocent, Mr. Miller. You're just another creep who got away with murder because a blindsided jury stopped thinking."

"I can live with that." He leaned deliberately against her door so she'd have to make him move before she could open it.

"Step away from my vehicle," she said.

"Make me."

He was trying to play her at her own game, pushing for a reaction. Like an alcoholic who presses drinks on others, he needed the affirmation of a shared weakness. He wanted to see her lose control just as he had. Only he thought he knew how far it would go. He thought she wouldn't really hurt him, but that there would be just enough contact for him to press charges and bleat about police harassment.

Jude almost laughed. Miller wouldn't be so cocky if he knew what she knew about her temper. That killing him would come easy. That with men like him, she had to fight the urge to inflict serious pain. Intellectually, she was aware that the dark places inside her had to remain shuttered. She had the self-discipline to keep herself in check, so she used it. But she was always conscious of a bomb ticking inside and a sense that when it exploded one day, she might not be able to hold herself back.

They stared at each other and Jude saw the violence in him, contorting the bland veneer of his features, straining for release. But he wasn't going to attack her. He was smart enough to know which one of them would end up without a pulse if things got serious.

"I was just thinking," she said coldly. "Every time you look in a mirror…every day for the rest of your life…you're going to see the face Corban saw that night. Ugly. Brutal. A disgrace to humanity."

"Fuck you."

Jude laughed. "Is that the best you've got? Jesus, you really are pitiful."

She swung the door open and got in her truck, allowing herself to picture him spread over her tires. She started the motor and backed around sharply, missing him by inches, forcing him to jump out of her way.

"I know what you are," he shouted.

Jude rolled her window down and granted the darkness inside some room. "Watch your back, Mr. Miller," she returned with chill threat. "Because one day—and you won't know when it's coming—you'll answer for Corban Foley. And you better hope it's not me with the knife to your throat."

CHAPTER TWENTY

"They're leaving town," Tulley said, poring over the *Durango Herald*.

Agatha topped up Jude's coffee. "You mustn't blame yourself, Detective. The prosecutor did everything he could after that shocking revelation."

"They're saying two guys on the jury bullied everyone else." Tulley fed a forkful of his scrambled egg to Smoke'm. "Shit like that happens. We do our job and the system lets us down."

Jude supposed she would be putting up with these assurances for the next six months until her colleagues convinced themselves that she wasn't planning to blow her brains out anytime soon.

"I'm okay," she told them.

"Everyone knows he did it," Tulley declared. "They know we had him fair and square."

Agatha sat down and stretched her feet out. She was wearing the UGG boots Jude had given her for her seventy-first birthday. Her extremities got cold even in the summer, she'd told Jude. "We can blame falling educational standards," she said. "Individuals are placed in a position beyond their mental capacity. I think at least three members of that jury were semiliterate at best."

"You got that right, Miss Benham." Tulley mopped egg from Smoke'm's jowls with a napkin. "Howie Nelson. He's a retard. How he made it through jury selection is a goddamned mystery."

"Language," Agatha chided. "As a matter of fact, I taught Howie. Now there was a child with learning challenges. The family environment didn't help. Cultural pygmies—that's what we're talking about."

Jude said, "We should have found Miller's buddy in Cahone."

"The guy hasn't lived around here for ten years," Tulley said. "No one knew he even had that boat anymore."

"Howie Nelson did."

"Like I said, Howie's ma dropped him on his head."

"Howie isn't the issue. We are. We investigated this case."

"You know what I don't understand," Tulley anguished. "That's how come the judge let Gums on the stand, anyways. He's bat-shit crazy."

"I think that was the point," Jude said. "His testimony spoke to reasonable doubt. And the fact is, he could have done it. He had the opportunity. And Griffin Mahanes knew how to imply that he had the motive and practice, too."

"Yeah, but he didn't do it." The buzzer sounded, and Tulley flipped his dark bangs away from his brow and angled his head expectantly toward the door.

The morning just got worse. Jude sighed as Bobby Lee Parker sauntered in. He tipped his fedora to Agatha, gave Tulley a broad wink, and placed a gift basket of fruit and nuts in front of Jude. He followed this with an ostentatious kiss that made Agatha beam and look away, then he relocated to the mirror where he removed his hat and rearranged his tousled blond hair.

"Don't tell me...you folks are still talking about the trial. Am I right?" he asked.

"What else has happened round here recently?" Tulley tossed back.

Bobby Lee shrugged off his buckskin jacket, arranged it carefully on a hanger, then took a small package from the breast pocket. He whistled for Smoke'm and the hound plodded over with more speed than usual.

"That dog sure loves you," Tulley said.

Bobby Lee unwrapped a few strips of bacon. "He's easy. Unlike some."

Tulley snickered.

"It's high time you gave the man an answer," Agatha reminded Jude indignantly.

"Don't you worry about me, Miss Agatha. I like a woman who's hard to get." Bobby Lee sniffed his hands. "Bacon grease and dog mouth. Oh, man."

Jude got to her feet and said, "I'm not going to sit here and listen to lectures about *my* personal life from a woman of seventy who made sure not to get tied down herself, a deputy who only sleeps with his dog, and a boyfriend who admits he's more faithful to his truck than to his women."

Her three companions stared.

"You're taking this trial too personally," Agatha said.

"Leave her be." Bobby Lee gave Jude a roguish smile. "She needs her space."

"And that's why I am taking the day off." Jude slid on her sunglasses and headed for the door.

"Where are you going?" Bobby Lee called after her.

Jude glanced back. "Hiking."

Predictably, he lost interest. Bobby Lee didn't see the point in scaling hills on foot when you could hire a horse for thirty bucks.

As she left the office she heard Tulley say, "Want to see *White Orphans* again?"

This was followed by a pathetic whine from Bobby Lee, who shared Jude's unease over movies with subtitles.

Before her official suitor could come after her with offers of better ways to spend the day, Jude got into her new purchase, a Land Rover LR3 she'd been promising herself all year, and hastily backed around. The sun was hot, the skies were blue, the earth was red again. Highway 145 had little traffic. Jude drove over the speed limit, as any cop was entitled to do, especially when in pursuit of nothing but the wind in her hair.

The morning sun glowed orange across the Uncompahgre Plateau behind her, and the San Juans rose ahead dappled pink and purple. In the months since Corban was found, the kayakers had returned to the Four Corners to take advantage of the snow-melt. Summer hikers were routinely getting lost again, or assaulting one another in campsite brawls. Telluride would soon be crawling with movie people and waiters who wanted to be movie people. There would be cattle missing from the Canyon Echo dude ranch roundup, and everyone would blame itinerant Mexican illegals. Then the cattle would be found and the locals would smirk over city slickers so busy listening to their iPods on the trail they can't keep a few large, slow-moving animals in sight.

"Life goes on," she said to the empty passenger seat. Chastity would look good sitting there, she thought and immediately swept the topic from her mind. She was not going to waste this day among gorgeous days agonizing over her personal life.

She cut across to Ridgeway and took the 550 south toward Silverton until she found the route to Mineral Creek. The gravel road she hit was easy until the turnoff to Clear Lake, which took her on a tortuous ascent over what passed for a road, but was only navigable if you were in a four-wheel drive. Fortunately there were no other vehicles making the climb, so she didn't have to worry about getting stuck behind a driver who would lose his nerve and roll backwards. The parking area at the switchback was empty. Jude reversed in carefully so that there was room for two or three more cars.

On weekends at this time of year, it wasn't unusual to find a line of Jeeps and Land Rovers from the trailhead back down the road. The Ice Lake Basin was a two-mile-wide valley encircled by sprawling ridges and 13,000 foot peaks. By late July it was idyllic, and the forested camping sites around the lower basin often had a constant population of six or seven tents.

She always came here early in the day so she could enjoy a long hike before the weather closed in, if it was going to. The afternoon storms across the mountains were thrilling to watch, in all their elemental fury, but Jude thought she'd save being struck by lightning for another life.

She followed a series of switchbacks higher and higher until it seemed there was no place to go but up, and then she found herself in a vast field of waist-high wildflowers—columbines, larkspur, and cow parsnip, rioting blues and yellows. The first time she'd ever ventured up here, this was as far as she got. She'd spent hours contentedly wandering through the aspens and spruce, then sprawling on her back in the meadows, cushioned by flowers and gazing up at the perfect blue sky and the shining white peaks.

She'd returned often after that, taking the time to explore the lush, wild beauty of the lower basin, with its waterfalls and astonishing views of the surrounding mountains. Only recently had she made the killer climb to the upper basin. There she'd waited the sun out, gazing at the brilliant apricot and gold of Fuller Peak and the Golden Horn, reflected in the dark sapphire blue of a tiny lake.

Ice Lake itself was just over the tundra shelf. Jude reached it after a solid ascent of almost two hours. Her calf muscles were beginning to burn and she was questioning her fitness level. Panting and wiping her face with her bandanna, she trod gingerly down toward the water, not even noticing at first that she'd stumbled into paradise.

The upper basin was a starker world than the slopes below. It spent most of the year under snow, but when the alpine flowers finally saw the sun, they blossomed furiously, carpeting the high tundra with every hue. Almost as soon as this happened, the ravens came. Hundreds of them, like envoys from another world, settling on rocks and terraces to wait and guard until called home. She could see none yet; perhaps it was too soon and they were still nesting below somewhere, teaching their young how to fly.

Jude lifted her head and slowly turned full circle, absorbing the perfect stillness and surrendering herself to a drunken splendor that defied description. The air was cold and chilled the sweat on her face and body. She climbed back up to the lake rim, dropped her backpack, and extracted a fleecy sweater. Everywhere she looked, small tarns dotted the undulating red and gray landscape. Many were ringed with snowbanks all year round.

Huge boulders and precipitous rock faces loomed above. Jude picked up her pack and wove a convoluted path along charcoal crags until she reached a high meadow awash with ivory flowers. Cloud misted around her and she stood there for a long while, gazing down on the crystalline perfection of Ice Lake, thankful that all this was on her doorstep and wishing she could stay here forever. Taking deep, controlled breaths, she felt something lift from her body and realized it was rage that had driven her up the mountain so fast, she thought she might have a heart attack if she didn't slow down.

Her legs felt weak suddenly and she sank down into the flowers, closing her eyes against the slight spinning of her head. As she lay, unmoving and exhausted, her tension draining away, something tugged at the belt of her hiking shorts. Blinking herself fully conscious again, Jude stared down at a large raven perched on a stone next to her.

Dark, nerveless eyes bored into hers, and Jude felt herself drawn to the bird by their shared presence in this otherworld between heaven and earth. They were the only two living creatures she could see.

Struck by the sinister wisdom of the visitor's black diamond gaze, she said, "Hello."

The raven replied, "Quork."

Moving slowly, Jude opened her pack and took out some provisions. She and the raven ate a ham sandwich, then occupied a placid silence.

Eventually, Jude said, "I have something for you."

She took a small tissue parcel from her breast pocket and unwrapped a strand of fair hair. Like a thief in the night, she had stolen this from Corban, lying to the funeral director about needing additional DNA samples.

She placed the silken lock in the palm of her hand and extended her arm toward the bird. It inspected the offering carefully, first studying it for several seconds, then moving it by a few degrees with its beak.

"Take it somewhere beautiful, far from here," she said.

Her companion made a soft sound in its throat, collected the curl, and left the earth with a rush of wings. Jude watched the sleek bird fly, until she could see only a black speck high above the shimmering bronze peaks.

Far in the distance, the San Juan Mountains stood watch over Cortez, and the angel on Corban's grave cast a shadow over dead floral tributes and faded teddy bears. The gods could not shelter him in life, and neither could his mother. For in the sleep of reason, monsters are made.

About the Author

Rose Beecham is the mystery pen name of romance writer, Jennifer Fulton. Born in beautiful New Zealand, Rose now resides in the Midwest with her partner and a menagerie of animals.

Her vice of choice is writing, however she is also devoted to her wonderful daughter, and her hobbies—fly fishing, cinema, and fine cooking. Rose started writing stories almost as soon as she could read them, and never stopped. Under pen names Jennifer Fulton, Rose Beecham, and Grace Lennox she has published fourteen novels and a handful of short stories.

When she is not writing or reading, she loves to explore the mountains and prairies near her home, a landscape eternally and wonderfully foreign to her.

Rose can be contacted at: rose_beecham@yahoo.com

PLACE OF EXILE

We all carry within us our places of exile, our crimes, and our ravages. But our task is not to unleash them on the world; it is to fight them in ourselves and in others.

–Albert Camus

A place like the Four Corners is the perfect exile for people escaping from something or someone. But when that someone is yourself, the problem with running away is that you bring your worst enemy with you. Sheriff's detective Jude Devine can relate. She thought she'd left her past in Washington, D.C., but when reclusive millionaire Fabian Maulle is found murdered in Paradox Valley, and a photograph of Jude's missing brother Ben is among his possessions, Jude finally has a chance to solve the mystery that has stalked her since childhood.

Sandy "Lonewolf" Lane, a former paratrooper Jude suspects of being a domestic terrorist, has called the Four Corners home since the suicide of her lover, whose son was killed in Iraq. She's planning to kill the Vice-President, and her determination to carry out her mission, and Jude's to stop her, draws the two women into a lethal game of cat and mouse. Meantime local white supremacist splinter faction, the Aryan Sunrise Stormtroopers, are threatening a chemical attack on the Telluride Film Festival.

All of this is quite a distraction from Jude's love life, which is probably just as well, since it's not going the way she was hoping. Jude is in a dilemma when Dr. Mercy Westmoreland's wife, actress Elspeth Harwood, is away shooting a movie and Mercy feels like company.

Books Available From Bold Strokes Books

Sleep of Reason by Rose Beecham. Nothing is as it seems when Detective Jude Devine finds herself caught up in a small town soap opera. And her rocky relationship with forensic pathologist Dr. Mercy Westmoreland just got a lot harder. (1-933110-53-8)

Passion's Bright Fury by Radclyffe. When a trauma surgeon and a filmmaker become reluctant allies on the battleground between life and death, passion strikes without warning. (1-933110-54-6)

Broken Wings by L-J Baker. When Rye Woods, a fairy, meets the beautiful dryad Flora Withe, her libido, as squashed and hidden as her wings, reawakens along with her heart. (1-933110-55-4)

Combust the Sun by Andrews & Austin. A Richfield and Rivers mystery set in L.A. Murder among the stars. (1-933110-52-X)

Of Drag Kings and the Wheel of Fate by Susan Smith. A blind date in a drag club leads to an unlikely romance. (1-933110-51-1)

Tristaine Rises by Cate Culpepper. Brenna, Jesstin, and the Amazons of Tristaine face their greatest challenge for survival. (1-933110-50-3)

Too Close to Touch by Georgia Beers. Kylie O'Brien believes in true love and is willing to wait for it. It doesn't matter one damn bit that Gretchen, her new and off-limits boss, has a voice as rich and smooth as melted chocolate. It absolutely doesn't. (1-933110-47-3)

The 100th Generation by Justine Saracen. Ancient curses, modern day villains, and a most intriguing woman who keeps appearing when least expected lead Archeologist Valerie Foret on the adventure of her life. (1-933110-48-1)

Battle for Tristaine by Cate Culpepper. While Brenna struggles to find her place in the clan and the love between her and Jess grows, Tristaine is threatened with destruction. Second in the Tristaine series. (1-933110-49-X)

The Traitor and the Chalice by Jane Fletcher. Without allies to help them, Tevi and Jemeryl will have to risk all in the race to uncover the traitor and retrieve the chalice. The Lyremouth Chronicles Book Two. (1-933110-43-0)

Promising Hearts by Radclyffe. Dr. Vance Phelps lost everything in the War Between the States and arrives in New Hope, Montana with no hope of happiness and no desire for anything except forgetting—until she meets Mae, a frontier madam. (1-933110-44-9)

Carly's Sound by Ali Vali. Poppy Valente and Julia Johnson form a bond of friendship that lays the foundation for something more, until Poppy's past comes back to haunt her—literally. A poignant romance about love and renewal. (1-933110-45-7)

Unexpected Sparks by Gina L. Dartt. Falling in love is complicated enough without adding murder to the mix. Kate Shannon's growing feelings for much younger Nikki Harris are challenging enough without the mystery of a fatal fire that Kate can't ignore. (1-933110-46-5)

Whitewater Rendezvous by Kim Baldwin. Two women on a wilderness kayak adventure—Chaz Herrick, a laid-back outdoorswoman, and Megan Maxwell, a workaholic news executive—discover that true love may be nothing at all like they imagined. (1-933110-38-4)

Erotic Interludes 3: Lessons in Love ed. by Radclyffe and Stacia Seaman. Sign on for a class in love…the best lesbian erotica writers take us to "school." (1-933110-39-2)

Punk Like Me by JD Glass. Twenty-one year old Nina writes lyrics and plays guitar in the rock band, Adam's Rib, and she doesn't always play by the rules. And, oh yeah—she has a way with the girls. (1-933110-40-6)

Coffee Sonata by Gun Brooke. Four women whose lives unexpectedly intersect in a small town by the sea share one thing in common—they all have secrets. (1-933110-41-4)

The Clinic: Tristaine Book One by Cate Culpepper. Brenna, a prison medic, finds herself deeply conflicted by her growing feelings for her patient, Jesstin, a wild and rebellious warrior reputed to be descended from ancient Amazons. (1-933110-42-2)

Forever Found by JLee Meyer. Can time, tragedy, and shattered trust destroy a love that seemed destined? When chance reunites two childhood friends separated by tragedy, the past resurfaces to determine the shape of their future. (1-933110-37-6)

Sword of the Guardian by Merry Shannon. Princess Shasta's bold new bodyguard has a secret that could change both of their lives. He is actually a *she*. A passionate romance filled with courtly intrigue, chivalry, and devotion. (1-933110-36-8)

Wild Abandon by Ronica Black. From their first tumultuous meeting, Dr. Chandler Brogan and Officer Sarah Monroe are drawn together by their common obsessions—sex, speed, and danger. (1-933110-35-X)

Turn Back Time by Radclyffe. Pearce Rifkin and Wynter Thompson have nothing in common but a shared passion for surgery. They clash at every opportunity, especially when matters of the heart are suddenly at stake. (1-933110-34-1)

Chance by Grace Lennox. At twenty-six, Chance Delaney decides her life isn't working so she swaps it for a different one. What follows is the sexy, funny, touching story of two women who, in finding themselves, also find one another. (1-933110-31-7)

The Exile and the Sorcerer by Jane Fletcher. First in the Lyremouth Chronicles. Tevi, wounded and adrift, arrives in the courtyard of a shy young sorcerer. Together they face monsters, magic, and the challenge of loving despite their differences. (1-933110-32-5)

A Matter of Trust by Radclyffe. JT Sloan is a cybersleuth who doesn't like attachments. Michael Lassiter is leaving her husband, and she needs Sloan's expertise to safeguard her company. It should just be business—but it turns into much more. (1-933110-33-3)

Sweet Creek by Lee Lynch. A celebration of the enduring nature of love, friendship, and community in the quirky, heart-warming lesbian community of Waterfall Falls. (1-933110-29-5)

The Devil Inside by Ali Vali. Derby Cain Casey, head of a New Orleans crime organization, runs the family business with guts and grit, and no one crosses her. No one, that is, until Emma Verde claims her heart and turns her world upside down. (1-933110-30-9)

Grave Silence by Rose Beecham. Detective Jude Devine's investigation of a series of ritual murders is complicated by her torrid affair with the golden girl of Southwestern forensic pathology, Dr. Mercy Westmoreland. (1-933110-25-2)

Honor Reclaimed by Radclyffe. In the aftermath of 9/11, Secret Service Agent Cameron Roberts and Blair Powell close ranks with a trusted few to find the would-be assassins who nearly claimed Blair's life. (1-933110-18-X)

Honor Bound by Radclyffe. Secret Service Agent Cameron Roberts and Blair Powell face political intrigue, a clandestine threat to Blair's safety, and the seemingly irreconcilable personal differences that force them ever farther apart. (1-933110-20-1)

Protector of the Realm: Supreme Constellations Book One by Gun Brooke. A space adventure filled with suspense and a daring intergalactic romance featuring Commodore Rae Jacelon and a stunning, but decidedly lethal, Kellen O'Dal. (1-933110-26-0)

Innocent Hearts by Radclyffe. In a wild and unforgiving land, two women learn about love, passion, and the wonders of the heart. (1-933110-21-X)

The Temple at Landfall by Jane Fletcher. An imprinter, one of Celaeno's most revered servants of the Goddess, is also a prisoner to the faith—until a Ranger frees her by claiming her heart. The Celaeno series. (1-933110-27-9)

Force of Nature by Kim Baldwin. From tornados to forest fires, the forces of nature conspire to bring Gable McCoy and Erin Richards close to danger, and closer to each other. *(*1-933110-23-6)

In Too Deep by Ronica Black. Undercover homicide cop Erin McKenzie tracks a femme fatale who just might be a real killer…with love and danger hot on her heels. (1-933110-17-1)

Erotic Interludes 2: Stolen Moments by Stacia Seaman and Radclyffe, eds. Love on the run, in the office, in the shadows…Fast, furious, and almost too hot to handle. (1-933110-16-3)

Course of Action by Gun Brooke. Actress Carolyn Black desperately wants the starring role in an upcoming film produced by Annelie Peterson. Just how far will she go for the dream part of a lifetime? (1-933110-22-8)

Rangers at Roadsend by Jane Fletcher. Sergeant Chip Coppelli has learned to spot trouble coming, and that is exactly what she sees in her new recruit, Katryn Nagata. The Celaeno series. (1-933110-28-7)

Justice Served by Radclyffe. Lieutenant Rebecca Frye and her lover, Dr. Catherine Rawlings, embark on a deadly game of hide-and-seek with an underworld kingpin who traffics in human souls. (1-933110-15-5)

Distant Shores, Silent Thunder by Radclyffe. Doctor Tory King—and the women who love her—is forced to examine the boundaries of love, friendship, and the ties that transcend time. (1-933110-08-2)

Hunter's Pursuit by Kim Baldwin. A raging blizzard, a mountain hideaway, and a killer-for-hire set a scene for disaster—or desire—when Katarzyna Demetrious rescues a beautiful stranger. (1-933110-09-0)

The Walls of Westernfort by Jane Fletcher. All Temple Guard Natasha Ionadis wants is to serve the Goddess—until she falls in love with one of the rebels she is sworn to destroy. The Celaeno series. (1-933110-24-4)

Erotic Interludes: *Change of Pace* by Radclyffe. Twenty-five hot-wired encounters guaranteed to spark more than just your imagination. Erotica as you've always dreamed of it. (1-933110-07-4)

Honor Guards by Radclyffe. In a wild flight for their lives, the president's daughter and those who are sworn to protect her wage a desperate struggle for survival. (1-933110-01-5)

Fated Love by Radclyffe. Amidst the chaos and drama of a busy emergency room, two women must contend not only with the fragile nature of life, but also with the irresistible forces of fate. (1-933110-05-8)

Justice in the Shadows by Radclyffe. In a shadow world of secrets and lies, Detective Sergeant Rebecca Frye and her lover, Dr. Catherine Rawlings, join forces in the elusive search for justice.(1-933110-03-1)

shadowland by Radclyffe. In a world on the far edge of desire, two women are drawn together by power, passion, and dark pleasures. An erotic romance. (1-933110-11-2)

Love's Masquerade by Radclyffe. Plunged into the indistinguishable realms of fiction, fantasy, and hidden desires, Auden Frost is forced to question all she believes about the nature of love. (1-933110-14-7)

Love & Honor by Radclyffe. The president's daughter and her lover are faced with difficult choices as they battle a tangled web of Washington intrigue for...love and honor. (1-933110-10-4)

Beyond the Breakwater by Radclyffe. One Provincetown summer three women learn the true meaning of love, friendship, and family. (1-933110-06-6)

Tomorrow's Promise by Radclyffe. One timeless summer, two very different women discover the power of passion to heal and the promise of hope that only love can bestow. (1-933110-12-0)

Love's Tender Warriors by Radclyffe. Two women who have accepted loneliness as a way of life learn that love is worth fighting for and a battle they cannot afford to lose. (1-933110-02-3)